ALFRED HITCHCOCK'S BOOK OF HORROR STORIES No. 9

Another spellbinding collection of tales worthy of the master of suspense.

Ex Libris
otting Hill
and
Ealing
h School

**Also by the same author,
and available from Coronet:**

Alfred Hitchcock's Book of Horror
  Stories – No. 5
Alfred Hitchcock's Book of Horror
  Stories – No. 6
Alfred Hitchcock's Book of Horror
  Stories – No. 7
Alfred Hitchcock's Book of Horror
  Stories – No. 8

About the author

Alfred Hitchcock was born in London in 1900.
The most celebrated master of suspense in
motion pictures, he started his career as an
assistant layout man in advertising. Soon
afterwards, however, he won a job as title
writer with Famous-Players-Lasky – now
Paramount – and from 1925 onwards his film
career was meteoric. He died in 1980.

Eleanor Sullivan is editor of *Alfred Hitchcock's
Mystery Magazine*.

Alfred Hitchcock's Book of Horror Stories No. 9

Alfred Hitchcock
Edited by Eleanor Sullivan

CORONET BOOKS
Hodder and Stoughton

Copyright © Davis Publications Inc. 1976

First published in Great Britain in 1985 by Max Reinhardt Ltd as the second half of a hardback edition entitled TALES TO KEEP YOU SPELLBOUND

British Library C.I.P.

Alfred Hitchcock's book of horror stories; no. 9.
  I. Hitchcock, Alfred *1899-1980*
  II. Sullivan, Eleanor
  III. Hitchcock, Alfred. *1899-1986*
  Alfred Hitchcock's tales to keep you spellbound
  813'.01'0816 FS

ISBN 0-340-48765-8

The characters and situations in this book are entirely imaginary and bear no relation to any real person or actual happening.

This book is sold subject to the condition that it shall not, by way of trade or otherwise, be lent, re-sold, hired out or otherwise circulated without the publisher's prior consent in any form of binding or cover other than that in which it is published and without a similar condition including this condition being imposed on the subsequent purchaser.

No part of this publication may be reproduced or transmitted in any form or by any means, electronically or mechanically, including photocopying, recording or any information storage or retrieval system, without either the prior permission in writing from the publisher or a licence, permitting restricted copying. In the United Kingdom such licences are issued by the Copyright Licensing Agency, 33-34 Alfred Place, London WC1E 7DP.

Printed and bound in Great Britain for Hodder and Stoughton Paperbacks, a division of Hodder and Stoughton Ltd., Mill Road, Dunton Green, Sevenoaks, Kent TN13 2YA, (Editorial Office: 47 Bedford Square, London, WC1B 3DP) by Cox & Wyman Ltd., Reading, Berks.

Acknowledgments

Grateful acknowledgment is hereby made for permission to reprint the following:

'A HOME AWAY FROM HOME' by Robert Bloch; © 1961 by H. S. D. Publications, Inc.; reprinted by permission of Scott Meredith Literary Agency, Inc.

'DEATH OF A DERELICT' by Joseph Payne Brennan; copyright H. S. D. Publications, Inc., 1967; reprinted by permission of the author.

'PRESENT FOR LONA' by Avram Davidson; copyright 1985 by H. S. D. Publications, Inc.; reprinted by permission of Kirby McCauley Agency.

'THE LONG TERRIBLE DAY' by Charlotte Edwards; © 1968 by H. S. D. Publications, Inc.; reprinted by permission of the author.

'PANTHER, PANTHER IN THE NIGHT' by Paul Fairman; copyright 1959 by H. S. D. Publications, Inc.; reprinted by permission of the author.

'MURDER 1990' by C. B. Gilford; © 1960 by H. S. D. Publications, Inc.; reprinted by permission of the author.

'WINTER RUN' by Edward D. Hoch; © 1964 by H.S.D. Publications, Inc.; reprinted by permission of the author.

'THE HANDYMAN' by Clayton Matthews; copyright H. S. D.

Publications, Inc., 1967; reprinted by permission of the author.

'MURDERER #2' by Jean Potts;   1960 by H. S. D. Publications, Inc., reprinted by permission of McIntosh & Otis, Inc.

'THE THIRD CALL' by Jack Ritchie; © 1961 by H. S. D. Publications, Inc.; reprinted by permission of Larry Sternig Literary Agency.

'YOU CAN'T BLAME ME' by Henry Slesar; © 1961 by H. S. D. Publications, Inc.; reprinted by permission of the author.

'JUST A MINOR OFFENSE' by John F. Suter; copyright 1960 by H. S. D. Publications, Inc.; reprinted by permission of the author.

'KILLED BY KINDNESS' by Nedra Tyre; © 1963 by H. S. D. Publications, Inc.; reprinted by permission of Scott Meredith Literary Agency, Inc.

'NOTHING BUT HUMAN NATURE' by Hillary Waugh; copyright H. S. D. Publications, Inc., 1969; reprinted by permission of Ann Elmo Agency, Inc.

'CICERO' by Edward Wellen; copyright 1959 by H. S. D. Publications, Inc.; reprinted by permission of the author.

Contents

Killed by Kindness	Nedra Tyre	9
Just a Minor Offense	John Suter	18
The Long Terrible Day	Charlotte Edwards	31
Cicero	Edward Wellen	61
Winter Run	Edward D. Hoch	66
You Can't Blame Me	Henry Slesar	80
Death of a Derelict	Joseph Payne Brennan	89
Present for Lona	Avram Davidson	101
Murderer #2	Jean Potts	110
The Third Call	Jack Ritchie	125
A Home Away From Home	Robert Bloch	135
The Handyman	Clayton Matthews	144
Nothing But Human Nature	Hillary Waugh	157
Murder, 1990	C.B. Gilford	167
Panther, Panther in the Night	Paul W. Fairman	181

Killed by Kindness

by Nedra Tyre

John Johnson knew that he must murder his wife. He had to. It was the only decent thing he could do. He owed her that much consideration.

Divorce was out of the question. He had no grounds. Mary was kind and pretty and pleasant company and hadn't ever glanced at another man. Not once in their marriage had she nagged him. She was a marvelous cook and an excellent bridge player. No hostess in town was more popular.

It seemed a pity that he would have to kill her. But he certainly wasn't going to shame her by telling her he was leaving her; not when they'd just celebrated their twentieth anniversary two months before and had congratulated each other on being the happiest married couple in the whole world. With pink champagne, and in front of dozens of admiring friends, they had pledged undying love. They had said they hoped fate would be kind and would allow them to die together. After all that John couldn't just toss Mary aside. Such a trick would be the action of a cad.

Without him Mary would have no life at all. Of course she would have her shop, which had done well since she had opened it, but she wasn't a real career woman. Opening the shop had been a kind of lark when the Greer house, next door to them in a row of town houses, had been put up for sale. No renovation or remodeling had been done except to knock down part of a wall so that the two houses could be connected by a door. The furniture shop was only something to occupy her time, Mary said, while her sweet husband worked. It didn't mean anything to her, though she had a good business sense. John seldom went in the shop. Come to think of it, it was a jumble. It made him a little uneasy; everything in it seemed so crowded and precarious.

Yes, Mary's interest was in him; it wasn't in the shop. She'd have to have something besides the shop to have any meaningful existence.

If he divorced her she'd have no one to take her to concerts and plays. Dinner parties, her favorite recreation, would be out. None of their friends would invite her to come without him. Alone and divorced, she would be shunted into the miserable category of spinsters and widows who had to be invited to lunch instead of dinner.

He couldn't relegate Mary to such a life, though he felt sure that if he asked her for a divorce she'd give him one. She was so acquiescent and accommodating.

No, he wasn't going to humiliate her by asking for a divorce. She deserved something better from him than that.

If only he hadn't met Lettice on that business trip to Lexington. But how could he regret such a miracle? He had come alive only in the six weeks since he'd known Lettice. Life with Mary was ashes in comparison. Since he'd met Lettice he felt like a blind man who had been given sight. He might have been deaf all his life and was hearing for the first time. And the marvel was that Lettice loved him and was eager to marry him, and free to marry him.

And waiting.

And insisting.

He must concentrate on putting Mary out of the way. Surely a little accident could be arranged without too much trouble. The shop ought to be an ideal place, there in all that crowded junk. Among those heavy marble busts and chandeliers and andirons something from above or below could be used to dispatch his dear Mary to her celestial reward.

'Darling, you must tell your wife,' Lettice urged when they next met at their favorite hotel in Lexington. 'You've got to arrange for a divorce. You have to. You've got to tell her about us.'

Lettice's voice was so low and musical that John felt hypnotized.

But how could he tell Mary about Lettice?

John couldn't even rationalize Lettice's appeal to himself.

Instead of Mary's graciousness, Lettice had elegance. Lettice wasn't as pretty or as charming as Mary. But he couldn't resist her. In her presence he was an ardent, masterful lover; in Mary's presence he was a thoughtful, complaisant husband. With Lettice life would always be lived at the highest peak; nothing in his long years with Mary could approach the wonder he had known during his few meetings with Lettice. Lettice was earth, air, fire and water, the four elements; Mary was – no, he couldn't compare them. Anyway, what good was it to set their attractions off against each other?

Then, just as he was about to suggest to Lettice that they go to the bar, he saw Chet Fleming enter the hotel and walk across the lobby toward the desk. What was Chet Fleming doing in Lexington? But then anyone could be anywhere. That was the humiliating risk illicit lovers faced. They might be discovered anywhere, anytime. No place was secure for them. But Chet Fleming was the one person he wanted least to see, and the one who would make the most of encountering John with another woman. That blabbermouth would tell his wife and friends, his doctor, his grocer, his banker, his lawyer. Word would get back to Mary. Her heart would be broken. She deserved better than that.

John cowered beside Lettice. Chet dawdled at the desk. John couldn't be exposed like that any longer, a single glance around and Chet would see him and Lettice. John made an incoherent excuse, then sidled over to the newsstand where he hid behind a magazine until Chet had registered and had taken an elevator upstairs.

Anyway, they had escaped, but only barely.

John couldn't risk cheapening their attachment. He had to do something to make it permanent right away, but at the same time he didn't want to hurt Mary.

Thousands of people in the United States had gotten up that morning who would be dead before nightfall. Why couldn't his dear Mary be among them? Why couldn't she die without having to be murdered?

When John rejoined Lettice and tried to explain his panic, she was composed but concerned and emphatic.

'Darling, this incident only proves what I've been insisting. I said you'd have to tell your wife at once. We can't go on like this. Surely you understand.'

'Yes, dear, you're quite right. I'll do something as soon as I can.'

'You must do something immediately, darling.'

Oddly enough, Mary Johnson was in the same predicament as John Johnson. She had had no intention of falling in love. In fact, she thought she was in love with her husband. How naive she'd been before Kenneth came into her shop that morning asking whether she had a bust of Mozart. Of course she had a bust of Mozart; she had several busts of Mozart, not to mention Bach, Beethoven, Victor Hugo, Balzac, Shakespeare, George Washington and Goethe, in assorted sizes.

He had introduced himself. Customers didn't ordinarily introduce themselves, and she gave him her name in return, and then realized that he was the outstanding interior designer in town.

'Quite frankly,' he said, 'I wouldn't be caught dead with this bust of Mozart and it will ruin the room, but my client insists on having it. Do you mind if I see what else you have?'

She showed him all over the shop. Later she tried to recall the exact moment when they had fallen in love. He had spent all that first morning there; toward noon he seemed especially attracted to a small back room cluttered and crowded with chests of drawers. He reached for a drawer pull that came off in his hands, then he reached for her.

'What do you think you're doing?' she said. 'Goodness, suppose some customers come in.'

'Let them browse,' he said.

She couldn't believe that it had happened, but it had. Afterward, instead of being lonely when John went out of town on occasional business trips, she yearned for the time when he gave her his antiseptic peck of a kiss and told her he would be gone overnight.

The small back room jammed with the chests of drawers became Mary's and Kenneth's discreet rendezvous. They added a chaise longue.

One day a voice reached them there. They had been too engrossed to notice that anyone had approached.

'Mrs. Johnson, where are you? I'd like some service, please.'

Mary stumbled out from the dark to greet the customer. She tried to smoothe her mussed hair. She knew that her lipstick was smeared.

The customer was Mrs. Bryan, the most accomplished gossip in town. Mrs. Bryan would get word around that Mary Johnson was carrying on scandalously in her shop. John was sure to find out now.

Fortunately, Mrs. Bryan was preoccupied. She was in a Pennsylvania Dutch mood and wanted to see butter molds and dower chests.

It was a lucky escape, as Mary later told Kenneth. Kenneth refused to be reassured.

'I love you deeply,' he said. 'And honorably. I've reason to know you love me too. I'm damned tired of sneaking around. I'm not going to put up with it any longer. Do you understand? We've got to get married. Tell your husband you want a divorce.'

Kenneth kept talking about a divorce, as if a divorce was nothing at all – no harder to arrange than a dental appointment. How could she divorce a man who had been affectionate and kind and faithful for twenty years? How could she snatch happiness from him?

If only John would die. Why couldn't he have a heart attack? Every day thousands of men died from heart attacks. Why couldn't her darling John just drop dead? It would simplify everything.

Even the ringing of the telephone sounded angry, and when Mary answered it Kenneth, at the other end of the line, was in a rage.

'Damn it, Mary, this afternoon was ridiculous. It was insulting. I'm not skulking any more. I'm not hiding behind doors while you grapple around for butter molds to show customers. We've got to be married right away.'

'Yes, darling. Do be patient.'

'I've already been too patient. I'm not waiting any longer.'

She knew that he meant it. If she lost Kenneth life would end for her. She hadn't ever felt this way about John.

Dear John. How could she toss him aside? He was in the prime of life, he could live decades longer. All his existence was centred on her. He loved to give her pleasure. They had no friends except other married couples. John would have to lead a solitary life if she left him. He'd be odd man out without her; their friends would invite him to their homes because they were sorry for him. Poor, miserable John was what everyone would call him. He'd be better off dead, they'd say. He would neglect himself; he wouldn't eat regularly; he would have to live alone in some wretched furnished apartment. No, she mustn't condemn him to an existence like that.

Why had this madness with Kenneth started? Why had that foolish woman insisted on having a bust of Mozart in her music room? Why had Kenneth come to her shop in search of it when busts of Mozart were in every second-hand store on Broad Street and at much cheaper prices?

Yet she wouldn't have changed anything. Seconds with Kenneth were worth lifetimes with John.

Only one end was possible. She would have to think of a nice, quick efficient, unmessy way to get rid of John. And soon.

John had never seen Mary look as lovely as she did that night when he got home from his business trip. For one flicker of a second, life with her seemed enough. Then he thought of Lettice, and the thought stunned him into the belief that no act that brought them together could be criminal. He must get on with what he had to do. He must murder Mary in as gentlemanly a way as possible, and he must do it that very night. Meantime he would enjoy the wonderful dinner Mary had prepared for him. Common politeness demanded it, and anyhow he was ravenous.

Yet, he must get on with the murder just as soon as he

finished eating. It seemed a little heartless to be contriving a woman's death even as he ate her cheese cake, but he certainly didn't mean to be callous.

He didn't know just how he would murder Mary. Perhaps if he could get her into her shop, there in that corner where all the statuary was, he could manage something.

Mary smiled at him and handed him a cup of coffee.

'I thought you'd need lots of coffee, darling, after such a long drive.'

'Yes, dear, I do. Thank you.'

Just as he began to sip from his cup he glanced across the table at Mary. Her face had a peculiar expression. John was puzzled by it. They had been so close for so many years that she must be reading his mind. She must know what he was planning. Then she smiled; it was the glorious smile she had bestowed on him ever since their honeymoon. Everything was all right.

'Darling, excuse me for a minute,' she said. 'I just remembered something in the shop that I must see to. I'll be right back.'

She walked quickly out of the dining room and across the hall into the shop.

But she didn't come back right away as she'd promised. If she didn't return soon John's coffee would be cold. He took a sip or two, then decided to go to the shop to see what had delayed her.

She didn't hear him enter. He found her in the middle of the room where the chandeliers were blazing. Her back was turned toward him and she was sitting on an Empire sofa close to the statues on their stands. She was ambushed by the statues.

Good lord, it was as he had suspected. She had been reading his thoughts. Her shoulders heaved. She was sobbing. She knew that their life together was ending. Then he decided that she might be laughing. Her shoulders would be shaking like that if she were laughing to herself. Whatever she was doing, whether she sobbed or laughed, it was no time for him to speculate on her mood. This was too good a chance to miss. With her head bent over she would be directly in the path of the bust of Victor Hugo or Benjamin Franklin or whoever it was towering above her. John would have to topple it only slightly and it would hit her skull. It needed only the gentlest shove.

He shoved.

It was so simple.

Poor darling girl. Poor Mary.

But it was all for the best and he wouldn't ever blame himself for what he'd done. Still, he was startled that it had been so easy, and it had taken no time at all. He would have tried it weeks before if he had known that it could be done with so little trouble.

John was quite composed. He took one last affectionate glance at Mary and then went back to the dining room. He would drink his coffee and then telephone the doctor. No doubt the doctor would offer to notify the police since it was an accidental death. John wouldn't need to lie about anything except for one slight detail. He would have to say that some movement of Mary's must have caused the bust to fall.

His coffee was still warm. He drank it unhurriedly. He thought of Lettice. He ached for the luxury of telephoning her that their life together was now assured and that after a discreet interval they could be married. But he decided he had better not take any chances. He would delay calling Lettice.

He felt joyful yet calm. He couldn't remember having felt so relaxed. No doubt it came from the relief of having done what had to be done. He was even sleepy. He was sleepier than he had ever been. He must lie down on the livingroom couch. That was more urgent even than telephoning the doctor. But he couldn't wait to get to the couch. He laid his head on the dining table. His arms dangled.

None of Mary's and John's friends had any doubt about how the double tragedy had occurred. When they came to think of it, the shop had always been a booby trap, and that night Mary had tripped or stumbled and had toppled the statue onto her head. Then John had found her and grief had overwhelmed him. He realized he couldn't live without Mary, and his desperate sense of loss had driven him to dissolve enough sleeping tablets in his coffee to kill himself.

They all remembered so well how, in the middle of their last anniversary celebration, Mary and John had said they hoped they could die together. They really were the most devoted couple any of them had ever known. You could get sentimental just thinking about Mary and John, and to see them together was an inspiration. In a world of insecurity nothing was so heartening as their deep, steadfast love. It was sweet and touching that they had died on the same night, and exactly as they both had wanted.

Just a Minor Offense

by John Suter

They must have come up with their lights cut off, because I didn't know they were there until one of them shone his flash right behind me and said, 'All right. What seems to be the trouble?'

He caught me standing there like a knucklehead, with the spring-leaf in my hand, staring at the coins spilling out of the pay phone. There was silver all over the floor of the booth and the shelf under the phone. A coin or two hung pinched in the twisted metal.

I didn't turn around. I figured the flashlight would be right in my eyes, and I didn't want things to be worse than they were going to be. I just stood still, watching his big arm go up and his big hand tighten the light bulb overhead. He crowded into the phone booth, ramming me against the wall while he shut the door. The light came on.

He grunted as though he'd seen what he expected to see. 'Jackpot, huh? All right, kid, let's get outside and talk a little.'

He opened the door, and the light went out. I started to turn, when his flash came on again.

'Hold it. Don't move or do a thing.' He raised his voice. 'Andy, take that hamburger out of the bag and bring the bag over here.'

In a few seconds, I heard the car door slam and the other cop came up. The one who was keeping me pinned said to his buddy, 'Thanks. Junior, here, is gonna clean up his mess for the phone company.' He spoke to me. 'Turn around. Okay. Now, hand over that hunk of steel. Lay it here.'

A big hand came out in front of me, a handkerchief spread across the palm.

I laid the spring-leaf on the handkerchief. My prints would be on the metal. They sure had me cold.

'Look,' I said, 'I didn't do this. I just came in to phone, and –'

'Sure,' he said. His outline was big and bulky against the streetlight. 'They never do, not even when you catch 'em red-handed.'

'If you'll listen a minute –'

'The only thing I'll listen to is that money jingling in the bag. Get to it.'

I'd always been told that you don't argue with cops, and there were two of them, one of them bigger than I am. I closed up and began scooping up the nickels, dimes, and quarters. I took care not to miss any, not even a dime in a far corner, not even the stuff still hanging in the coinbox itself.

Finally, I straightened and turned around, passing over the bag.

'All right, officer,' I said, as evenly as I could. 'I've done what you wanted me to. If you'll listen a minute, I'll tell you something that'll prove I didn't do it.'

'You tryin' to tell me I didn't see what I saw?'

The other cop, the one he'd called Andy, cut in. His tone was a little quieter. 'Let's give him a minute, Mike. It looks better when we come in with all the angles accounted for. We don't want something flying up and hitting us in the face later.'

The big one was quiet for a second. 'Okay,' he said finally. 'Let's hear it.'

'It's this way,' I said, trying to keep the relief out of my voice. 'I've been out with three other guys. I'll give you their names –'

'Later.'

'I'd just taken the last one home, and I started across the park when the car pooped out on me. Right around the bend up there. It's my Dad's car. I can't get it started – acts like there's dirt in the needle-valve. Well, you know what happens if you leave a car on the street, especially in the park. It gets hauled in, and it costs you to bail it out. So I thought I'd better phone Dad, then call Brown's Garage.'

'And you didn't have the change, so you thought you'd just help yourself to some –'

This Andy cut in again. 'If he'd done that, it might knock out the phone, Mike. Let him finish.'

I went on: 'When I came in sight of the booth, I thought I saw somebody step out and disappear, but I wasn't sure. And when I got here, it was the way you saw it. The spring-leaf was on the shelf. Like a meathead, I picked it up. Then you came along. And that's it.'

The other cop said, 'It wouldn't hurt to check out this thing about the car. Only take a few minutes. Which way is it, kid?'

I pointed. 'Over that way, half a block. It's a '57 Chevvy.'

The big one took me by the arm.

'Let's go.'

I walked out to the cruiser with them. They put me in front beside Andy, the driver. Mike got in behind me. As we came out under the streetlight, I saw that he had a sort of blocky face, pitted here and there. His buddy was shorter, thinner, with sandy eyebrows and a sharp nose.

We were over by the Chevvy almost before I got settled. We pulled up alongside. Andy held out a hand. 'The keys.'

I gave them to him. 'To start it, you –'

'I know,' he said, slipping from behind the wheel.

He went and turned the starter of the Chevvy over two or three times, then got out and lifted the hood. He flashed his light at the motor for a minute, then closed the hood and came back.

'It's like he says.' He returned the keys.

I felt better. I was pretty sure they'd check me, but you can't count on dirt. Sometimes it works loose in a valve when you don't think it can.

Mike cleared his throat. 'So how does this let him off the hook?'

Andy drummed on the wheel. 'He'd never use that buggy for a getaway the way it is. Incidentally, what's your name, kid?'

'David Carey.'

'Your father's name?'

'Samuel E. Carey.'

Andy nodded. 'The registration was in that name. Let me see your driver's license.'

I handed it over. He glanced at it and gave it back. 'It checks.'

'Sure,' I said. 'It's on the level, all the way. Look, I've given it to you straight. Why don't you let me go, then hunt out this other guy? I still have to call home, and I'd better phone the garage.'

Mike hefted the bag of money. 'How do we know you're not in Sergeant Jensen's file on a couple of counts already?'

'I'm not. I've never been in trouble in my life. I'm not wanting to start now.'

Andy said, 'I'm not out to make it rough for anybody, kid. Neither one of us is. But we'd be pretty poor cops if we didn't take you in. They probably won't do a thing but they like to be the ones to make the decisions.'

'But the car –'

'Don't worry about the car. If you're clean, we'll see you don't get bit for something you couldn't help.'

He moved the stick over to *Drive*, and we took off.

We were at the station in less than ten minutes. They took me into a room with several straightback chairs around the walls, a worn hardwood floor, and a cop behind a desk who seemed to match the room. He had thin brown hair and a hatchet face. I found out that he was the night sergeant, Driscoll.

He stared at me poker-faced and pulled out some kind of form, then started asking questions. When he got to my age and I said, 'Sixteen,' he looked at Mike.

Then he said, 'Better call his family and get 'em down here. What's he done?'

'Looks like he smashed a pay phone for the chicken feed. Here.' Mike plunked down the bag.

Driscoll's face didn't change a bit. 'They won't need a lawyer, then. His old man'll be enough.'

Mike picked up the phone. 'What's the number, kid?'

I turned to Sergeant Driscoll. 'You're going to book me?'

'It has to go on the record, son. They brought you in. I haven't heard it all yet. But whatever comes in here, it goes down on the sheet.'

I didn't say anything, trying to figure a way to keep my name clean. Driscoll prodded me again. 'If you didn't do it, it can't count against you. You're sixteen. We're not in the habit of blabbing all over town who the kids are who come in here. Now let's get on with this. There's enough other things to keep me more than busy.'

Andy, who was standing beside me, dropped a match into an ashtray on the desk. 'What's going on?'

'Some kind of fight started five minutes ago,' Sergeant Driscoll said, 'over near Locust and Third. And some girl's family called in around that same time to say their kid's overdue getting home – not with her friends, not in the hospital. Out parked somewhere, probably.' He looked at me. 'Her name's Joyce Reynolds. Know her?'

'I know who she is. She's a year ahead of me in school.'

'Who's she go with?'

'I hear she goes steady with Herb Blackwood.'

He looked at a note pad. 'That one hasn't seen her – he says.'

Andy asked idly, 'Any of these kid gangs breaking and entering tonight?'

'No reports. Well – back to business.' He looked at Andy, then at Mike. 'Tell me about his one.'

In about half an hour, Dad came down. He didn't storm in, like some of the old boys you see on TV, and he didn't come in, hat in hand, to let them walk all over him. He just looked at me, then at Driscoll (the other two had gone back to work) and said, 'The officer who called said Dave was caught breaking into a pay phone.'

The sergeant tapped the paper with his pen. 'That's the way it looks, Mr. Carey. There's some business about your car that might be in his favor.'

'What do you want us to do?'

Us.

The sergeant was matter-of-fact. 'We'll turn this report over to Sergeant Jensen, of Juvenile, and let him check it out. Right now, we'll release the boy in your custody. I suggest that he comes back here tomorrow to talk to Sergeant Jensen.'

'He'll be here. What time?'

Driscoll considered. 'It'll take a little time. No sense in making him miss school. Say, about four o'clock.'

'He'll be here at four. Shall I come too?'

'As you like. Jensen doesn't chew 'em up and spit 'em out in little pieces. Sometimes it works out better when the kid's alone. Why not leave it to him?'

'All right.' Dad turned and looked at me. 'Well – you don't seem to be the worse for wear. But your mother's liable to say something about the dirt on your knees. How'd that happen?'

I brushed at my pants. It didn't brush off too well. 'I guess I got it kneeling in that booth picking up the money.'

Driscoll had a faint frown on his face. His voice had a slight rasp. 'He wasn't roughed up, if that's what you're getting at.' He made a note on the paper in front of him.

Dad seems pretty average sometimes, but he wasn't so average just then. His eyes glinted, and I almost thought his hair bristled. 'Nobody *will* bring it up if it's not necessary. But *somebody* will drag it out into the open if it *is* necessary.'

He turned back to me. 'Now, let's hear about the car, so we can straighten that part out and go home.'

In the morning, school was about as usual, but toward the end of lunch period Jack Burton stopped me in the hall. He halfway hung that head of his with the peroxided widow's peak, so that he was looking up, a habit of his. His eyes looked a little worried.

'I'm glad you called me, even if it was awful early in the morning. The cops talked to me, the way you said they would.'

I kept up a front of confidence. Better not scare my best witness. 'You told 'em straight about what time I left you, I hope? You live right by the park, and they'll be able to figure that I was telling the whole truth about the car and all.'

He stuck his thumbs in the corners of his pants pockets. 'Sure. We gotta stick together. I know that. Look, Dave, when you let me out, did you see any sign of Joyce Reynolds?'

'Joyce Reynolds? No. How come?'

'She lives the second house from me, remember? She's missing.'

'I heard them mention it last night. What's this got to do with you?'

'She was out with Tom Fisher. Mad at Herb Blackwood, I hear, and had this date with Tom, instead. Tom says he brought her home around 12:15, close to the time you let me out. He didn't see her to the door – what a birdbrain! – and he doesn't know whether she got in or not. She didn't. So where'd she get to? The cops asked me, did I see her? I had to tell 'em no.'

'Well, I didn't either,' I said. 'I have enough to do, trying to get out from under this phone business. You'll stick with me?'

He grinned quickly. 'Beat the phony rap? I'll do what I can.'

'Stick to the truth, that's all. Stick to the truth.'

I went down alone to Police Headquarters to see Sergeant Jensen at four o'clock, the time they'd set. Mom tried to get Dad to go along, but he thought it over and said I'd have to learn to face things alone more often now. He'd checked on Jensen and I'd get a fair break.

Jensen's office wasn't much more than a desk, three chairs, and a lot of filing cabinets. The sergeant was a short cop, looking something like Franchot Tone, with a good bit of gray in his hair. He seemed sort of good-natured, but when he looked at me with those hazel eyes of his, I felt he'd known me all of my life, that he knew everything about me.

He waved me to a chair beside his desk and sat looking at me without talking for a minute or two. Finally, he decided to open up.

'David Carey. I've never run into you before, Dave.'

'It's not my fault that you have this time, Sergeant.'

'I wonder how you mean that,' he said quietly.

This put me off-balance a little. Getting double meanings out of what I'd said, when I'd hardly opened my mouth.

'All I mean is I've always tried to keep out of things that cause trouble. And here things have turned on me, and I get pulled in for something I didn't do.'

'There're a lot of kids breaking and entering these days who aren't getting pulled in. For all we know, you might be a member of one gang we're after. You see?' Jensen fingered some papers. 'I have a number of reports on you, Dave. Good reports. That's in your favor. Of course,' he said with a little more bite in his tone, 'we had a kid in here about three months ago just your age. What they called a "model boy". He decided to steal a car and did – but he was caught.'

I kept quiet.

'That boy, and these vandals we haven't caught yet, think that they don't amount to anything if they're being normal citizens. If they're not leaders, or something, they have to prove themselves some other way. Maybe that could be you. Could it?'

I tried to figure out what to say.

He studied me. 'Dave, if you have anything at all to say about this affair that you haven't told us, I'd advise you to tell us now. It'll make things a lot easier if we decide to carry this further.'

'Sergeant, I don't know what you want me to say, but all I can tell you is I didn't do it. It doesn't matter how bad it looks.'

He shrugged. 'All right.' He looked at those papers again. 'Against you is the fact that you were caught in a phone booth with the box pried open and money all over the place. You had an automobile spring-leaf in your hand. Your fingerprints were on the metal. *They were also on the phone box.* What about that?'

In spite of myself, I began to sweat some. 'I put my hands on the box when they asked me to gather up all the money. Some of it was still in the box. I couldn't help it. Did they mention that?'

He made a note. 'No. I'll verify it.'

'Did you find any other prints on that spring-leaf?'

'Yes, but they weren't any good. Yours blurred them.'

'Isn't that in my favor?'

He compressed his lips briefly. 'It could be. It could also be that you just picked up that hunk of steel somewhere, knowing that somebody else's prints would be on it.'

'Sergeant,' I said, trying to get through to him, 'if that's the case, why'd I be fool enough to use the thing barehanded? Why should I want to put my own prints on it?'

His answer was mild. 'It doesn't add up. Now – in your favor. Your story about the boys you were out with checks. We talked to them all, and you did just what you said. You did seem to be heading back across the park after you let the Burton kid out.'

'And the car – doesn't that help?'

He nodded. 'The car. Yes. We called the garage. There was dirt in the needle-valve as you guessed. The officers who brought you in verify that it wouldn't start. All of this, plus good character references, add up in your favor. The question now is, do these things weigh more than our finding you practically in the act?'

'But, Sergeant,' I said, 'the phone company didn't lose any money. All they have to do is fix the phone. It means a lot to me to keep my name clean. Why don't you give me the benefit of the doubt?'

His eyes became cold all of a sudden. 'The phone company helps to pay my salary, the same as everybody else does. Any decisions I make had better be good ones, no matter who's involved.'

He just sat there and let me fidget. Finally, he spoke in a mild voice again.

'Let's talk about something else for a minute. Do you know a Joyce Reynolds?'

'Some. I see her around school. She's a Senior, I'm a Junior.'

'See her last night?'

'No, I hear she's missing.'

He looked at me directly again. 'Yes. You could have seen her.' It was a flat statement, but it sounded almost accusing.

He had me worried. 'She lives near Jack Burton,' I said, 'sure, but I didn't see her last night.'

He turned his attention to the tips of his fingers. 'What's she like?'

'I don't know too much about her, except in a general way. About five feet four, real black hair, not built quite as much as some – but you might look twice. She's been steadying with Herb Blackwood, but maybe that's over. I hear she was out with Tom Fisher last night.'

He said casually, 'I understand you're a little interested yourself.'

I got sort of hot. Jack Burton must have – 'Who says?'

'Somebody.'

'Well, you tell somebody he doesn't know what he's talking about! Look, she's a Senior, and Senior girls hardly ever look at Junior boys. Besides, she's going steady.'

'You go steady?'

'No.'

He considered his notes. 'You're what? Sixteen? Then it may be understandable that you don't go steady. Run around with three or four other boys, no girls? The way it was last night?'

'Usually.'

'But Joyce Reynolds – Did you ever make any passes?'

I felt like squirming, but I sat still. 'She's about a year older than I am. Why should I?'

'Why not?'

'I'd seem like a kid to her. Don't you get it?'

He shrugged. 'I didn't say she'd reciprocate – though that's not impossible, either.'

I imagine he could tell that I was simmering, the way my voice must have sounded. 'Sergeant, why're we beating in time on this? What's it got to do with a busted pay phone?'

He was stiff-faced when he answered. 'They found Joyce Reynolds' body this morning. In the park, in a crevice under some big rocks. Not too far from that phone booth where they picked you up.'

I couldn't say a thing.

'She was strangled and beaten,' he went on. 'Maybe somebody made a pass and got mad when he didn't get anywhere. Maybe it was somebody she looked on as sort of a kid. Maybe she even laughed at him when he got serious. *How about it?*'

I finally found my voice. 'Me? First you say I wreck a pay phone, then you say I killed Joyce Reynolds. What am I supposed to be – a one-man crime wave?'

'It's not so crazy as you might think, boy.'

'Me? Why me?' I almost yelled. 'How do you know Herb Blackwood wasn't hanging around waiting for her when Tom Fisher brought her home? How do you know Tom even brought her home? How about Jack Burton? All that stuff you said about me you could say it about him – and he lives close to her house. How do you know he didn't walk her over to the park after I left him? What time was she killed, anyway?'

Jensen looked away. 'This much I'll give you: we don't know yet.'

'Then –'

He stared coldly at me. 'I'll tell you what could have happened in your case. Not Fisher's, Blackwood's, or Burton's case. Yours. You pick up this girl and drive to the park. You make a pass, but you get nowhere. You get mad and slug her, then you strangle her. You try to hide the body – temporarily, anyway. Then you go to leave – and you can't start the car. You begin to sweat. That car is close to the body. It can tie you to what you've done. So you decide to fake a smash on that pay phone, maybe you even hang around until you're sure of being picked up. This is to fix our attention on you for a minor offense, instead of murder. Who'd be robbing a phone if he'd just committed murder? A neat trick, if somebody doesn't see through it. Now that's the case we can build against you. *Can you prove otherwise?*'

My brain had been busy while he was piling things on. 'Sergeant, you'd better be thinking about those others. Listen, if I did what you just said, where'd that spring-leaf come from? The one that was used on the phone?'

'How should I know?'

'If I smashed that phone to draw attention away from Joyce, I'd have to get that hunk of steel in a hurry, wouldn't I? You know how clean they keep the park. Where'd that leaf come from?'

'Out of the trunk of your car. Where else?'

I snorted. 'Are you kidding? You take a look in that trunk, the way Dad keeps it. You could eat off the floor. All that're in it are the spare tire, jack, and lug wrench. Chains in the winter, not now.'

Jensen looked thoughtful. 'What kind of tires have you?'

'Tubeless.'

'Okay. With inner tubes, a lot of drivers used to carry a spring-leaf to pry the tire off the rim if they fixed a flat themselves. That doesn't sound likely here.'

He shut up and thought. Then he said, 'All the same, I'm going to check with your Dad about that spring-leaf. In the meantime, I guess we'd better have you tell me about this Jack Burton.'

He pulled some papers over in front of him.

'Where shall I start?' I asked, feeling easier.

He didn't answer. He was staring at two papers lying next to each other. He studied one, then the other. Finally, he looked up.

'You and Jack Burton run around with several other boys quite a bit?'

'That's right.'

'Sort of a gang?'

'I wouldn't call it that, Sergeant. You know how that sounds nowadays. Why do you always –'

'Look at the bad side? I'll tell you why, Carey. You don't drive your Dad's car every night. I don't think he'd let you. So, if he keeps the trunk so clean, the spring-leaf wouldn't be in it all the time. Why not? You know – a spring-leaf makes a pretty good jimmy, especially if the end's filed down. I'll have to look at your little toy to see about that. Now, if your gang had been breaking and entering, you'd have a spring-leaf with you on certain nights, all right.'

I pointed to the papers on his desk. 'I suppose it says so in there.'

He tapped them. 'Oh, no. It doesn't say a word about that. But one of them says that whoever tried to shove Joyce Reynolds' body under those rocks had to kneel to do it. The other report has a note on it that your father was concerned about some dirt on the knees of your pants when they brought you in last night.'

He stood up suddenly. 'Now, I wonder if we went out to your house and brought back those pants for the lab to test, would they find the same kind of dirt as that by the rocks?'

I couldn't say a thing. The pants hadn't gone to the cleaner's. And I knew where the dirt on the knees came from.

The Long Terrible Day

by Charlotte Edwards

The long terrible day started at exactly eight o'clock. The siren hooted from the paper mill and the chimes of the church on Main Street clanged in the steeple, telling the time as they always did.

Ernie's chair scraped as he pushed it back. Clearing his throat, he said, 'Time to be off,' which he announced every workday morning.

I sat at the table in the breakfast nook, a cup of coffee halfway to my lips. The paper was spread before me, but my eyes were on my husband.

What I had just seen in the middle of the front page formed an after-image that fitted over his features; fitted perfectly, neatly, in every detail – except the mustache, crewcut and twenty extra pounds.

Ernie leaned across the table and patted four-year-old Steve on the head. 'Mind Mama,' he commanded.

Steve nodded, his mouth too full to answer.

Ernie walked around in back of me, his steps heavy and sure, to the high chair. 'Daddy's girl be good today,' he coaxed.

Liz chortled and offered him a spoon of oatmeal from which the overload dropped rhythmically.

'Some kid,' Ernie gloated, then moved behind my chair. His hand lay, heavy as his footsteps, warm and sure, on my shoulder. 'You're going to spill your coffee.' Large, broad-shouldered, powerful, he looked down at me.

I smiled up at him.

Eyes, amber, green-flecked. Small scar dividing the right eyebrow, tilting it up.

32 *The Long Terrible Day*

I lowered my gaze, set the coffee cup back in the saucer, picked up the paper. 'Ernie,' I said, 'there's the craziest thing here –'

He didn't look, but bent to kiss me. His lips were warm and gentle. His mustache tickled a moment against my mouth and was gone – the red mustache, small, neatly clipped, almost rusty; grown the first year of our marriage.

'Gotta rush, kid,' he said. 'Big day. Save it, eh?'

'But it will only take –'

He rumpled my hair, then he was gone.

I was alone in the house with my children. The long terrible day was fifteen minutes old – only I didn't know it was going to be a long terrible day, not then.

He'd have gotten a bounce out of it. Ernie could take a joke, even when it was on him – if he wasn't upset, wasn't angry, wasn't hurt.

I stood up abruptly. Maybe he was still upset about last night. Maybe that's why he wanted to hurry. I shook my head. Ernie didn't have to have a reason for rushing to work, for cat's sake. He did that often.

I began to clear the table, ignoring the paper, awkwardly folded there beside my plate. I rinsed the dishes carefully and wiped around Steve's comic book, around the *Daily Express*, leaving them like two puddles to be mopped up later. I pulled Liz from the high chair, washed the accumulated debris from around the smiling mouth, and carried her into the living-room, setting her carefully in the playpen, handing her an assortment of soft toys.

For a moment then, I stood still, as if waiting for something. As if it needed only physical quiet to start it in motion, a hammer, a deep slow, heavy-swinging hammer, started pounding inside the cave of my left ribs. Thud, bong, thud, boom, it picked up tempo faster and faster, heavier, louder. When it filled my ears, filled the neat small room, the word came out, sharp, sudden. 'No!'

The hammer slowed almost to a stop. 'All I have to do,' I said to myself, 'is go back to the kitchen and pick up the paper. Look at the drawing again, carefully, don't snatch impressions.'

Shame began to crawl through me. I hated women who checked for lipstick, notes, phone numbers; suspicious, untrusting wives.

With sudden determination I walked briskly to the kitchen, but instead of picking up the paper, I found myself washing the dishes. Sounds came remotely: Liz gibbering, Steve rumbling, the roar of cars on the freeway.

'I *will* look.' I went to the table, propelled by my own loud words. The headline was louder than my voice in its grim declaration:

GIRL FOUND BLUDGEONED TO DEATH ON GOLF COURSE

'The body of Marylee Adams, 18, was discovered early this morning, head gashed by repeated heavy blows, in bushes by the 16th hole of the Arnaughton Golf Course. There was no sign of the murder weapon.

Miss Adams, who lived at 1617 Central Street with her mother, had many suitors, according to the information so far obtained.

Police Chief J. Hampton Jones remarked upon the similarity of this crime and that of the killing of one Sandra Hims, also 18, on a public golf course in Kansas City about five years ago. At that time the murder weapon was found, a heavy car jack.

The drawing (at right) was forwarded from that city, and is based on a witness' description of the suspect, the man with whom Miss Hims was last seen leaving a Kansas City bar.'

My eyes pulled from the words, fastened on the four-column picture centred on the page. The hammering started again.

I began at the wavy hair, growing clean and straight above the broad forehead, followed the line of the nose with its rounded tip, the cheeks that hollowed in a little just above the square chin. I traced the thin, determined curves of the mouth.

Heat rose in me until I was scorched with panic. I stared, horror blazing through me, at the face of Ernie, my husband,

34   *The Long Terrible Day*

staring back at me from the printed page of the *Daily Express*. Except for the mustache, the crewcut, and the twenty extra pounds, it was Ernie as I first knew him, when I first met him.

The chimes from the church on Main Street spoke out nine times.

I stared out of the window at the two orange trees showing in the yard. Ernie took good care of the trees.

The picture was a thing to laugh at, and over, with Ernie, a product of an artist's imagination five years ago. So what? Nobody else would notice except a fantasy-ridden, silly wife. Ernie'd had a mustache ever since we came here, and extra flesh and short hair. Talk about lipstick-crazy wives!

'You done any killin' lately?' I could hear Jim, Ernie's boss, roar; Jim, who wouldn't take a mint from Ernie.

Everybody loves Ernie – kids, dogs, men, old ladies, neighbors. No one would believe it for a moment.

I love him and I don't believe it for a moment, either. You don't love a man who could smash a girl to death. You'd know about a thing like that. It wouldn't be in a gentle, quiet man like Ernie. When things close in on him, he just gets up and walks out. A couple hours of walking around and he's back – sweet, trouble forgotten – like last night.

I closed my eyes and leaned forward. The chair squeaked, like the squeak I'd heard during the night and had just barely roused to notice.

When was that? What hour? What time?

Eighteen is just beginning to live. Was Marylee Adams blonde? Was her hair freshly set in rollers and pin curls, the way kids go around, and a scarf?

Eighteen – I was eighteen five years ago when I first met Ernie, first saw his hands, square and strong and clean. He didn't work in a garage then. He was dapper and a bachelor, and he came to the door of my mother's house selling appliances.

Mama liked him at once, and when Papa came home from his sales trip, he and Ernie talked half the night and ate nearly a whole cake, baked by me with love. Yes, it was love, even that first week.

Every weekend for over two months he came to the white house in the small town, and Sunday evening came too soon.

'I don't like to say goodbye to you. I don't like going back to the city anymore,' Ernie would say.

Then one Saturday he came, breathless in his quiet way. 'This man in California advertised in the city paper, a good steady job in a garage. I wrote him, and he called clear across country – and hired me!'

That week we were married. On the train, Ernie was already sprouting the mustache above his firm upper lip.

Eighteen – five years ago – the white house was left behind, the city left behind. The city; what city?

Did she have rollers, and pin curls? Oh, it would hurt worse with pin curls, all those little steel clips ground into the bones of her head...

Like the lost morning hour, I had no recollection of leaving the house, of starting the old jalopy which ran like new because of Ernie's skill. Liz was beside me. Steve stood in back, eager, talking. I started to make a grocery list in my mind.

Bread, margarine, the city, eggs, cereal, what city, shortening, Kansas City. That's the city. Kansas City, sugar – twenty-five miles from the white house and Mama and Papa –

Steve began to count the bongs in the steeple. Ten o'clock, two hours since eight. 'Eight – nine – ten,' Steve said it for me.

The doors of the supermarket flashed open in that miraculous way that intrigued Steve.

I walked through, lopsided, to hold Liz's hand. The store was so bright I felt as if I'd emerged from a tunnel. The normalcy, the bustle, the clang of registers and rustle of bags slowly oozed into me.

Sorting, pricing, watching the basket pile high behind Liz, the displays were walls protecting me from the morning, the paper awkwardly folded over on the kitchen table.

There was a bad moment at the meat counter.

'Round for Swiss?' I asked.

The butcher nodded. 'Okay, Mrs. Cochran. Pounded like usual?'

'Like usual.'

I stared into the big mirror lining the wall behind the butcher: like usual, short brown hair, brown, seemingly untroubled eyes; typical young mother, typical week's shopping.

Then, beside my reflection an arm rose. In the hand was a hammer-hatchet. It went up. It came down with a dull thud. Up, down, up, down – BLUDGEON.

'That's enough, Peppy,' I called sharply.

The arm stopped. 'Heck, it ain't pounded half as much –' He shrugged, wrapped the gummy red meat in thick white paper, wrote red numerals on it, and shoved it toward me.

It took all my self-control to pick up the package.

At the cheese case Jim's wife called to me. 'See you tonight.'

'Tonight, Eloise?'

'Pot luck, remember?'

Every other Friday we got together with seven other couples. Eloise's house was the meeting place this time.

'I'm not sure. Baby-sitter trouble –'

'Bring 'em along. Tuck 'em in.'

I moved toward the checkout counter. 'Ernie wouldn't like –'

Eloise laughed. 'Ernie likes whatever you want.'

I swallowed. It hurt. The truth hurts.

What he couldn't buy, Ernie made up for in effort, like feeding the kids on Sunday, emptying the rubbish, scrubbing the kitchen. And bigger things, like not being a bachelor in a good-looking suit anymore, but wearing coveralls, for all the greasy dirty work he did. And the hard work was for me, wasn't it?

Or was it – my mind talked straight at me – because a well-dressed salesman with amber eyes and curly hair couldn't be so easily traced if he were a garage mechanic in a city a couple of thousand miles away?

I looked for Steve at the checkout. He was sitting on the magazines, doubled over a comic book. My eyes slid from him and lighted on the paper stand.

BLUDGEONED yammered out at me. Ernie's five-years-ago face yammered out at me, the cashiers, Eloise – I gripped the counter edge.

Eloise's arm went around me. 'Kid, you're white. What's the matter? You scared? She laughed. 'That guy's five hundred miles away by this time, honey.'

I pulled myself together, said, 'I'm all right. It's really nothing.'

I followed the boy with the carry-out basket. The sun hit me without heat. Funny, the market had seemed so bright. Now the market was a tunnel, and the outdoors brazen.

'You want these in the trunk, ma'am?'

I nodded.

'Then I gotta have the keys.'

I pulled out my case and walked to the back of the car. I inserted the round key, noticing impersonally that my hand shook. I turned the key. The boy reached over to lift the trunk lid, then transferred the cartons. I lifted my arm to bring the trunk lid down.

Suddenly, my hand was halted. My heart was halted. Even with the cartons, the trunk looked – different, not right.

I stared at the boxes, at the spare tire, waiting for it to hit me, to know what was missing from the rear trunk of the jalopy.

I stared, seeing where it should be. I tried desperately to see it there. I leaned forward, finally, and pushed the heavy cartons aside, one knee on the back bumper to put myself closer. I peered into the corners and felt behind the spare.

The car jack was gone! The heavy, solid old jack that Ernie insisted should be there because the tires were recapped was gone.

Roars hit against me, bruising and sharp. Eleven of them bounced and hurt before they faded. I was pulling into our driveway before I realized they weren't roars at all, but the chimes of the church steeple striking the hour before noon.

All right, so the morning was almost gone. See, world? I'd washed the dishes and done the shopping. Now I'd burn the rubbish. The *Daily Express* on the table would catch quickly, burn the crazy ideas, the weird wicked thoughts; ashes and dust – and Marylee Adams was pretty as a picture.

I got my scissors from the sink drawer and sat down at the kitchen table. Carefully I cut out the front piece from the *Express*, picked up my purse from the drainboard, folded the clipping into a tidy square and tucked it into the zippered compartment. Then I crunched up the paper, put it on the top of the wastebasket and carried it to the back of the yard. I emptied the basket and struck a match. I was right. The *Daily Express* burned fast and set everything else on fire – but it burned away no evil thoughts.

As I went through the kitchen door the phone rang.

'Hello,' I heard a tinny voice but a close voice. 'That you, Sara?'

For a moment too sheer to hold, comfort oozed into me. 'Ernie?'

'I been ringing all morning.' He sounded worried.

'I went shopping.'

'Oh. You still mad? About last night?'

That depends, I thought calmly, on what happened last night. 'No. Why?'

He hesitated. 'You seemed so – kind of funny this morning.'

'Funny?'

'You still seem funny.' He sounded strange this time; on guard, yet prying.

'I'm all right.'

'Look, Sara,' he spurted, 'I took a walk is all. Got that? Sure, I was sore. So I took a walk.'

I held up my hand and studied it. 'A long walk?'

I could hear him breathe before his answer. 'Pretty long. You were asleep when –'

'I know.'

'Weren't you?'

I thought about that. 'Sort of – dozing.'

'Oh, I wish –'
'Why?'
'Never mind. You still sound funny. Look, I forgot my lunch, I have to work right through. I'm – I'm doing a paint job on old Tinsdale's car –'

'I'm sorry.' I was. 'I forgot to fix your lunch.' There *was* an hour then, before eight o'clock. 'Then I sat down to look at the paper –' I bit my lip, hard.

'What was that about the paper?' His voice was harsh, louder.

'Nothing.'

'Jim just rolled a cart through here. What was –'

'I'm sorry –'

'Well, look, could you bring it down to me? Like I said –'

'I heard you.'

Could I bring it down? Could I talk to him, with the square of paper in my purse and mind, and sound like Sara Cochran, the mother of his children, the wife of his bosom?

'Something is the matter.' He slowed his words. 'I think you better come on down here.'

'The kids –'

'I want to see you, Sara.' Ernie had never spoken like that; flat, in command.

I hung up slowly, slowly, cutting off his tone.

The phone rang again instantly.

'You hung up. Why?'

I grabbed for breath. 'Because I wanted to fix your lunch, silly.'

He grunted. 'Well, say, the other thing. Last night – you know when I took that walk – I well, I stopped in here. Thought I'd maybe try to mix the paint for Tinsdale –'

'Yes?' Oh please, no, not that!

'Well, I got a few spots on my gray slacks. Jim's all set for the shin-dig.' He made a funny sound. 'You know me. One-pants Cochran. Be a good kid and clean those spots out for me, will you?'

'All right.'

'And, Sara –'

'Yes?'

'If it's too much trouble – I'll ask somebody to bring me a hamburg.'

'You sure that's all right?' Calm and easy now. Get ready for the question. 'I've got a washing started – That sounds good, Sara.

'Sure, it's okay. Just that you were –'

'Funny, I know. Well, I'm not now.'

'Good. I'll see you tonight. And remember the gray pants, eh?'

'I'll remember, Ernie.' Now! Ask it now and fast. 'Ernie?'

'Yes?'

'Old Man Tinsdale? What color's he having you paint his car?'

Ernie did laugh this time, short. 'Bright red. Isn't that a howl?' He hung up.

I walked steadily back into the bedroom and opened the closet door. Ernie's slacks were on a hanger. I carried them, not glancing down, into the kitchen, to the window, to the brightest light, I held them out, letting the sun touch them shrewdly to be certain.

They were spotted all right, small spots, but a lot of them. Maybe Old Man Tinsdale's car was supposed to be bright red – but the paint didn't hold up on flannel. All those little spots were brown, rusty brown.

All hell broke loose suddenly, inside and outside of me. The noon whistle shrieked, Liz began to cry, Steve slammed into the house. The room, the house, reverberated with the noise.

But the biggest sound, the loudest yell, the highest whistle, came from inside myself, a noise that grew and grew and tore me apart.

Ernie Cochran, my husband, was a murderer!

When you are afraid something is true and you fight off the knowledge with everything in you, and when at last the proof of the truth seems indisputable, a stillness comes. I knew that stillness. It lasted until I had the kids in for their naps and bent to kiss them.

That was a mistake. That pushed the first tickle of the knife into the shock. These wonderful children – with a murderer for a father?

If he is, part of me staunchly cried. *If. If.*

I shut the door and went into the living-room to the little desk. The morning, I decided, was one segment of a continued play. The new hours, they would be the next installment.

What then?

I unzipped the compartment of my purse in the kitchen and pulled out the clipping.

How could I doubt it? There before my eyes?

I was, I knew, dodging a decision. 'Accessory after the fact,' came neatly to my mind. What do you do when you believe your husband is a murderer and nobody else suspects it?

Suppose nobody ever suspects it? My heart leaped with a strange looseness, a relief. Suppose you just go on, and every morning he leaves and every night he comes home to you and nobody ever dreams that Ernie Cochran has battered and crumpled and shattered and crushed – everybody loves Ernie.

The looseness tightened into a sudden knot. What if he does it again?

I went to the phone, compelled. I dialed quickly. After what seemed hours the voice came, heavy and remote.

'Police department.'

'Homicide,' I heard.

The voice lost its casualness. 'Homicide? Lady, you mean murder?'

'I mean murder.' Who said that in that strange easy way? Not Mrs. Cochran. Not about Mr. Cochran.

'Just a minute.'

In an office somewhere in the heart of the city men were moving and stirring, maybe pounding from door to door, asking and demanding, trying to get a clue.

My eyes landed on the gray flannel slacks, folded over the back of the kitchen chair. Come to the phone and I'll give you a clue, I thought, a little wild with the waiting, the hum in the line going right into my ear and brain.

'Sergeant Anderson speaking.' It was a new intense voice. 'Homicide.'

'I –' I began. 'I –' I swallowed. I lifted my head from the dial that seemed to be going around and around of its own free will. 'I want –' I swung my glance toward the door.

Ernie stood there. His shoulders seemed to fill the entire doorway, like Goliath, like Samson. His eyes looked all green, not amber and flecked. His mouth, under the mustache, was tight and small.

'Lady,' the sergeant's voice came again. 'Hey, lady –'

I felt the receiver slip from my hand and knew vaguely that I was slipping with it. All the way down to the floor into unconsciousness, my eyes were tied to Ernie's. I took them with me into the blackness – his eyes – and the simple unadorned sound of the church bell tolling a single note.

For what seemed an eternity I tried to climb up a black velvet ladder which sagged. It was unutterably difficult, but I had to try. Somewhere at the top a voice insisted, commanded, cajoled. Then, flashingly, the velvet was torn, the voice was loud, and all was bright. Ernie's face was so close to mine I could see the pores of his tanned skin. His arms were locked around me, holding me tight against the bed.

Relief filled my chest and eyes, and tears rolled down my cheeks. 'A nightmare,' I babbled. 'Just a bad dream. Oh, Ernie – honey – I dreamed that you – that you –' I looked at his eyes then. It was no nightmare.

'I never knew you to pass out like that before,' he said thoughtfully, his hands urgent on my shoulders. I felt the shudder begin where his fingers lay, and travel, secret and sick, all the way down my body to my toes.

'You're shivering. On a day like this.' He got up. 'You lie still. I'm going to call the doctor.'

Let him, the voice inside said quickly. The doctor is somebody in the house.

I listened to his heavy footsteps go down the hall to the kitchen, pause, then start back.

Ernie came toward me again. 'He's out, but I left a message.'

The most awful of all thoughts of this horrible day came to me then, as Ernie walked slowly toward me, his big hands extended. I had left the clipping on the kitchen table, naked and revealing. If he had seen it, had read it, and had picked up that receiver, had heard the voice of Sergeant Anderson – then Ernie would want me dead too!

Maybe not want – but most certainly need!

I began to talk fast. 'How did you happen to come home?'

'Spray gun jammed. Jim said we needed a new one. We hopped in the truck –'

Hope was a beat in my throat. 'Jim's here?'

He shook his head. 'Dropped me off for lunch.' He was beside me now, bending over.

More fear – if he kills me now, having already called the doctor, could he make it look natural – 'Don't!'

He pulled his hands away.

'I – my head aches.'

Steve called, 'Mama.'

I pushed myself up. Ernie pushed me down. 'Tell you what. I'll dress the kids and take them to Eloise's.'

It sounded fine. The children would be safe.

He paced out of the room.

I was out of bed instantly, tip-toeing to the kitchen grateful that Ernie had removed my shoes. The receiver sat crosswise in its cradle. The clipping was still on the table beside my purse. Had it been moved?

I snatched up the clipping and grabbed my purse, tucked the paper into it, zipped it shut again and carried it back to the bedroom to stuff it under my pillow. Then I lay down, breathing hastily.

Outside a shrill horn bleated and Ernie hurried into the room.

I sat up. 'You go along. I can take care of the kids. Honest.'

'You look funny,' he said slowly. 'You act funny. You got something on your mind?'

Maybe, then, the hope bubbled, he hadn't seen the

clipping. 'You go, Ernie. Don't worry. I'll be here when you come back.' It was a promise, strong and meant. I had to see what he would do. I had to know for sure, even if it killed me!

He said, 'Reason I couldn't get a hamburger, kid, I'm broke.'

I reached under my pillow and pulled out my purse.

'How did that get there? It wasn't there when I carried you in.'

I swallowed a thick lumpiness. 'Sure it was. You were – excited.'

I reached up and tucked the money into his coverall pocket and forced a smile.

Jim's horn sounded twice, roughly. As the kitchen door closed behind Ernie, the phone rang. By the time I picked up the receiver, the rings had synchronized with the two bongs of the church bell.

'Yes?' I sounded brusque.

'Sergeant Anderson speaking. 'You all right, lady?'

'Of course I'm, all right.'

'You hung up. You said murder and hung up.'

'Police? There must be some mistake.'

'We traced the call.'

'But I haven't used the phone.'

'Something's haywire here. There anybody else in your house?'

I laughed, high, strange. 'Two small children.'

He said something I could almost hear to somebody I couldn't see. Then, 'Don't see how it could happen, lady. Sorry to bother you. Some crank maybe. With a psycho on the loose –'

'Yes.' *Psycho*. That was the word I had been searching for all day!

'Okay then.'

I held the receiver for a long moment, listening to the remote hum.

So that was the way it was going to be. I couldn't turn the clipping, the slacks, and Ernie over to the police. Five years and two children – I couldn't point the finger.

Why couldn't I point the finger? It had to be proved. I had to be sure.

I called the doctor's office.

'Mrs. Cochran,' the girl said in answer to my question, 'there's no record of any call from your husband.'

I hung up.

Ernie hadn't called the doctor. Why? If I thought the doctor was coming I would stay home. I would be there whenever he could fix an alibi and sneak out of the garage to come to me – and with a 'psycho on the loose' – be safe.

Wait a minute, this is Ernie I'm thinking about, my Ernie. Please, the benefit of the doubt.

I called Eloise. 'I have to get to the bank before it closes. The kids – could you –?'

'Love it.'

'I'll be right over.'

Eloise's house looked very safe. I could stay here. Yet I drove on to the neighborhood bank, withdrew all the money in our joint account and turned it into traveler's checks. There wasn't a great deal, but there was enough to get my children and me back to the white house twenty-five miles from Kansas City, within the sanctuary of my parents' circle. Then maybe I could point the finger.

If I were a detective where would I start? Where Ernie started last night?

I drove back toward the house and cruised to the end of the block. To the right was the movie theater. I stopped before the marquee. Sandy, the ticket seller's name was.

'Sandy,' I said quickly, 'you know Mr. Cochran when you see him?'

She laughed. 'Everybody around here knows Ernie.'

'Sandy, last night – were you here last night?'

'Sure. You know me – Old Faithful.'

'Did you see Ernie – Mr Cochran? Did he come in here?' By the sudden ache in the pit of my stomach, I knew I had been hoping that Ernie had walked this far, been tired, had stepped inside and let the picture ride by until he was calm again.

'He didn't come in.'

'He didn't come in?' I repeated sharply. 'You mean you saw him?'

'Yeah, about nine-thirty, little earlier maybe. I give him a "hi," but he didn't seem to see me.'

'Thank you.' I went back to the car.

Sandy called. 'He went that-a-way.' She flipped a thumb to the left and I followed its gesture.

Halfway down the block I stopped the car again. Sometimes Ernie brought me to Joe's cafe for a sandwich and a glass of beer. Big deal.

It was dark inside after the glare of the sun. Joe's voice reached me before I saw him. 'Be with you in a sec.' His voice changed when he saw me. 'Mrs. Cochran.' He belched a hearty laugh. 'You taken to drink in the daytime?'

'What I wanted to know – well – I don't want to be a prying wife, Joe, but Ernie –'

'You checkin' up on that man of yours, eh?'

For a moment I wanted to turn, to run. This thing I was doing to Ernie was as bad as pointing the finger, planting suspicion. Sandy now, would she remember Sara Cochran trying to find out where her husband had been? Would Joe add two and two when the paper was tossed on the bar?

No, Ernie was too different now. I alone remembered how he looked five years ago – and Ernie, himself.

'It's a joke,' I said quickly. 'But was he – last night –'

He nodded definitely. 'Sure was.'

A funny looseness came around my heart again. If he sat here and tied one on until all hours – it would be an alibi. 'How long?'

The laugh bounced. 'In again, out again – one quick glass.'

This see-sawing. This up-and-down.

Joe reached to an intricately carved clock behind the bar. He began to wind it. 'I remember,' he said. 'Ten o'clock on the nose by Oscar here.' As if to seal it, a small bird popped quickly out above Joe's head. 'Cuckoo, cuckoo, cuckoo,' he crowed proudly, and snapped himself back inside.

I left the cafe and walked steadily toward the corner. Where next? Ernie left home about nine-thirty. Down the street, turn right by the movie, one beer at ten o'clock

What time did he get home?

I stared at my sandals following each other. If they could have a nose, like a dog on the scent, they could pick up one clear scent, of Ernie Cochran, to lead me where Ernie walked – and keep him away, away, away, from the Arnaughton Golf Course – but, of course, they couldn't. Six blocks, seven, ten, steadily forward, until the stores were gone, then on to the sign, a wide brown board with worn gold words; ARNAUGHTON MUNICIPAL GOLF COURSE.

I watched the doll-like figures tossed out over the course. Last night, when the Arnaughton Golf Course was black instead of green, a labyrinth to snare the feet, Marylee Adams, eighteen, was smashed down in the bushes by the sixteenth hole.

Suddenly I couldn't take any more. I couldn't walk onto that course and find the sixteenth hole. I wasn't a detective. I was the wife of Ernie Cochran, and had trusted him completely until today. I wanted him innocent with all my heart.

I ran, until there was pain in my side and a wild bumping in my chest, until I reached the jalopy. There I sat, blind haze before my eyes, my hand on the ignition key, and watched the rain begin.

When I could breathe I started the car and steered it carefully back home. I got the big suitcase from the top of the neat shelves Ernie had built in the garage. I gathered all the children's clean clothes, packed them in and clicked the case shut. I lugged it out to the back and shoved it into the trunk of the jalopy, avoiding the place where the jack should have been.

I stood still, knowing something was forgotten, something I would need.

I darted back into the house. They were still there, over the kitchen chair – the slacks I was supposed to clean, the little rusty spots. I rolled them up tightly and wrapped them in brown paper. My hand was on the door when the front chimes rang.

Instinctively, the brown package still in my hand, I went to answer it. A tall man stood there. Black patches of rain were soaked on the shoulders of his coat and the rim of his hat.

'Yes?' I clutched the package.

'Mrs. Cochran?'

I nodded.

He did a sleight-of-hand and a badge appeared in his open palm. 'Police. Sergeant Anderson. I'd like to talk to you.'

'Me?' It came out a croak. 'Come in.' I stepped back.

The wedding clock on the mantel, Mama's wedding present ('To keep track of happy times, Dollie') pinged in its breathless way, one, two, three, four pings.

'Nice little house you have here.'

Trying to throw me off the track? Trying to make me think everything's all right? Had he been to places I hadn't thought of? Because I'm a wife, you see; not a detective.

'Won't you sit down?'

'I don't intend to stay, ma'am.'

Suddenly the weight of the package under my arm turned from wool to lead, and I set it down on the planter, feeling each rusty brown spot as a pound, a ton, in my conscience.

Sergeant Anderson watched me. 'You look like a sensible woman,' he said abruptly.

'I do?' The croak was back.

'You look like a woman who, if she had information the police needed, would be telling it.'

I might have known. Somehow they'd traced Ernie. They'd come this close.

'Mrs. Cochran,' the sergeant said quietly, 'last night a young girl was beaten to death. Everybody knows that. She wasn't much, but nobody, good or bad, deserves to die like she did.'

I asked sharply, 'What has all this got to do with me? Do you think I killed her?'

He smiled. 'Of course not. I'm here because of that phone call. Like I told you when I called you back, somebody mentions murder, we hop on it. First when we traced your call –'

Did I let the receiver slip when I fainted? Did I hang it up myself, the way it was when I went back into the kitchen?

'When I talked to you first, I thought, some mistake. You sounded calm. But operators don't make mistakes.'

'Everybody make mistakes.'

He nodded. 'I think I made one. I got busy after I talked with you. Then, when I was going over the scene of the murder, your call came back to me.'

'I didn't call.'

'Okay. But somebody called. This woman said she wanted homicide. You remember what she said?'

I swallowed thickly. 'Don't try to trick me. I didn't call.'

He shrugged. 'She said, "I mean murder."'

'So?'

'So, I came to the phone. You – she – said, "I want – I want –" Then she shut up. The wire hummed a long time. Three, four minutes.'

I said, anger bright in my voice, 'What are you trying to prove?'

'That I'm a dope. You – she – could have been murdered, the way I loused around. Out on the course there, it came to me. When you – she – didn't hang up she sort of faded away. Then, after that hum, somebody picked up the receiver. I heard breathing.'

'Breathing?'

'Yeah. Not a woman's. A man's – heavy, lower breathing.'

Panic bit like teeth against the back of my throat. 'Did he – say – anything? Ask who –'

The sergeant shook his head. 'Not a word. You're okay, but you look me in the face and lie in your teeth. Why?'

I was wild with desire to tell Sergeant Anderson everything, before what he was afraid could have happened really did. Tell him, and not have to get in the packed jalopy with the brown package. I didn't even have to say it. I could just hand him the package and tell him, 'These slacks were worn by my husband last night.' He'd do the rest.

Then the pendulum swung again. I was equally wild with the desire to get him out of the house, and Liz and Steve out of the state, so I could run into my father's arms and ask him what to do.

'I'm so ashamed,' I heard myself say. 'I'm – a scaredy cat.' It sounded coy. 'Neither house beside us is occupied. The yard backs up to that orange grove.'

Suddenly I was really scared. It was true. Ernie could come after me and I could scream my head off and not be heard.

I took a big breath. 'Well, this morning I read all that. When I emptied the rubbish, I – I thought I heard a noise. I locked everything and called the police. When I heard your voice, so official, I nearly – fainted. If there was a man, it was the owner –'

Sergeant Anderson looked tired. 'Okay. I'll just take a look around outside.' He walked past me to the door.

I picked up the brown paper package and hurried to the bedroom. The phone rang as I tucked it on the top shelf of the closet.

'Honey,' Eloise cried, 'Ernie's rolled along home with Jim to unload the case of beer. He's taking Jim's truck to bring the kids home.'

'He's leaving?'

'He left.'

She hung up.

Left. How long ago? There was a knock on the back door.

'Everything looks okay around here,' Sergeant Anderson reported.

Go, I willed. Any minute Ernie will clank up in Jim's old truck and step out – the man in the picture, the face you have studied so hard that twenty extra pounds, a crewcut and a mustache wouldn't fool you a bit.

'I'm sorry I caused you so much trouble.'

'That's all right.' I started to close the door.

He turned. 'Mrs. Cochran,' he said. 'When you're scared you sure freeze at the receiver. You sure breathe like a man.' He walked quickly down the sidewalk to his car.

The start of his motor fitted itself with two other sounds: the church steeple bell striking the first of five strokes, and the clatter of Jim's old truck swinging into the back drive off the alley.

Softly now, all things softly. My hands gripped themselves together in a gesture that was both a wringing and a prayer.

Through the window Liz and Steve, being lifted from the truck by Ernie, made a pretty picture; Daddy and the kids, the sun just coming out after the rain, and all small human troubles drying up from the late afternoon heat. Seeing them, everything in me denied the events of the day and my mind. Then Ernie, with Liz on his shoulder, strode to the back door and we stood staring at each other.

Look at his eyes, I commanded myself. What is that hardness way in back, like a rock under soft water?

There was some of the hardness in his normally warm voice. 'Whose car was that out front?'

I stammered, 'Just a man, selling books for children.'

'You must have let him go through his whole spiel. The car was here when I came down Jim's street. I saw it from the corner.'

'He was quite a talker.'

Ernie looked at the clock. 'Ten after five. Time to do a couple jobs before we get dressed.'

Dressed! The slacks I was supposed to clean! 'Ernie,' I said carefully, 'you know those gray slacks you wore last night?'

Did his mouth tighten?

'I couldn't seem to get the – paint – out. I dropped them at the cleaners.'

He was still silent.

'I'll press your brown ones.'

He spoke then. 'You feel better?'

'Fine.'

'Eloise said you went to the bank. Why?'

I was the silent one.

'Was it to get money for the dress we talked about?'

I shook my head.

'It's your money too.'

'Forget the dress. It's caused enough trouble. Forget last night.' I fought the tears.

'I'd like to forget last night,' Ernie said, very softly.

'I'll press your brown pants. But I – my head – I still feel a little rocky. Anyhow, I couldn't find a sitter –'

Ernie said flatly, 'I won't go without you.'

My moves, then, were like the ones in the hour I couldn't remember before the long terrible day began. When it was all done I knew I was going to Eloise's and Jim's with Ernie. It was a way of buying time, putting off the hour when I would be alone with the man in the drawing, while dark pulled itself down around the tract house and the orange groves, and grew blacker and thicker.

I saw it all. I watched, Gulliver-high above a doll house, while a doll man leaned over a doll woman's bed and lifted a car jack with infinite slowness. I found myself, normal size, out on the street, running and running. As I ran, I knew for the first time exactly what I would do.

I would get old Mrs. Callahan to stay with the children. I would get dressed and go with Ernie to Eloise's and Jim's to laugh and talk. When the men got into the poker game in the dining room, which couldn't be seen from the patio, I would excuse myself to check on the children. I would take the jalopy, get them – and go.

When I was back in the white house, when my father knew the whole story, I would mail the slacks to Sergeant Anderson with a slip of paper reading: 'These belong to Ernie Cochran.' It would be settled.

When Mrs. Callahan agreed to come right away, I said I'd drive over and pick her up. At the open door of the garage a tiny noise broke the stillness.

Ernie stood with his back to me, whistling between his teeth contentedly. His right arm moved rhythmically. A greasy rag flipped back and forth.

I stood very still, but as if he sensed me, he swung around slowly, his arms never stopping. I forced my eyes to go with equal slowness from his face to his shoulder, down the length of his powerful arm, to his hands. Rub-a-dub-dub, smooth and gleaming in the maw of Ernie's strong greasy hands lay the missing jack from the trunk of the old jalopy!

Suddenly the church bells rang, grew louder and louder, until each of the oranges in the grove seemed to have a clapper in it, ringing, ringing, the news that it was six o'clock.

Ernie's whistle stopped. 'You look awful. Did the doctor come?'

'Did you call him?'

His eyelids flickered. 'You know I did. No, wait.' The rag fluttered. 'The line was busy. I called from the garage.'

'You told me you called him.'

'I didn't want to worry you. Did he come?'

'I told him not to. Anyway, I'm going to get Mrs. Callahan. I don't want you to stay home because of me.'

'Maybe we'd better. You look so – funny –'

I laughed. 'You've been saying that all day. Where did that jack come from?' It sounded casual.

Ernie came toward me suddenly. He put his hands on my shoulders and pulled me against him, hard. The greasy rag touched one of my arms and the jack felt long and cold and hard against the other. Ernie put his mouth against mine. I pursed my own lips, trying to keep them soft and responsive.

'That's better.' He let me go and once again the rag began to slick its way along the jack. 'It makes me feel – bad – when we quarrel.'

How bad, Ernie? Miles beyond my numbness a sort of pity stirred impersonally. There must be thousands like Ernie – people who had, deep and hidden, maybe even from themselves, a sickening twist of mind that turned them from the normal into hideous places of darkness and terror. When? When they felt bad. I remembered Sergeant Anderson's voice. 'Psycho.'

'Ernie,' I said as he started toward the back of the jalopy, 'what are you doing?'

'Putting the jack back where it belongs, of course.'

'No.' I ran to him. Was the trunk locked? It must be or Sergeant Anderson would have noticed –

Ernie tugged at it. 'Darn,' he said mildly. 'Where are your keys?'

I took his arm and smiled at him. 'Later, friend. We're going to a party, remember?'

'I don't get you.' He shrugged, walked back into the garage and laid the jack on the workbench. He seemed tired of the whole thing as we went into the house, he to the bedroom. When I heard the shower begin I picked up my purse from the kitchen shelf, took out the traveler's checks, put them into the zippered compartment along with the clipping. I bent to the lowest shelf and put the purse in the heavy Dutch oven, settling the cover on tightly. Ernie loved stew made in a Dutch oven.

'Let's go,' Ernie said when Mrs Callahan was in, briefed, and before the TV. 'We'll take Jim's truck back.'

I hadn't thought of that, and the gratitude went through me. No matter how engrossing the poker game, if I took the jalopy from the party Ernie would hear. He knew each cough of the motor.

High in the truck, he drove slowly. Over the noise I said, 'Funny, when I put the groceries in the trunk this morning, the jack – it wasn't there.' I snapped a glance at him.

'Of course it wasn't.'

'Why not?' I was afraid to ask but I had to find out.

'Because I took it out to clean it.' He stared straight ahead.

'Do jacks get dirty, even when you don't use them?'

'Anything gets rusty.'

'I didn't see it anywhere –'

He switched toward me. 'You mean you looked?'

'I thought, what if I get a flat tire?'

His laugh was short. 'You've never changed a tire in your life.'

'Oh, what's the difference?' I tried to laugh. 'Just making conversation is all.'

He waited a moment. 'I see.'

We parked in Jim's drive and Ernie cut the motor. The sound of the patio party reached thinly out to us.

If Ernie was pondering about me the way I had about him, then he knew that I knew. He could be deciding what move he should make – when we were alone, when the time was right.

'Seeing as how you're so interested,' Ernie said, opening the truck door, 'the jack was on the top shelf above the workbench for the last three days.'

We walked together through Jim's gate, and I could see the two of us, the Cochrans, Ernie and Sara, as nice a couple as you'd want to meet. Our feet made a matched scuffling, louder than the voices of greeting, louder than the church bells, sounding muffled this time, far away and muffled – seven o'clock in the evening.

Almost at once, though, it was better. There were all these people, these friends. They made a ring around me, as my father's house would make a ring if I could get there. They protected me, not only from Ernie – from actual physical Ernie – but for a little while from all of the thoughts that had tormented me. The things they said were so usual.

It was wonderful, like when a toothache stops. You know it will hurt again, and will have to be drilled and cleaned out and packed with something new to take the place of the diseased portion. But at the moment it doesn't ache, and that little respite is wonderful.

The toothache stayed away until I heard Jim's voice over supper. '... no clues yet. What kind of a monster would do a thing like that? And to think it's so close.'

Eloise cried, 'Oh, Jim – cut it out.'

Ernie said, close, just the width of the redwood table away, 'Sara?'

I kept my eyes down then. I pretended not to hear, and called to one of the girls.

We ate. We cleared the tables. We played records and danced on the uneven bricks. We drank beer. The dusk was gone. The spotlight beside the garage sent down a shaft of light that widened as it slanted, so that the movement, the rhythm, was light and dark, swift and shadowy. Ernie didn't come near me, not even to ask me to dance.

Then the men moved, as if on signal, into the dining room for poker. The women sat in the deep light chairs, feet high, heads back. I lay there, too, looking upward. It was as if I had never seen the sky before.

In these clothes, then, this yellow dress and this white stole, would I start the long ride home, two sleepy babies soft against my lap? From these friends, then, would I go up over the mountains, which had always frightened me, across the desert which always seemed unending, into the middle west country?

I thought suddenly, I could call Sergeant Anderson from the phone in Eloise's room. All these people would be around to protect me. Or I could tell Jim what I knew, let him carry the burden. But lying there, ankles crossed, my hands folded, too filled with tension to allow themselves the luxury of tenseness, I shook my head at the stars and I knew I could do neither.

I could run away from Ernie, even be caught by Ernie, but somehow, all day and now tonight, I could not stand up and tell these people, tell anybody, that Ernie Cochran was a monster – a murderer and a monster.

Eloise's hand came down on my shoulder. 'Let's go make the girls some lemonade.'

I pushed myself up out of the chair. After the bells, the sirens, the wedding clock, the cuckoo, had cut each hour off sharply with razor-like strokes, now, outdoors in the dark, cool, silvered night, I had been given this refreshment. Now, the time had come.

'I have to run home a minute,' I whispered to Eloise. 'Don't bother about me. Mrs. Callahan –'

She patted my shoulder. 'Okay. Bring back some ice cubes, will you?'

I nodded and moved toward the gate. The clock seemed loud. I walked quickly, silently around the house. The street stretched before me. In all of the tract there were no lights.

This was the way, then, that the world looked to Ernie on those nights when he was troubled. This was the way it was for Ernie last night – the darkness, widespread, acres of it, eighteen holes of it – with a stopping place at the sixteenth hole where the bushes were darker than the greens, where anything could happen and nobody would see. Not until dawn came and revealed –

It was then I heard the footsteps. They were unhurried, wider than mine. They grew closer, heavy, steady, closing in.

I walked faster. I trotted. Then I began to run. The footsteps ran too. Light exploded behind my eyeballs. Then I was on my own porch. My hand was on the knob – and Ernie's hand crashed solid and tight against my shoulder.

I screamed. Ernie put his other hand against my mouth.

Mrs. Callahan opened the door. 'Sakes' alive,' she yelped, 'you near scared the life out of me!'

Ernie said, breathlessly but quietly, 'I'm sorry. My wife was giving me a race.'

I pushed my heart down out of my throat. 'Ernie'll walk you home,' I managed. 'Then he's going back to the party. Me – I'm going to bed.'

Ernie said, 'Me, I'm going to bed too.' He slipped Mrs. Callahan's shawl over her shoulders. 'Let's go, Mrs. Callahan.'

I closed the door and leaned against it. Then I went, weak and shaky, into the kitchen and poured myself a glass of water. The jalopy sat in the drive, with its suitcase. 'What will I do now?' I asked aloud.

The front door opened and shut, quietly. I could hear Ernie's breathing, the click of the night lock. I listened to his feet, the heavy feet that had chased me down the street, had caught me, too late, on our own front porch.

What if those feet had caught me on the middle of the first block? Or the second?

I looked down at my yellow dress. These are not the clothes I will run away in, I thought with deep hopelessness. These are the clothes I shall die in. The yellow all smudged and stained. The white turned red. And my hair –

Ernie was in the doorway. 'That was a fool thing to do.'

I nodded dumbly.

'Where did you think you were going?'
'How did you know I was gone?'
'I went to the kitchen – Eloise told me.'
The silence closed in.
Ernie said, 'You should have known better. After last night.'
'What about last night?'
'A girl was killed on the golf course.'
'I know.'
'A man who can kill once can kill twice.'
'I know.'
Ernie moved. I gripped the slick tile of the sink, but he didn't come near me.
'I think we'd better settle this once and for all.'
'Settle what?'
'What's on your mind. What's been on your mind all day.'
The words were there to yell at him. Settle it, then, they screamed in my throat. Grab something. A knife, or get the jack. It's cleaned and ready again. Kill me. Go on. Murder me. But – get – it – over – with! But the words stayed inside me.
'I'm going to bed,' Ernie announced surprisingly. 'I'll wait for you.'
In the dark then, like the doll house.
When he was gone, I walked weakly into the living-room and sank down in the nearest chair. A reprieve. Maybe he would fall asleep. Maybe he was in no hurry. Maybe he wanted me to sleep first.
If he would sleep, I could call Sergeant Anderson. Or perhaps, by a miracle, by prayer, I could get the children out to the jalopy. I closed my eyes and let the prayer fill me.
After a while I leaned forward and switched on the TV, keeping it soft. The grayness came and the hum, and finally the eleven o'clock news face, its mouth moving quickly.
The words that tumbled from the fast mouth made no sense at first. Then they caught me like a tossed lariat.
'... brilliant police work. The young man – he's just turned seventeen – was recently released from a mental institution. He admits having followed Marylee Adams for the past

week. Last night he stole a car. He offered her a ride when she left work. He says she did not object to driving up the back road behind the Arnaughton Golf Course. He became chaotic about the actual crime, but he took the police to the place where he threw away the murder weapon – a golf club given him by a man for whom he caddied, which he'd hidden in the back of the car. His reason? 'I don't like pretty girls.'

'And now to the weather picture for southern –'

Seventeen! I leaned forward and turned off the TV. My body felt as if warm milk flowed sleepily through my veins. I lay back in the chair and floated for a long long time.

The trip back to reality was short and brutal. I sat up, pain all through me.

In the bedroom was Ernie Cochran. He was waiting for his wife. He was wondering, and hurt, by her actions of the day. Good, kind Ernie Cochran.

The pain grew and spread. A murder had been committed. And Sara Cochran had committed it. By suspicion, by lack of faith, I had killed the goodness of Ernie, my husband. I had turned him from the man he was into a monster.

That was the reason I couldn't point a finger. A deep instinct had kept me from telling Sergeant Anderson or Jim or anybody. The knowledge that Ernie Cochran was good.

I began to cry then, the day's thousand tears streamed down my face and choked in my throat. Filled with them, I stumbled down the hall. I went directly to Ernie's bed and flung myself down.

'Forgive me.' I heard myself murmur over and over. 'Forgive me.'

Then I was pulled into Ernie's arms. 'Forgive you for what, darling?'

That moment was the worst of all the moments of the day. I couldn't tell him. I could never tell him. The shame and the guilt were mine to hold alone all the rest of our years together. What man could live with the thought that his wife believed him, even for one day, capable of brutal murder?

After a while my sobs slowed.

'All day,' Ernie was saying, 'I've felt awful. You looked at me so strangely. On the phone you were so cold. This noon –

oh, honey, you scared me silly.'

His kiss was long now, an interlude and a promise.

'Then I called this afternoon and you were gone. I saw the man – quite close. He looked smart, sure of himself. The suitcase was gone from the shelf – and you didn't want me to look in the trunk of the car –'

It was all there. Ernie had been puzzled too. He had added up the strangeness of my actions, words, looks, and had persuaded himself that his wife no longer loved him – was leaving him – was unfaithful.

Such tenderness filled me that it beat with an ache against my skin. I wanted to help, but if I eased his mind in one way I would kill him again in another. I kissed him instead.

I lay in the circle of Ernie's arm and listened to his contented breathing beside me. I closed my eyes and drew my breath easily through lungs that could now breathe without fear.

Far away, gentle, sweet, silver, the bells of the church steeple chimed slowly, the long count, from one to twelve.

I drifted with the chimes: Tomorrow I'll make Ernie a stew. He loves stew made all day in the Dutch oven –

In the Dutch oven. The traveler's checks –

I can take them back in the morning.

The long terrible day was over.

On the brink of sleep, on the very cliff, ready to fall softly into nothing. I sat bolt upright, awake, staring into the dark, the now familiar clawing of my heart tearing at my chest – the Dutch oven!

'Police Chief J. Hampton Jones remarked upon the similarity of this crime and that of the killing of one Sandra Hims, also 18, on a public golf course in Kansas City about five years ago. At that time the murder weapon was found, a heavy car jack.

The drawing (at right) was forwarded from that city, and is based on a witness' description of the suspect, the man with whom Miss Hims was last seen leaving a Kansas City bar.'

Cicero

by Edward Wellen

'Know somethin'?' Cicero seemed almost shy confessing it, an alarming thing in a man of his bulk. 'I got a itch in my trigger finger to do the rubbin' out by myself.'

Brains didn't glance up from his chess problems, but Lefty dropped his scratch sheet and his jaw.

'Yourself?' Lefty finally said. 'Now, Chief. You can't help bein' aware of the fact that you got where you are today by knowin' when and how to delegate responsibility.'

'Yeah. Still and all, Herrin is my one big mistake. Who'd ever figure a guy like Herrin, a guy that seems to have nothin' on his mind but dressin' swell and keepin' his self neat, to have the gall to cross me, who give him his start, and set him up on his own?'

'Nobody'd figure that, Chief.'

'Yeah, I just itch to do this one myself personal.' He looked wistful. 'Be like in the good old days when I was just startin' out myself and workin' my way up.'

'I hear you sure had the gift, Chief.'

'Yeah. The steady hand and the steely eye. And most important – the sense of timin'.'

There was a moment of silence as Cicero gazed feelingly back across the years. A growing firmness of purpose showed on his face.

Lefty took alarm. 'Now, listen, Chief.'

'Yeah?'

'You ain't serious. I mean about doin' the rubbin' out yourself?'

'No?'

62 *Cicero*

'You can't be. You know yourself you're kinda rusty now, Chief. You know that.'

'Yeah?'

'Well, you know I wouldn't wanna wound your feelin's for the world, Chief, but –'

'No, go on. That's all right, Lefty. I ain't in the least bit touchy. You go on ahead and say it.'

'Okay, let's face it, Chief. Your eye ain't what it used to be, and neither is your hand.'

Lefty failed to get out of the way in time.

'Ow! I thought you said you wasn't touchy.'

'I ain't. That's for negative thinkin'. Maybe my eye ain't what it used to be and maybe my hand ain't what it used to be –'

'The hell it ain't,' Lefty said under his breath.

'But my sense of timin' is just as good as ever. And as long as my sense of timin' stays sound I ain't licked. Brains. Brains!'

Brains shoved the board back and got up with a sigh.

'Brains, I'm gonna run Herrin out myself. But I got tobacco tremor and bum glims. To you I delegate the responsibility for figurin' out how I score a bull's eye.'

Brains drew nourishment from something challenging. His eyes lit, but he didn't waste energy pacing. He leaned against the wall and walled his eyes in speculation.

Cicero and Lefty tensed like hawks when Brains cleared his throat.

'You know, it might not work out bad at all,' Brains said. 'You'll have the element of surprise going for you. They count you out. They know Lefty is a muscle man, but a torpedo he ain't. They know I'm no killer. And the rest of the bunch – I won't even waste my breath. Herrin will be expecting that if and when you make your move, it'll be in the shape of hiring a gun. Local talent is out. He'll be looking for out-of-town talent. He'll know the minute it blows in. Until he hears that word, he'll feel safe. He won't break routine. Lefty, what's Herrin's routine?'

Lefty closed his eyes and began to recite. 'At ten on the nose, Herrin comes outa the hotel and crosses to the beanery. He could have room service breakfast in bed, but he has his eye on one of the waitresses at the beanery. After breakfast he –'

'That's enough. That does it.'

The interruption discomfited Lefty for an instant; he could have gone on and on. Then he smiled. 'I know. You figure to get to the dame and set Herrin up. The Chief'll be waitin' behind the door of her room and when Herrin and the dame walk in – Sure, how can the Chief miss with the gun right in Herrin's ribs?'

Brains stepped over to his chess problem, picked up the red queen, grinned at it, then set it down. 'No.'

Lefty was hurt. 'No?'

'Never trust a dame. No, what I have in mind is a whole lot safer and surer.'

Lefty leaned forward. 'I know. We clout a heap and drive past when Herrin starts to cross the street. The Chief blasts him, when we're right alongside, just like that.'

'No.'

'No?'

'The car is out.' Brains first made sure he was out of range of a possible punch from Cicero; then he said, 'In the Chief's case we can't risk a moving triggerman. That would be compounding the difficulty. What I mean is, here we already got a moving target. No, the Chief has to be stationary. But we can't sit waiting in a car. Herrin would spot us.'

'I know –'

'We gotta get a room overlooking the street, shoot Herrin from a window.'

'But the Chief's eye, his hand –'

Brains raised an eyebrow and put up a hand of his own. Lefty subsided. Brains cleared his throat and the others held their breath.

'You know how they put "X marks the spot" when they print the picture of the scene of the crime?'

'So?'

'So why not put the X in first? Before the crime. This X will be like cross-hairs in a sight. Only big. So big you can't miss it, Chief. See, we paint a big X on the crosswalk, clamp a high-powered rifle in the window, zero it in on the X, and when

Herrin is crossing over it you pull the trigger. You don't have to worry about aiming or holding. You don't need a steely eye or a steady hand. All you need is a sense of timing to tell you when to squeeze the trigger. Then out the room, up the stairs, across the roofs.'

Cicero smiled. 'Sounds great.' Then he frowned.

'What is it, Chief?'

'That X. Seems to me a bull's eye'd be more in keepin'.'

'Anything you say, Chief. Be easy enough to lay out the circles with string and chalk.' Brains' enthusiasm had begun to peter out now that he had the answer all cut-and-dried, and his voice took on a mocking tone. 'Of course we want to get things like the circumferences of the circles all squared away. It'll take a bit of working out with pi – the three point fourteen sort – but we'll put your man on the spot.'

'But to paint a big target on the street –'

'Don't fret about that, Chief. That's the easiest part.'

It may have seemed easy to Brains, who whistled as he wielded his brush, but Lefty was sweating. Wooden horses detoured early morning traffic around the two men painting big bright-red concentric circles in the center of the crosswalk. Brains and Lefty had smeared their faces with paint to hide their identity and wore old coveralls for the same reason. The cop on the beat had given them a perfunctory glance as he went by. But under the makeup Lefty was pale.

Brains grinned one of his rare grins. 'Take it easy, Lefty. Just go ahead and behave as though you know what you're doing and no one will ask questions.'

Lefty grunted and went on painting. He painted mighty furiously.

'Boy, you're sloppy, Lefty. Look at mine, nice and neat.'

Lefty grunted and went on painting.

They heard one passerby say to another, 'What is it? Why, there's going to be a helicopter landing here. I think I read something about it.'

Brains grinned.

They were getting there, working from the inside out.

Lefty paused and said in a whisper, 'I can feel the Chief lookin' down at us.'

Brains said deadpan, 'Yeah, Lefty, we must be making a perfect target out of ourselves. Be a good joke on us if the Chief was thinking of wiping us out.'

'Let's finish up and get outa here.'

They worked silently and swiftly and soon Brains was straightening with a groan. He eyed their work.

'It's quick-drying paint, but we'll lay down these wet-paint signs to keep pedestrians from rubbing it out. Okay, Lefty, everything's in order, let's go. Ten minutes before Herrin comes out we return, take away the horses...'

Cicero had to tell himself to hold his horses, his trigger finger was itching that bad. Herrin was stepping out of the hotel. He was nearing the target, one foot over the rim.

Cicero was happy. He liked it now with the finger on the trigger, the squeeze of flesh and metal, and now the tightness of no more give, and the shock, and the hot metal.

Brains and Lefty were at Cicero's shoulder and they saw Herrin, at the last instant, dance his spotless white shoes away from the target. Cicero didn't see this. At the last instant, Cicero blinked, anticipating the noise and recoil of the shot.

When the blink was over, he saw Herrin still alive, still moving – moving fast for cover.

Cicero was numb, wholly numb. Lefty and Brains had to drag him to get him away before the police got there. They hauled him home, got him safe behind his steel doors and steel shutters.

Outside his bedroom they whispered.

'I know what it is. He's in shock. He thinks he's lost his sense of timin'.'

'And he'll pine away into a pine box.'

'You gonna stand by and let the Chief think he's a has-been?'

'I sure won't be the one to tell him Herrin sidestepped the target because we forgot to remove the wet-paint signs.'

'Me neither.'

Brains eyed Lefty shrewdly before making up his mind to say, 'Before the word gets out Cicero is through, we'd better throw in with Herrin.'

Winter Run

by Edward D. Hoch

Johnny Kendell was first out of the squad car, first into the alley with his gun already drawn. The snow had drifted here, and it was easy to follow the prints of the running feet. He knew the neighborhood, knew that the alley dead-ended at a ten-foot board fence. The man he sought would be trapped there.

'This is the police!' he shouted. 'Come out with your hands up!'

There was no answer except the whistle of wind through the alley, and something which might have been the desperate breathing of a trapped man. Behind him, Kendell could hear Sergeant Racin following, and knew that he too would have his gun drawn. The man they sought had broken the window of a liquor store down the street and had made off with an armload of gin bottles. Now he'd escaped to nowhere and had left a trail in the snow that couldn't be missed, long running steps.

Overhead, as suddenly as the flick of a light switch, the full moon passed behind a cloud and bathed the alley in a blue-white glow. Twenty feet ahead of him, Johnny Kendell saw the man he tracked, saw the quick glisten of something in his upraised hand. Johnny squeezed the trigger of his police revolver.

Even after the targeted quarry had staggered backward, dying, into the fence that blocked the alley's end, Kendell kept firing. He didn't stop until Sergeant Racin, aghast, knocked the gun from his hand, kicked it out of reach.

Kendell didn't wait for the departmental investigation, Within forty-eight hours he had resigned from the force and was headed west with a girl named Sandy Brown whom he'd been planning to marry in a month. And it was not until the little car had burned up close to three hundred miles that he felt like talking about it, even to someone as close as Sandy.

'He was a bum, an old guy who just couldn't wait for the next drink. After he broke the window and stole that gin, he just went down the alley to drink it in peace. He was lifting a bottle to his lips when I saw him, and I don't know what I thought it was – a gun, maybe, or a knife. As soon as I fired the first shot I knew it was just a bottle, and I guess maybe in my rage at myself, or at the world, I kept pulling the trigger.' He lit a cigarette with shaking hands. 'If he hadn't been just a bum I'd probably be up before the grand jury!'

Sandy was a quiet girl who asked little from the man she loved. She was tall and angular, with a boyish cut to her dark brown hair, and a way of laughing that made men want to sell their souls. That laugh, and the subdued twinkle deep within her pale blue eyes, told anyone who cared that Sandy Brown was not always quiet, not really boyish.

Now, sitting beside Johnny Kendell, she said, 'He was as good as dead anyway, Johnny. If he'd passed out in that alley they wouldn't have found him until he was frozen stiff.'

He swerved the car a bit to avoid a stretch of highway where the snow had drifted over. 'But I put three bullets in him, just to make sure. He stole some gin, and I killed him for it.'

'You thought he had a weapon.'

'I didn't think. I just didn't think about anything. Sergeant Racin had been talking about a cop he knew who was crippled by a holdup man's bullet, and I suppose if I was thinking about anything it was about that.'

'I still wish you had stayed until after the hearing.'

'So they could fire me nice and official? No thanks!'

Johnny drove and smoked in silence for a time, opening the side window a bit to let the cold air whisper through his blond hair. He was handsome, not yet thirty, and until now there'd always been a ring of certainty about his every action. 'I guess I just wasn't cut out to be a cop,' he said finally.

'What *are* you cut out for, Johnny? Just running across the country like this? Running when nobody's chasing you?'

'We'll find a place to stop and I'll get a job and then we'll get married. You'll see.'

'What can you do besides run?'

He stared out through the windshield at the passing banks of soot-stained snow. 'I can kill a man,' he answered.

The town was called Wagon Lake, a name which fitted its past better than its present. The obvious signs of that past were everywhere to be seen, the old cottages that lined the frozen lake front, and the deeply rutted dirt roads which here and there ran parallel to the modern highways. But Wagon Lake, once so far removed from everywhere, had reckoned without the coming of the automobile and the postwar boom which would convert it into a fashionable suburb less than an hour's drive from the largest city in the state.

The place was midwestern to its very roots, and perhaps there was something about the air that convinced Johnny Kendell. That, or perhaps he was only tired of running. 'This is the place,' he told Sandy while they were stopped at a gas station. 'Let's stay a while.'

'The lake's all frozen over,' she retorted, looking dubious.

'We're not going swimming.'

'No, but summer places like this always seem so cold in the winter, colder than regular cities.'

But they could both see that the subdivisions had come to Wagon Lake along with the superhighways, and it was no longer just a summer place. They would stay.

For the time being they settled on adjoining rooms at a nearby motel, because Sandy refused to share an apartment with him until they were married. In the morning, Kendell left her to the task of starting the apartment hunt while he went off in search of work. At the third place he tried, the man shook his head sadly. 'Nobody around here hires in the winter,' he told Kendell, 'except maybe the sheriff. You're a husky fellow. Why don't you try him?'

'Thanks, maybe I will,' Johnny Kendell said, but he tried two more local businesses before he found himself at the courthouse and the sheriff's office.

The sheriff's name was Quintin Dade, and he spoke from around a cheap cigar that never left the corner of his mouth. He was a politician and a smart one. Despite the cigar, it was obvious that the newly arrived wealth of Wagon Lake had elected him.

'Sure,' he said, settling down behind a desk scattered casually with letters, reports, and wanted circulars. 'I'm looking for a man. We always hire somebody in the winter, to patrol the lake road and keep an eye on the cottages. People leave some expensive stuff in those old places during the winter months. They expect it to be protected.'

'You don't have a man yet?' Kendell asked.

'We had one, up until last week.' Sheriff Dade offered no more. Instead, he asked, 'Any experience in police work?'

'I was on the force for better than a year back East.'

'Why'd you leave?'

'I wanted to travel.'

'Married?'

'I will be, as soon as I land a job.'

'This one just pays seventy-five a week, and it's nights. If you work out, though, I'll keep you on come summer.'

'What do I have to do?'

'Drive a patrol car around the lake every hour, check cottages, make sure the kids aren't busting them up – that sort of thing.'

'Have you had much trouble?'

'Oh, nothing serious,' the sheriff answered, looking quickly away. 'Nothing you couldn't handle, a big guy like you.'

'Would I have to carry a gun?'

'Well, sure!'

Johnny Kendell thought about it. 'All right,' he said finally. 'I'll give it a try.'

'Good. Here are some applications to fill out. I'll be checking with the people back East, but that needn't delay your starting. I've got a gun here for you. I can show you the car and you can begin tonight.'

Kendell accepted the .38 revolver with reluctance. It was a different make from the one he'd carried back East, but they were too similar. The very feel and weight and coldness of it against his palm brought back the memory of that night in the alley.

Later, when he went back to the motel and told Sandy about the job, she only sat crossed-legged on her bed staring up at him. 'It wasn't even a week ago, Johnny. How can you take another gun in your hand so soon?'

'I won't have it in my hand. I promise you I won't even draw it.'

'What if you see some kids breaking into a cottage?'

'Sandy, it's a job! It's the only thing I know how to do. On seventy-five a week we can get married.'

'We can get married anyway. I found a job myself, down at the supermarket.'

Kendell started out the window at a distant hill dotted here and there with snowy spots. 'I told him I'd take the job, Sandy. I thought you were on my side.'

'I am. I always have been. But you killed a man, Johnny. I don't want it to happen again, for any reason.'

'It won't happen again.'

He went over to the bed and kissed her, their lips barely brushing.

That night, Sheriff Dade took him out on the first run around the lake, pausing at a number of deserted cottages while instructing him in the art of checking for intruders. The evening was cold, but there was a moon which reflected brightly off the surface of the frozen lake. Kendell wore his own suit and topcoat, with only the badge and gun to show that he belonged to the sheriff's car. He knew at once that he would like the job, even the boredom of it, and he listened carefully to the sheriff's orders.

'About once an hour you take a swing around the lake. That takes you twenty minutes, plus stops. But don't fall into a pattern with your trips, so someone can predict when you'll be passing any given cottage. Vary it, and, of course, check these bars along here too. Especially on weekends we get a lot of underage drinkers. And they're the ones who usually get loaded and decide to break into a cottage.'

'They even come here in the winter?'

'This isn't a summer town any more. But sometimes I have a time convincing the cottagers of that.'

They rode in silence for a time, and the weight of the gun was heavy on Johnny Kendell's hip. Finally, he decided what had to be done. 'Sheriff,' he began, 'there's something I want to tell you.'

'What's that?'

'You'll find out anyway when you check on me back East. I killed a man while I was on duty. Just last week. He was a bum who broke into a liquor store and I thought he had a gun so I shot him. I resigned from the force because they were making a fuss about it.'

Sheriff Dade scratched his balding head. 'Well, I don't hold that against you. Glad you mentioned it, though. Just remember, out here the most dangerous thing you'll probably face will be a couple of beered-up teenagers. And they don't call for guns.'

'I know.'

'Right. Drop me back at the courthouse and you're on your own. Good luck.'

An hour later, Kendell started his first solo swing around the lake, concentrating on the line of shuttered cottages which stood like sentinels against some invader from the frozen lake. Once he stopped the car to investigate four figures moving on the ice, but they were only children gingerly testing skates on the glossy surface.

On the far side of the lake he checked a couple of cottages at random. Then he pulled in and parked beside a bar called the Blue Zebra. It had more cars than the others, and there was a certain Friday night gaiety about the place even from outside. He went in, letting his topcoat hang loosely over the badge pinned to his suit lapel. The bar was crowded and all the tables were occupied, but he couldn't pinpoint any under-age group. They were young men self-consciously trying to please their dates, beer-drinking groups of men fresh from their weekly bowling, and the occasional women nearing middle age that one always finds sitting on bar stools.

Kendell chatted a few moments with the owner and then went back outside. There was nothing for him here. He'd turned down the inevitable offer of a drink because it was too early in the evening, and too soon on the job to be relaxing.

As he was climbing into his car, a voice called to him from the doorway of the Blue Zebra. 'Hey, Deputy!'

'What's the trouble?'

The man was slim and tall, and not much older than Kendell. He came down the steps of the bar slowly, not speaking again until he was standing only inches away. 'I just wanted to get a look at you, that's all. I had that job until last week.'

'Oh?' Kendell said, because there was nothing else to say.

'Didn't old Dade tell you he fired me?'

'No.'

'Well, he did. Ask him why sometime. Ask him why he fired Milt Woodman.' He laughed and turned away, heading back to the bar.

Kendell shrugged and got into the car. It didn't really matter to him that a man named Milt Woodman was bitter about losing his job. His thoughts were on the future, and on Sandy, waiting back at the motel...

She was sleeping when he returned to their rooms. He went in quietly and sat on the edge of the bed, waiting until she awakened. Presently her blue eyes opened and she saw him. 'Hi. How'd it go?'

'Fine. I think I'm going to like it. Get up and watch the sunrise with me.'

'I have to go to work at the supermarket.'

'Nuts to that! I'm never going to see you if we're both working.'

'We need the money, Johnny. We can't afford this motel, or these two rooms, much longer.'

'Let's talk about it later, huh?' He suddenly realized that he hadn't heard her laugh in days, and the thought of it made him sad. Sandy's laughter had always been an important part of her.

That night passed much as the previous one, with patrols around the lake and frequent checks at the crowded bars. He saw Milt Woodman again, watching him through the haze of cigarette smoke at the Blue Zebra, but this time the man did not speak. The following day, though, Kendell remembered to ask Sheriff Dade about him.

'I ran into somebody Friday night – fellow named Milt Woodman,' he said.

Dade frowned. 'He try to give you any trouble?'

'No, not really. He just said to ask you sometime why you fired him.'

'*Are* you asking me?'

'No. It doesn't matter to me in the least.'

Dade nodded. 'It shouldn't. But let me know if he bothers you any more.'

'Why should he?' Kendell asked, troubled by the remark.

'No reason. Just keep on your toes.'

The following night, Monday, Johnny didn't have to work. He decided to celebrate with Sandy by taking her to a nearby drive-in where the management kept open all winter by supplying little heaters for each car.

Tuesday night, just after midnight, Kendell pulled into the parking lot at the Blue Zebra. The neoned juke box was playing something plaintive and the bar was almost empty. The owner offered him a drink again, and he decided he could risk it.

'Hello, Deputy,' a voice said at his shoulder. He knew before he turned that it was Milt Woodman.

'The name's Johnny Kendell,' he said, keeping it friendly.

'Nice name. You know mine.' He chuckled a little. 'That's a good-looking wife you got. Saw you together at the movie last night.'

'Oh?' Kendell moved instinctively away.

Milt Woodman kept on smiling. 'Did Dade ever tell you why he fired me?'

'I didn't ask him.'

The chuckle became a laugh. 'Good boy! Keep your nose clean. Protect that seventy-five a week.' He turned and went toward the door. 'See you around.'

Kendell finished his drink and followed him out. There was a hint of snow in the air and tonight no moon could be seen. Ahead, on the road, the twin tail lights of Woodman's car glowed for a moment until they disappeared around a curve. Kendell gunned his car ahead with a sudden urge to follow the man, but when he'd reached the curve himself the road ahead was clear. Woodman had turned off somewhere.

The rest of the week was quiet, but on Friday he had a shock. It had always been difficult for him to sleep days, and he often awakened around noon after only four or five hours' slumber. This day he decided to meet Sandy at her job for lunch, and as he arrived at the supermarket he saw her chatting with someone at the checkout counter. It was Milt Woodman, and they were laughing together like old friends.

Kendell walked around the block, trying to tell himself that there was nothing to be concerned about. When he returned to the store, Woodman was gone and Sandy was ready for lunch.

'Who was your friend?' he asked casually.

'What friend?'

'I passed a few minutes ago and you were talking to some guy. Seemed to be having a great time.'

'Oh, I don't know, a customer. He comes in a lot, loafs around.'

Kendell didn't mention it again. But it struck him over the weekend that Sandy no longer harped on the need for a quick marriage. In fact, she no longer mentioned marriage at all.

On Monday evening, Kendall's night off, Sheriff Dade invited them for dinner at his house. It was a friendly gesture, and Sandy was eager to accept at once. Mrs. Dade proved to be a handsome blonde woman in her mid-thirties, and she handled the evening with the air of someone who knew all about living the good life at Wagon Lake.

After dinner, Kendell followed Dade to his basement workshop. 'Just a place to putter around in,' the sheriff told him. He picked up a power saw and handled it fondly. 'Don't get as much time down here as I'd like.'

'You're kept pretty busy at work.'

Dade nodded. 'Too busy. But I like the job you're doing, Johnny. I really do.'

'Thanks,' Kendell lit a cigarette and leaned against the workbench. 'Sheriff, there's something I want to ask you. I didn't ask it before.'

'What's that?'

'Why did you fire Milt Woodman?'

'He been giving you trouble?'

'No. Not really. I guess I'm just curious.'

'All right. There's no real reason for not telling you, I suppose. He used to get down at the far end of the lake, beyond the Blue Zebra, and park his car in the bushes. Then he'd take some girl into one of the cottages and spend half the night there with her. I couldn't have that sort of thing going on. The fool was supposed to be guarding the cottages, not using them for his private parties.'

'He's quite a man with the girls, huh?'

Dade nodded sourly. 'He always was. He's just a no-good bum. I should never have hired him in the first place.'

They went upstairs to join the ladies. Nothing more was said about Woodman's activities, but the next night while on patrol Kendell spotted him once again in the Blue Zebra. He waited down the road until Woodman emerged, then followed him around the curve to the point where he'd vanished the week before. Yes, he'd turned off into one of the steep driveways that led down to the cottages at the water's edge. There was a driveway between each pair of cottages, so Kendell had the spot pretty much narrowed down to one of two places, both big rambling houses built back when Wagon Lake was a summer retreat for the very rich.

He smoked a cigarette and tried to decide what to do. It was his duty to keep people away from the cottages, yet for some reason he wasn't quite ready to challenge Milt Woodman. Perhaps he knew that the man would never submit meekly to his orders. Perhaps he knew he might once again have to use the gun on his hip.

So he did nothing that night about Milt Woodman.

The following day Sheriff Dade handed him a mimeographed list. 'I made up a new directory of names and addresses around town. All the houses are listed, along with the phone numbers of the bars and some of the other places you check. Might want to leave it with your wife, in case she has to reach you during the night.' Dade always referred to Sandy as Kendell's wife, though he must have known better. 'You're still at that motel, aren't you?'

'For a little while longer,' Kendell answered vaguely.

Dade grunted. 'Seen Woodman around?'

'Caught a glimpse of him last night. Didn't talk to him.'

The sheriff nodded and said no more.

The following evening, when Johnny was getting ready to go on duty, Sandy seemed more distant than ever.

'What's the matter?' he asked finally.

'Oh, just a hard day, I guess. All the weekend shopping starts on Thursday.'

'Has that guy been in again? The one I saw you talking to?'

'I told you he comes in a lot. What of it?'

'Sandy –' he went to her, but she turned away.

'Johnny, you're different, changed. Every since you killed that man you've been like a stranger. I thought you were really sorry about it, but now you've taken this job so you can carry a gun again.'

'I haven't had it out of the holster!'

'Not yet.'

'All right,' he said finally. 'I'm sorry you feel that way. I'll see you in the morning.' He went out, conscious of the revolver's weight against his hip.

The night was cold, with a hint of snow again in the air. He drove faster than usual, making one circuit of the lake in fifteen minutes, and barely glancing at the crowded parking lots along the route. The words with Sandy had bothered him, more than he cared to admit. On the second trip around the lake, he tried to pick out Woodman's car, but it was nowhere to be seen. Or was his car hidden off the road down at one of those cottages?

He thought about Sandy some more.

Near midnight, with the moon playing through the clouds and reflecting off the frozen lake, Johnny drove into town, between his inspection trips. There wasn't much time, so he went directly to the motel. Sandy's room was empty, the bed smooth and undisturbed.

He drove back to the lake, this time seeking lights in the cottages he knew Woodman used. But all seemed dark and deserted. There were no familiar faces at the Blue Zebra, either. He accepted a drink from the manager and stood by the bar sipping it. His mood grew gradually worse, and when a college boy tried to buy a drink for his girl Kendell chased them out for being under age. It was something he had never done before.

Later, around two, while he was checking another couple parked down a side road, he saw Woodman's familiar car shoot past. There was a girl in the front seat with him, a concealing scarf wrapped around her hair, Kendell let out his breath slowly. If it was Sandy, he thought that he would kill her.

'Where were you last night?' he asked her in the morning, trying to keep his voice casual. 'I stopped by around midnight.'

'I went to a late movie.'

'How come?'

She lit a cigarette, turning half away from him before she answered. 'I just get tired of sitting around here alone every night. Can't you understand that?'

'I understand it all right,' he said.

Late that afternoon, when the winter darkness had already descended over the town and the lake, he left his room early and drove out to the old cottages beyond the Blue Zebra. He parked off the road, in the hidden spot he knew Woodman used, and made his way to the nearer of the houses. There seemed nothing unusual about it, no signs of illegal entry, and he turned his attention to the cottage on the other side of the driveway. There, facing the lake, he found an unlatched window and climbed in.

The place was furnished like a country estate house, and

great white sheets had been draped over the furniture to protect it from a winter's dust. He'd never seen so elaborate a summer home, but he hadn't come to look at furniture. In the bedroom upstairs he found what he sought. There had been some attempt to collect the beer bottles into a neat pile, but they hadn't bothered to smooth out the sheets.

He looked in the ash tray and saw Sandy's brand. All right, he tried to tell himself, that proved nothing. Not for sure. Then he saw on the floor a crumpled ball of paper, which she'd used to blot her lipstick. He smoothed it out, fearing, but already knowing. It was the mimeographed list Sheriff Dade had given him just two days before, the one Sandy had stuffed into her purse.

All right. Now he knew.

He left it all as he'd found it and went back out the window. Even Woodman would not have dared leave such a mess for any length of time. He was planning to come back, and soon – perhaps that night. And he wouldn't dare bring another girl, when he hadn't yet cleaned up the evidence of the last one. No, it would be Sandy again.

Kendell drove to the Blue Zebra and had two quick drinks before starting his tour of duty. Then, as he drove around the lake, he tried to keep a special eye out for Woodman's car. At midnight, back at the bar, he asked the manager, 'Seen Milt around tonight?'

'Woodman? Yeah, he stopped by for some cigarettes and beer.'

'Thanks.'

Kendell stepped into the phone booth, and called the motel. Sandy was not in her room. He left the bar and drove down the road, past the cottage. There were no lights, but he caught a glimpse of Woodman's car in the usual spot. They were there, all right.

He parked further down the road, and for a long time just sat in the car, smoking. Presently he took the .38 revolver from his holster and checked to see that it was loaded. Then he drove back to the Blue Zebra for two more drinks.

When he returned to the cottage, Woodman's car was still

there. Kendell made his way around to the front and silently worked the window open. He heard their muffled, whispering voices as he started up the stairs.

The bedroom door was open and he stood for a moment in the hallway, letting his eyes grow accustomed to the dark. They hadn't yet heard his approach.

'Woodman,' he said.

The man started at the sound of his name, rising from the bed with a curse. 'What the hell!'

Kendell fired once at the voice, heard the girl's scream of terror and fired again. He squeezed the trigger and kept squeezing it, because this time there was no Sergeant Racin to knock the pistol from his hand. This time there was nothing to stop him until all six shots had been blasted into the figures in the bed.

Then, letting the pistol fall to the floor, he walked over and struck a match. Milt Woodman was sprawled on the floor, his head in a gathering pool of blood. The girl's body was still under the sheet, and he approached it carefully.

It wasn't Sandy.

It was Mrs. Dade, the sheriff's wife.

This time he knew they wouldn't be far behind him. This time he knew there'd be no next town, no new life.

But he had to keep going. Running.

You Can't Blame Me

by Henry Slesar

Now it was Beggs' turn. A generation had grown to manhood since he went behind the gates, and now they were opening for him. As he stood in the Warden's office, his skin itching in civilian tweed, he thought, First twenty-year-old I see, I'll go up to him and say, kid, I'm one guy you never laid eyes on before, I'm one guy you can't blame for anything, because I've been sitting out your lifetime.

Twenty years!

'Fifty's not old,' the Warden said. 'Plenty of men get new careers at fifty, Beggs. Don't go getting discouraged, because you know what that leads to.'

'What?' Beggs said dreamily, knowing the answer, only wanting to keep the talk going, to delay the moment.

'You know. Trouble. You wouldn't be the first I've said goodbye to one day and hello to the next.'

He cleared his throat and shuffled papers. 'I see you have a family.'

'Had,' Beggs said, not with bitterness.

'Your wife wasn't much for visiting, was she?'

'No.'

'That money you stole –'

'What money?'

'All right,' the Warden sighed. 'I remember now. You're one of the innocent ones. Well, fine. That's the kind I like to see leave.' His hand was out. 'Good luck, Beggs. I hope you find what you want out there. Only wish I had some good advice for you.'

'That's all right, Warden. Thanks just the same.'
'I'll give you one tip.' He smiled benignly. 'Dye your hair.'
'Thanks,' Beggs said

He was out. He knew Edith wouldn't be waiting on the other side of the wall, but he stopped and looked up and down and sat on a hydrant to smoke a cigarette within ten yards of the prison gates. He heard a guard chuckle on the catwalk overhead. Then he got up, and walked to the bus stop. He sat in the rear seat of the bus and watched his white-haired reflection all the way into town. I'm an old man, he thought. But that's all right.

He used up most of the rehabilitation money in two days. Some went for shelter, for new clothes, for food, and for train fare. When he stepped onto the platform at Purdy's Landing, a taxi man solicited his business. He said yes, and got into the front seat. 'Do you know the Cobbin farm?' he said.

'Nope,' the cab driver said. 'Never heard of it.'
'Used to be on Edge Road?'
'Heard of Edge Road.'
'That's where I want to go. I'll tell you where to stop.'

He told him, within sight of a small housing development. He paid the man, but waited until he was driving off before he approached one of the houses. When the car was out of sight, he turned out of the driveway and started walking down the road. Nothing seemed familiar but he wasn't worried. Everything changes. Latitudes remain. Stone endures.

He saw the jagged rim of the rocky slope ahead of him, and he knew he was in the right place. He slid down the small embankment, braving himself against a fall. He had been nimbler twenty years ago. There was a steep woodland at the end of the slope, and he entered the thick of it. He stumbled around until he saw the rough circle of stacked stones, the old blackened tree stump, and the spot where he had hidden the money.

He began removing the stones. There were many of them. He had no fear that his hiding place had been discovered in his absence. His confidence was as strong as faith.

It was there, still in the leather suitcase, all in cash, neatly bundled up by denomination, slightly damp but still new-looking and spendable. He wiped off the suitcase – it had cost forty dollars, new – and clucked when he saw the mold damage on its edge. But it was sturdy still, and hefted well by its stout handle.

He returned to the road, carrying the suitcase. This time, he did stop at one of the houses, and knocked on the door. A woman answered, looked dubiously at his suitcase as if expecting a sales pitch, and then relaxed when she saw his snowy hair and heard his question. Could he have a drink of water? Of course. Could he please call a taxi? Go ahead, phone's right over there. She was a nice woman, not young. With a shock, Beggs remembered that Edith would be the same age now.

He reached the old neighborhood at dusk. The light dab of rouge on the tenements didn't improve their appearance; it was like makeup on a trollop. Not much change here, he thought, only for the worse. Dilapidation and decay, another twenty-year layer of dirt on the pavements and building stones. Then he saw the differences: an all-glass front on the corner drugstore; an empty lot where a candy warehouse had been; a change in nationality in the street urchins; a new sign, neon, in front of Mike's Bar and Grill. The sign read 'Lucky's,' and when it blinked, the 'L' fizzled and crackled and seemed ready to burn out.

He went into the bar. He had spent plenty of hours there in his youth, even after his marriage. But only the latitude and longitude were the same. Mike's place had been rough-furnished, honestly lit, and the bartender had had sweat on his forearms. Lucky's was another sort of place altogether. It was dark, too dark for an old pair of eyes, jeweled up with chrome and colored glass, a lousy cocktail lounge. There were even women: he saw a black dress and a string of pearls and heard hard, feminine laughter. The bartender wore a white uniform and had a ferret's face. He played the cash register like a Hammond organ.

'Yes, sir?' the barman said.

'Phone?' Beggs said hoarsely.

Contempt. 'Back there.'

He stumbled on something, righted himself, found the phone booth. He searched clumsily through the directory, marveling at its thickness, the smell of alcohol around him almost strong enough to make his head spin; there hadn't been whiskey past his throat in two decades. He found her listing, BEGGS, EDITH, the number different but the address the same. He felt almost weepy with gratitude toward his wife for being stubborn and changeless.

He went into the booth, forcing the suitcase in between his legs, dug a nickel out of his pocket, and then saw that rates were different. He found a dime, but he didn't deposit it. His hands were shaking too much. He couldn't face the moment, couldn't sit here in this glass cell and hear the voice from yesterday tinny and disembodied in the receiver. He came out of the booth, sweating.

At the bar, he sat on a plush stool and placed his elbows on the bar and rested his head in his hands. There was nobody drinking. The barman moved in on him like a bird of prey. 'What'll it be?' he said seductively. 'You look like you need one, friend.'

Beggs looked up. 'Whatever happened to Mike?' he said.

'Who?'

'I'll – I'll have a whiskey.'

The glass was in front of him, paid for, easing the strain between them. The barman relaxed and said: 'You mean Mike Duram? Used to be his bar once?'

'Yes.'

'Six feet under,' the man said, jerking his thumb downwards. 'Maybe ten years ago. Place's had four owners since then. You a friend of Mike's or something?'

'I knew him,' Beggs said. 'A long time ago.' He downed the drink and it exploded in his head like a grenade. He coughed, choked, almost fell forward on the mahogany counter. The bartender cursed and got him water.

'What are you, a wise guy?' he said. 'Tryin' to make out my whiskey's no good?'

'I'm sorry; it's been a long time.'

'Yeah, don't give me that.'

He walked off, injured. Beggs covered his face with his hands. Then he felt a touch in the middle of his back, and turned to see the cheap dead-white pearls and the slim throat severed by a low black neckline.

'Hello, Pop, you got a cold or something?'

'It's nothing,' he said. She came and sat on the opposite stool, a young pale, pretty girl, her skin even whiter than the fake necklace she wore. 'I'm not used to it,' he said. 'Can't take he stuff anymore.'

'You need practice,' she smiled. Then he realized that this wasn't amateur cordiality; the girl worked there. He reached for the suitcase handle. 'Stick around, Pop, you can't fly on one wing.'

'I don't understand.'

'Have another drink. It'll taste better this time.'

'I don't think so.'

'I'll tell you what. You buy one and try it; if you don't like it, I'll finish it for you. It's like a moneyback guarantee, only you don't get your money back.' She laughed gaily.

He started to refuse, but he hated to see even the false smile disappear.

'All right,' he said gruffly.

The bartender returned, all prepared. He set two shot glasses in front of them, and filled both to the rim. He placed the bottle in front of Beggs, turning it to display the brand name. Beggs, chastised, gave him a small grin. The girl's thin white fingers closed around her glass, and she lifted it.

'Here's to you,' she said.

The second went down easier. It didn't relax him, but it made his depression easier to bear. It made him remember what a drink was for. He looked shyly at the girl, and she patted his shoulder. 'Nice man,' she said, cute, patronizing. 'Such nice white hair.'

'You're not drinking,' he said.

'Come to think of it, I'd like mine with ginger ale. Couldn't we sit at a table?'

Beggs looked to the end of the bar; the bartender was wiping glasses and appeared contented.

'Sure, why not?' he said. He picked up the suitcase and climbed off the stool. His foot didn't feel the ground when he touched it, and he laughed. 'Hey, what's going on here? My foot's asleep.'

She giggled, and looked at the suitcase. Then she put her arm through his. 'Gee, you're cute,' she said. 'I'm glad you came in.'

He was in the prison shop, the machines roaring, his body stiff with fatigue, his head hurting. He rested it on the cool surface of the lathe, and the guard gripped his shoulder and shook it.

'Wake up, buddy.'

'What?' Beggs said, lifting his head from the micarta tabletop. His hand was still around a glass, but the glass was empty. 'What did you say?' he said.

'Wake up,' the bartender grumbled. 'This ain't a hotel. I got to close up.'

'What time is it?' He straightened and gongs rang in his ears. His fingertips were tingling and there was glue in his mouth. 'I must have fallen asleep,' he said.

'It's after one,' the bartender said. 'Go on home.'

Beggs looked down at the other side of the booth. It was empty. He reached down for the suitcase handle and clutched air. 'My suitcase,' he said calmly.

'Your what?'

'Suitcase? Maybe I left it at the bar' He got up, stumbled toward the stools and started pushing them around. 'It's got to be here someplace,' he said. 'Didn't you see it?'

'Look, buddy –'

'My suitcase,' Beggs said distinctly, facing the man. 'I want my suitcase, you understand?'

'I didn't see any suitcase. Listen, you accusing me of –'

'The girl I was with. The one who worked here.'

'No girl works here, fella. You got the wrong idea about the kind of place I run.'

Beggs put his hand on the man's lapel, not rough. 'Please don't fool around,' he said. He even smiled. 'Look, don't joke. I'm an old man. See my white hair? What did you do with it? Where's the girl?'

'Mister, I'll tell you this once more.' The barman plucked off his fingers. 'I didn't see your lousy suitcase. And no girl works here. If you got rolled by somebody, that's your business, not mine.'

'You *liar*!'

Beggs hurled himself forward. It wasn't an attack; his arms were spread out in pleading, not violence. He shouted at the man again and the man walked away, disdainful. He followed him, and the man turned and said nasty words. Then Beggs started to sob, and the bartender sighed wearily and said, 'Oh, that did it, that's too much.' He grabbed Beggs' arm and began propelling him to the doorway. He scooped up his overcoat from the rack and threw it at him. Beggs shouted, but he kept moving. At the door, the barman gave one final shove that sent him into the street. The door slammed shut and Beggs pounded on it with his fist, only once.

Then he stood on the sidewalk, and put on his overcoat. There were cigarettes in the pocket, but they were crushed and worthless. He threw the crumpled pack into the gutter.

Then he walked off.

He remembered the stairs. There were three flights of them, easy to take when he had been young and newly married and Edith was waiting for him upstairs. Steeper when he had been drinking at Mike's after a jobless day. Now they were endless, a wooden Everest. He was puffing by the time he reached the apartment door.

He knocked, and in a little while a woman who could have been Edith's mother opened the door. But it was Edith. She stared at him, pushing back the limp yellow-gray strands from her face, a bony hand fumbling with the dangling button of a soiled housecoat. He wasn't sure if she recognized him, so he said, 'It's Harry, Edith.'

'Harry?'

'It's kind of late,' he mumbled. 'I'm sorry to come so late. They let me out today. Could I come in, maybe?'

'Oh, my God,' Edith said, putting her hands flat over her eyes. She didn't move for almost thirty seconds. He didn't know whether to touch her or not. He shifted from one foot to another, and licked his lips dryly.

'I'm awful thirsty,' he said. 'Could I have a glass of water?'

She let him in. The room was in darkness; so his wife lit a table lamp. She went into the kitchen and came out with the water. She brought it to him, and he sat down before drinking it.

When he handed her the empty glass, he smiled shyly and said, 'Thanks. I sure was thirsty.'

'What do you want, Harry?'

'Nothing,' he said quietly. 'Only a glass of water. I couldn't expect nothing else from you, could I?'

She walked away from him, fooling with her hair. 'My God, I look terrible. Why couldn't you give me some warning?'

'I'm sorry, Edith,' he said. 'I better get going.'

'Where to?'

'I don't know,' Beggs said. 'I haven't thought about it.'

'You got no place to go?'

'No.'

She took the empty glass to the kitchen, and then came out. She remained in the doorway, folding her arms and leaning against the doorframe.

'You could stay here,' she said flatly. 'I couldn't turn you out, without no place to go. You could sleep on the couch. Do you want to do that, Harry?'

He rubbed his palm over the cushion.

'This couch,' he said slowly. 'I'd rather sleep on this couch than in a palace.' He looked at her, and she was crying. 'Aw, Edith,' he said.

'Don't mind me –'

He got up and went to her side. He put his arms around her.

'Is it okay if I stay? I mean, not just tonight?'

She nodded.

Beggs held her tighter, the embrace of a young lover. Edith must have realized how foolish it looked, because she laughed brokenly and pushed a tear off her cheek with the heel of her hand.

'My God, what am I thinking of?' she said. 'Harry, you know how old I am?'

'I don't care –'

'I'm a woman with a grown daughter. Harry, you never even saw your daughter.' She freed herself and went to a closed bedroom door. She knocked, and her voice trembled. 'Harry, you never saw Angela. She was only a baby when – Angela! Angela, wake up!'

A moment later the door opened. The blonde girl in the loose-fitting nightgown was yawning and blinking. She was pretty, but her expression was cross.

'What the heck's going on?' she said. 'What's all the yellin' about?'

'Angela I want you to meet somebody. Somebody special!'

Edith clasped her hands together and looked at Beggs. Beggs was looking at the girl, smiling foolishly, in embarrassment. The smile didn't last. Edith saw it go, and made a sound of disappointment. They looked at each other, the old man and the girl, and Angela tugged nervously at the strand of cheap dead-white pearls still around her throat.

Death of a Derelict

by Joseph Payne Brennan

One afternoon in early summer I sat supping cold sarsaparilla in the Victorian living-room of my investigator friend, Lucius Leffing. Shades were drawn against the sun; the room was cool and quiet. Leffing sprawled in his favorite chair.

As I glanced around at the gaslight fixtures, the mahogany furniture, and Leffing's favorite pieces of Victorian pressed glass, I smiled. 'I suppose,' I said, 'that two gentlemen must have sat much like this in somebody's parlor back in the so-called Gay Nineties. If I should hear the clop of horses' hooves outside, it would not surprise me.'

Just then the doorbell rang.

Leffing got up reluctantly. 'I fear a little reminiscent trip backward into time must be delayed for a more propitious moment. The present seems to be intruding.'

I heard conversation at the door and then Leffing ushered in an individual who was not conducive to moods of gentle nostalgia.

He was short, fat and fiftyish with a large-toothed smile which in the dimly lighted room seemed to switch on and off like a neon sign. A suit with a pattern of large checks did nothing to enhance his pot-bellied presence.

Leffing introduced him as Mr. Clarence Morenda and waved him to a chair.

Glancing around, Mr. Morenda favored us with another flashing grin. 'Well, well, you gentlemen have got yourselves a cozy little hideaway here.' He laughed uproariously.

'Mr. Morenda,' Leffing informed me when the storm had

subsided, 'is manager of the entertainment concession at Frolic Beach. He is here on business.'

Mr. Morenda, recalled to the purpose of his visit, scowled portentiously. 'Crummy nuisance, that's what it is!' He cleared his throat. 'But first you better tell me what this will cost.'

'That depends on the particular circumstances, the time consumed, expenses and so on,' Leffing told him. 'But compensation can be decided later. I do not press my clients.'

Mr. Morenda seemed momentarily confused by such an unbusinesslike attitude, but then he shrugged and grinned again. 'Okay, Mr. Leffing, I like a man who don't make too much of money.'

Leffing nodded. 'Quite so. And now, what is your case?'

Morenda's shaggy eyebrows stitched together again. 'About a month ago we found a stiff in an alley which runs alongside the Cyclone. Head all bashed in. Couldn't figure out whether he'd fallen off the Cyclone or got slugged. The coroner said he "came to his death in a manner at present unknown" – or something like that. We'd seen this bum hangin' around for quite a while, but nobody knew his name or anything. They took pictures and then kept him on ice, but nothing turned up so finally they planted him in Potter's.'

He paused, took out a large purple handkerchief and wiped the perspiration from his face. 'Then a week ago this nutty dame shows up. Claims this stiff was her cousin, Joel Karvey, says he fell off the Cyclone. Claims it was our fault. Now she's gettin' ready to sue us for $100,000!' He snorted. 'Imagine that! Why that bum wasn't worth two cents!'

'I appreciate your problem, Mr. Morenda,' said Leffing, 'but I fear you need an astute attorney, not a private investigator.'

Morenda shook his head vigorously. 'Those finky shysters! They'd keep the case goin' for five years. I want the suit thrown out before they start chewin' on it. That bum didn't fall at all – he was murdered! If I can prove that, the suit comes apart at the seams.'

Leffing winced at the metaphor. 'Mr. Morenda, is there any definite evidence to indicate that it was murder – or are you just engaged in wishful thinking?'

'Sure it was murder! The guy's head was all bashed in, but there wasn't another mark on him. If he'd fallen off the Cyclone, he'd be banged up all over.'

'Perhaps he landed on his head,' I suggested.

Morenda scowled at me impatiently. 'It ain't likely. He'd have to take a real swan dive off the top of the Cyclone and drop directly into that little alley. If he fell off, he'd hit at every tier, bang into the railings and bounce around.'

'Assuming you are correct,' Leffing put in, 'why should anyone murder a penniless drifter? Can you suggest a motive?'

Morenda hesitated. 'Well, I ain't sure. Maybe somebody thought he had a few bills. You know how it is – they'll cosh you for a quarter these days. Or maybe he got in a fight with some drunk.' He spread his hands. 'Could be lots of things.'

Leffing sat silently for a minute or two. 'I will take the case,' he said at length. 'The motive intrigues me. We cannot at this point, of course, rule out the possibility that the drifter's death was an accident.'

After assuring Mr. Morenda that he would start work on the case the next day, Leffing conducted his new client to the door.

'Well, Brennan, what do you think?' he asked as he settled back in his chair.

I set down my sarsaparilla glass. 'The whole sordid business looks pretty obvious to me. This female cousin had the drifter murdered and left near the Cyclone so that she could bring a suit against the Frolic Beach. Some rat-trap lawyer is calling the plays for her.'

'Well, well, you may already have solved the case!' Leffing replied with a touch of sarcasm. 'However, your solution must bear up under investigation. Much remains to be done.'

I did not see Leffing again until several days had passed. One evening I stopped in to ask how the case was moving along.

Leffing leaned back in his chair and put his fingertips together. 'I am now convinced that the drifter, Joel Karvey, was murdered. I studied the morgue photographs and talked to the coroner, who, incidentally, does not agree with me. I believe Karvey was struck over the head by a lead pipe. The coroner thinks he struck his head against the iron railings which parallel the Cyclone's track along both sides of the structure.'

'If Karvey fell,' I asked, 'wouldn't he have been seen?'

Leffing shook his head. 'Quite possibly not. Not if he fell at night. The Cyclone is not too well lighted and the alley in which he was found is dark. There is also the possibility, as the coroner pointed out, that he climbed up on the Cyclone after closing hours – midnight – as a lark, or just to get a view of the harbor lights.'

'Highly unlikely!'

'Where murder is suspected, or where $100,000 lawsuits are pending, one cannot dismiss possibilities.'

I grunted.

'I can't believe a drifter would be riding around on the Cyclone or climbing up to see the harbor lights. I still think this female cousin had him killed.'

'The female cousin,' Leffing said, 'is a charwoman living in New Bridge, a drab unimaginative creature with no criminal connections that I can discover. She mentioned to someone that the dead drifter was a distant relative; an opportunistic attorney learned the circumstances and descended upon her. He will obviously be rewarded only if he wins the case.'

'You are convinced Karvey was murdered?'

'The head wounds indicate assault so far as I can judge from the photographs and autopsy descriptions. What baffles me is the motive. Why should anyone murder such a nondescript beggar?'

I had no further suggestions to offer but the case began to interest me and I made Leffing promise to keep me informed. When I stopped back a week later, he was restless and fretful.

'You have made no progress?'

He stopped pacing the floor and sat down. 'The motive, Brennan! The motive! I am now more firmly convinced that the female cousin is innocent, but we have no other suspect.'

'How about Morenda himself?'

'He had no reason to kill Karvey.'

'Suppose,' I said, 'Karvey fell off the Cyclone, was found injured but conscious, and threatened to bring suit? Maybe Morenda finished him off to avoid getting hauled to court.'

Leffing frowned. 'An unpleasant possibility I must admit I had not entertained. But if Morenda "finished off" Karvey, as you say, why would he seek help to prove Karvey was murdered? Is he brash enough to risk his own life or freedom in order to nullify a lawsuit?'

I nodded. 'I believe he may be bold and callous enough to take the risk. All he wants you to do is establish the fact that Karvey was murdered, in order to end the lawsuit. If he himself is guilty, he must be confident that you can never prove it. Probably he believes he would never be suspected.'

'I intend to question him again, in any case,' Leffing said. 'We will see then what turns up.'

'You have learned nothing more at all?' I asked presently.

'Only one minor thing, insignificant perhaps, yet puzzling. Karvey never did any work at the concessions and he was never seen panhandling, yet he always seemed to have a little money – enough for hamburgers, chips, soda and so forth. Morenda hoped to get him arrested for begging and thus get rid of him. He even had the Frolic Beach watchman, Henry Marnault, spy on him at intervals, but Marnault never caught him panhandling.'

'He may have been a pickpocket.'

'Doubtful. If he picked pockets, he must have been an accomplished professional. He'd never been arrested for anything except vagrancy. A professional of his age – he was about sixty – would certainly have a police record.'

'What is your next move?'

'Tomorrow afternoon I am going to make another visit to Frolic Beach. I will see Morenda again and then perhaps just prowl about. Would you care to accompany me?'

Frolic Beach, south of New Haven along the Sound, is a cluster of carnival-like concessions, interspersed with hamburger stands, popcorn palaces, lemonade stalls, and several surprisingly good restaurants.

Early afternoon found Leffing and myself walking down Lavender Street, the main thoroughfare which bisects the beach area. Morenda's office was located in a dingy building behind the merry-go-round.

He glanced up from a sheaf of greasy-looking sales slips as Leffing and I entered. 'You got any news for me, Mr. Leffing?'

Leffing shook his head. 'Nothing fresh, Mr. Morenda. Can you take time out to stroll about a bit? Perhaps another visit to the scene of the crime might be helpful.'

'Sure, sure. But we been there before.' He left his sales slips with obvious reluctance to accompany us.

Screaming couples were rocketing about on the Cyclone's track when we arrived. The alley in which Karvey had been found ran along one side of it, a dim, narrow little lane, empty except for sandy wrappers, bottle caps and a piece of yellowed newspaper.

We followed Leffing inside. He poked about for a time and then stood looking up at the Cyclone. Suddenly he pointed. 'A section of the railing up there was recently replaced. Mr. Morenda? Correct?'

Both Morenda and I squinted upward. Most of the iron-pipe railing looked old and rusty, but there was one small section which appeared shiny and bright.

Morenda nodded his head. 'Yeah, a piece got loose up there, so we had a new section put in a couple of months ago.'

'Where was the old piece of railing left?' Leffing asked. 'Was it by any chance discarded in this alley?'

Morenda scratched his chin. 'Might be. I never paid any attention. You think that bum got bashed with it, Mr. Leffing?'

'I believe it highly possible. That may be why the coroner thinks Karvey fell. The wounds on his head would indicate that that pipe railing caused them, but in my opinion it was the discarded piece, left lying in the alley here, which did the job.'

'If we could locate it, we might have fingerprints!' I exclaimed.

'Possibly. But the murderer probably walked a few yards down to the beach and hurled it into the breakers. We would have a herculean task recovering it, and any fingerprints would be scoured off by now.'

Morenda shook his head. 'You sure got all the answers, Mr. Leffing!' Suddenly he broke into a roar of laughter. 'All except the big answer. Who killed Karvey?' He went on laughing like an hysterical hyena.

If Leffing was annoyed, he gave no sign. 'You are right, Mr. Morenda,' he said quietly when the raucous hee-hawing had subsided. 'The big answer still eludes me.'

As we walked back toward Morenda's office, Leffing inquired about Henry Marnault, the Frolic Beach watchman.

'We got a real bad worry about fire,' Morenda explained. 'After midnight, when we close, Henry checks up on all the rides and stands. You know how it is – a smouldering butt could bring down the works.'

'That is the extent of Marnault's duties?' Leffing asked.

'His night tour takes about two hours. Then he goes off and doesn't come on again till four the next afternoon. He sweeps my office and does a few odd jobs, but mostly he just drifts around picking up soda bottles and stuff. Sometimes if a stand runs out of change, he'll bring a bill to my office. We don't push Henry. It's hard to get a man for that night tour.'

'Where does he live?' Leffing asked.

'Lives in a barn down off the end of Lavender Street. We fixed it up for him and we don't charge any rent. He's got all he needs in there.'

Leffing nodded. 'Well, we may just have a chat with him, if you've no objection.'

'Sure, sure. Leave no stone unturned, as they say, Mr. Leffing!'

We left Morenda and walked down Lavender Street, stopping for a lemonade along the way.

Henry Marnault's barn was situated in a salt meadow off the end of the street. It was not much more than an oversized shack, but the roof looked new and storm windows had been fitted into the front.

We walked around to the rear, but Marnault was not in sight. As we came back around to the front, we noticed someone walking down the near end of Lavender Street. He was hunched over with his head bent down, and for a moment we thought he was searching the road for something he had lost. As he turned in toward the barn, however, we saw that this was his habitual way of walking.

Marnault looked up at us suspiciously out of somewhat bloodshot eyes, but he became friendly when Leffing explained his errand.

'Karvey? Yeah, sure. I knew who he was. Mr. Morenda had me watchin' him for a while. We figured he was panhandlin', but I never did catch him at it. Slippery cuss. But I ain't got no information about him. He just hung around, never talked to nobody.'

'You think he was murdered?'

Marnault ran a hand through his ragged hair. 'Naw. Who'd want to kill him? He wasn't worth killin', a bum like that. But I don't think he *fell* off the Cyclone. I figure he just climbed up there one night and *jumped*!'

'What reason had he for suicide?' Leffing asked.

Manault tapped his head.

'He was loose up here. Those kind of people get crazy urges like that.'

Leffing nodded. 'Well, you may be right, Mr. Marnault. You may be right.'

He could tell us nothing more. Leffing thanked him and we started back up Lavender Street.

'If Karvey committed suicide,' I pointed out, 'we are wasting our time.'

'Well, there are worse ways of wasting it, Brennan. We have the tang of sea air, and fresh lemonade is just at hand.'

Leffing then began a series of inquiries which exasperated me and eventually left me exhausted. He stopped at every stand and stall along Lavender Street and inquired about Karvey. Did they remember him? Did he ever buy food or drink from that particular stand? How did he pay for it?

By the time I fell into my car for the drive back to New Haven, my legs were literally aching. Leffing, apparently immune to fatigue, was in an optimistic mood.

'Well, well, Brennan, I think the case is clearing.'

'I can't recall that you learned anything of consequence from the various vendors along Lavender Street.'

'You attach no significance to the fact that Karvey invariably paid for his food or drink with coins – usually nickels and dimes?'

'The only significance I attach to it,' I replied, 'is that he was an elusive and hard-working panhandler.'

Leffing would say no more. He began humming an old English music hall ballad. This went on until we arrived back at Autumn Street.

He turned to me as I stopped the car in front of his small house. 'Brennan, are you willing to drive me down to Frolic Beach tomorrow morning – about five o'clock?'

I groaned. 'Good grief, are we going in pursuit of a murderous milkman?'

He laughed. 'I think not, but we must have an early start.'

'I'll be right here at five o'clock.' I told him.

I knew it would be useless to question him. He loved being both melodramatic and secretive, and I had come to accept the irritating fact that apparently he could not be cured of this deplorable childishness.

I set my alarm for four-thirty and was still sleepy as I stopped in front of seven Autumn Street. It was just beginning to get light. A heavy fog filled the streets.

Moments after I pulled up, a disreputable-looking figure appeared out of nowhere, slouched up to the car and yanked open the door.

I turned in alarm. 'What do you want?'

The tramp leered at me. 'I want a lift down to Frolic Beach. That's where you're headed, ain't it – Brennan?'

I stared at him for a full half minute before the import of his words came through. 'Leffing! You've given me another gray hair!'

He got in the car. 'Sorry, Brennan. Did my little disguise take you in?'

I shook my head. 'I had no idea you were a master of makeup. Where did you learn the art?'

'In my distant youth I was identified with several amateur theatrical groups. At various times my early stage experience has proved invaluable.'

98 *Death of a Derelict*

Traffic was light, but the fog slowed us up considerably. Leffing chatted about everything except the case at hand. I remained completely mystified as to the reason for his disguise.

We parked a few blocks from the beginning of Lavender Street. Leffing peered cautiously through the fog. 'No more talking, Brennan, and remain close to the buildings. We must not be seen.'

We skulked down Lavender Street single file, like a pair of thieves. About halfway down, Leffing nudged me into a doorway.

'We will take our stand here,' he whispered.

The light strengthened and the fog lifted a bit as we waited. Suddenly Leffing squeezed my arm and nodded.

Inching out, I looked down Lavender Street. At the far end a shambling figure came into sight. In the fog he looked like a wraith beginning to materialize. He kept his head bent forward and down. Twice, as we watched, he bent swiftly and seemed to pick something out of the street.

This weird behavior was repeated several more times as he approached. When he drew closer, Leffing edged slowly onto the street and began to stroll toward him.

I watched, puzzled but fascinated, and now Leffing stooped and appeared to pick up something. He seemed to be entirely oblivious to the figure coming toward him from the other end of the street.

As the other figure slowly emerged from the fog, I finally recognized the features of Henry Marnault, the Frolic Beach watchman. He kept his head bent and his eyes on the ground most of the time, so he did not see the disguised form of Leffing until they were less than a block apart.

He stopped in his tracks and stared. Leffing continued shuffling forward. At intervals he bent to pluck something from the gutters.

Marnault watched him like a man bewitched. He seemed frozen into immobility. When he found his voice, it was high-pitched, frantic, filled with rising hysteria!

'Karvey! Get back! You're dead, you crazy bum, I killed you! Get away from me!'

As Leffing continued toward him, Marnault turned with a scream and began to run down Lavender Street. Leffing straightened up, drew something from a pocket and put it into his lips. The shrill blast of a police whistle cut through the foggy morning air. A moment later a blue-clad figure came pounding from somewhere out of the fog and collared the terrified Marnault.

Leffing called out in his own voice, 'Splendid work, Sergeant Corliss! Arrest that man for the murder of Joel Karvey!'

Marnault signed a full confession later in the day, admitting that he had slugged Karvey over the head with a piece of pipe railing found in the alley next to the Cyclone. He had dragged Karvey into the alley, walked to the shore and thrown the murder weapon into the ocean. This had occurred just at daybreak, when the Frolic Beach area was still deserted.

He had killed Karvey, he explained, because Karvey, in spite of repeated threats, had continued to 'muscle in' on his territory. Marnault had found that an early-morning inspection of the Frolic Beach streets, gutters and sidewalks almost invariably yielded a modest crop of coins. The area, which was open until midnight, was not well lighted; many coins dropped during the evening remained waiting to be picked up on the following morning. Marnault averaged enough to pay for his weekly bottle of gin.

Then Karvey had drifted in. One morning Marnault had run into him prowling the gutters in search of coins. The watchman had warned him to leave, but Karvey had remained. Morning after morning Marnault ran into the drifter, and the watchman's daily harvest of coins dwindled ever lower. The amount involved was small, but so was Marnault's salary, and the bottle of gin was important to him. At length his irritation had turned to murderous rage. Finally, one foggy morning he had waited in the little alley next to the Cyclone, where he had picked up the length of pipe railing. Karvey's coin collecting had come to an abrupt end.

That evening I sat in Leffing's gaslit Victorian living-room while he poured a generous portion of his choice, cask-mellowed brandy.

I sampled it with relish. 'It certainly was a bizarre murder motive,' I commented, 'but two things still puzzle me. Why was Marnault so terrified when he saw you approaching in the fog? And how did you figure out the business in the first place?'

Leffing smiled. 'Marnault was terrified,' he replied, 'because I had made up to resemble Karvey. I had studied the morgue pictures you know. I made up my face to look like his and I had even scoured the secondhand shops to get some rags of clothing which resembled his own. It was a gamble, of course, but it worked.'

He set down his glass. 'From the beginning the motive interested me. It eluded me for some time. Then I began to speculate as to Karvey's source of money. He never worked and was never seen begging, yet he always seemed to have a few coins. I was still groping in the dark until that day when we went to see Marnault. When I saw him approaching, I immediately tagged him as a "stooper" – a tramp term for a person who scrounges around looking for coins in the gutters and streets. Marnault had no physical deformity; the bent head and constantly downcast eyes, therefore, could mean only one of two things: atrocious posture arising out of sloth and indifference, or the habitual stance of a confirmed "stooper." I was not sure of myself at first, but when I canvassed the stall operators and found that Karvey almost invariably paid for his snacks with small coins, I felt that I had found the motive for his murder.'

I shook my head. 'It seems unbelievable to me that a man would murder for a few miserable coins snatched out of the gutter!'

Leffing shrugged. 'Those "miserable coins" meant a regular weekly bottle of gin. To a person such as Marnault, alcohol can become pretty important.'

A whimsical grin touched his thin face, 'Speaking of alcohol, Brennan, would you care for another brandy?'

I held out my glass.

Present for Lona

by Avram Davidson

There was sawdust – just like in a butcher shop – on the floor of the long room where Jack Clauson stood waiting for the man he was going to kill. Whatever the man had done, Clauson did not hate him for it. But he had to die, and Clauson had to kill him. Not out of hate, but for love – for love of Lona.

I won't be the only one, he kept telling himself. It won't just be me... And he has it coming to him anyway... But it was no use. He felt an unfamiliar rigidity in his throat, struggled against nausea.

Bright lights, terribly bright lights, bore down from overhead on the far end of the long room. The near end was dark. The men there shifted from foot to foot, coughing nervously. The coughing stopped abruptly as the door at the far end opened.

Clauson tensed, fighting against the impulse to drop what he held in his hands and run.

A group of people entered, but Clauson had his eyes only on the one in the open shirt. As he watched, the man – his face paper-white – blinked and ran the tip of his tongue along his lips. I can't do this... Clauson's thoughts darted around frantically, like rats cornered in a pit. I never saw him before... I won't do it; they can't hurt me if I refuse... The man walked steadily enough and his head was up and he didn't say anything. But there was suddenly the sharp fresh smell of his sweat; it was the odor of fear.

Clauson started to move. Then he remembered. I must. I have to. He'll die anyway. He deserves to die. He killed an innocent man.

Present for Lona

The guards bound the arms of the man in the open shirt swiftly, tightly. The chaplain murmured from his little book. A target was pinned over the heart.

The man's head began to move from side to side. It was still moving when the bullets hit him.

Jack Clauson counted his money. Twenty-five dollars. Not a lot, not for killing a man. His hand jerked suddenly at the thought. Why, he could earn that much from his regular work in a single morning, and work six days a week – to say nothing of overtime. So what was twenty-five dollars?

Not much. Only a man's life. Only another man's marriage. Clauson loved his wife. Now he'd killed for her. This was the first money he'd made in over a month, and it was for just a few minutes' work too. He'd buy Lona something. Something nice. She loved to get presents. He'd make her smile; she'd come into his arms, and things would be all right between them, again... Or would they?

He drove along the new road on his way back. It was really longer. There was a quicker route to reach the trailer camp, but he liked to ride along the new one. He'd helped build it. It was finished a month ago. He and Lona really should have been moving on long ago. She couldn't have much left out of the last of his earnings – the money he'd given her when everything was all right between them. But everything wasn't all right between them anymore. He was moody; she was moody; they quarreled and yelled at one another. *She* wanted to settle down and *he* wanted to keep moving; *that* was the trouble. And so they rubbed each other raw, and it had been sullen and ugly and apart that they'd spent the last week. They both knew that a split was coming, knew the other knew. It had been hell. Because he wanted her. Badly.

Jack knew he had to *do* something to show he wanted her. Words would no longer be enough. There had to be something from outside the two of them.

How the man's head had weaved from side to side! As if he was looking for an out – and knowing there wasn't any. Then the bullets, smashing into him –

Recalling it made Jack hunch over the wheel, drive faster and faster, sorry he'd taken the longer route, anxious to be back at the trailer camp, eager to show her his token of love – the present. Lona had always loved to get presents. He laughed – why, he hadn't even bought it yet! But it wouldn't take long; it was Late Closing Night at the stores in the little town. The neon signs beckoned to him as he carefully parked the car. They were mostly red. Red. The color of blood. Blood soaking into sawdust. When the bullets hit, the man didn't even yell. He just grunted. And then the blood...

Seeing the lights out in the trailer, Jack thought Lona might be asleep. If she was, he'd wake her up. He couldn't just turn in by himself, not *now*, not with *this* on his mind and heart. He'd done it for Lona and Lona alone could make it all right. He could forget, in her arms. Maybe she was just lying awake in the dark as she sometimes did. Softly, he opened the door. 'Lona?' he called, making his voice gentle. There was no answer, and his eyes, adjusting to the dark, saw she wasn't in bed. He grunted, flicked on the lights.

He jumped at the sudden flood of brightness, swore. For a moment he'd thought he'd seen a man under the lights, a man with bound arms and a bloody target on his chest. Badly frightened. Clauson stood still, waiting for his racing heart to slow down. He looked around him.

The place was a mess, clothes scattered all around, bed unmade, a paper bag of garbage spilling on the floor. Lipstick-smeared tissues and a scattering of face-powder told him that she'd gone somewhere she expected to meet people. But – he hastily checked – her things were still there. She'd be back – but he wasn't going to wait! Not alone.

'Why couldn't you be here?' he asked the empty trailer, aloud. 'I wanted to give you the present I got for you.' His face twisted in disappointment as he looked down at the fancy-wrapped package. The money had gone just far enough – two crisp tens and one new crisp five. Twenty for the present. A bottle of bourbon used up all but some loose change out of the remainder.

A man's life = a present + a bottle of bourbon = a happy

couple and a saved marriage. *Or does it?* Because it was as close as that with them. It was as close as that...

There was an almost-empty half-pint on the table. That was something Lona had taken to again. She did that when things were bad between them. If only she'd drink *with* him – but she wouldn't, not with that black mood on her. And afterwards they were certain to quarrel, screaming at each other the empty threats that made no more sense than the rest of their quarreling.

'You like it so much here?' his own voice rang in his ears. 'Then you can stay – all by your lonesome! I'm getting out!'

And her voice, shrill, 'I'll kill you! I'll kill you!'

Each knowing the other didn't mean it... With a sigh, Jack went out and walked over to the Roanes' trailer. Ed and Betty Roane were the only friends they had left in the trailer camp; most of the construction workers had moved away as soon as work on the new road was over. Jack envied them; he longed for the feeling of freedom, the long trips across the state and even into a different part of the country, perhaps. But not Lona.

He sighed again.

There was a heavy weight on his chest. How much of it, he half-formed the question, was his wife – and how much of it was the man he'd helped kill?

The sounds of radio and TV, the smell of late suppers cooking, the murmur of conversations, children's voices... Maybe if they'd had children, but each had wanted to be modern and wait. Suddenly bitter, he muttered, 'Wait for what?' and then he was at the Roanes' trailer, knocking.

And with each knock, he felt it was no use. It had all been for nothing. His heart sank, and he felt he was sinking with it. The gap between him and Lona was too wide by now for any gift to bridge. He'd done a terrible thing, and it was all for nothing.

Ed and Betty never fought. They were easy going, and it was always 'Yes, dear' and all that sort of thing.

Lona was there. She smiled briefly and tightly as she saw him. He was right: it *was* too late. No – she wouldn't snap or snarl if others were present, but neither would she pretend. And old Mrs. Cheener was there too: Mrs. Cheener who owned the camp, a tiny little woman with wild white hair. Her age and position made her a privileged character and she now at once proceeded to take advantage of it.

'Well, so you finally got here, did you?' she rattled away at him. 'I suppose you were boozing it up while your poor little wife sits here with us. If she takes a notion to walk out on you, nobody'd be to blame but you there, Clauson, I'm speaking to you. The way you yell and threaten her!'

Jack asked, with a forced grin, 'But what about the way she threatens *me*, Mrs. Cheener?'

Lona looked up. Jack noticed that she didn't appear to be taking his remark as an affront. Could it possibly be that it wasn't too late, after all?

Mrs. Cheener's bright eyes turned to the Roanes. The implication, that she didn't want to waste any more of her valuable time on Jack.

'Turn on the television,' she directed, as if it were *her* place. 'I want the news.' Betty obeyed – reluctantly, it seemed to Jack. Ed avoided his eye.

The newscaster's face flowed into focus. '– the only State which allows such a choice or uses such a means of execution –' his voice boomed out. Betty, grimacing, hastened to soften it.

'There, we tuned in late and missed the beginning,' the old lady fretted.

'– a target was pinned over the condemned man's heart and –'

'Ah, it's that no-good from down the state that killed his partner,' the old woman remarked grimly.

'– the firing-squad was, as is customary, composed of paid civilian volunteers, who –'

Betty shuddered. 'Oh, I'd rather not listen to this!' She screwed up her face and put her hands over her ears. She and Ed stared at each other. Mrs. Cheener gazed avidly at the screen, as if expecting it to reveal the death-event itself. Jack Clauson sat stiff, saying nothing. Then he reached across to where Lona was sitting and took her hand, held it though she did make an attempt to free it.

'Meanwhile, the death toll continues to mount in the California floods,' the announcer was saying, in his smooth, rich voice, summing up the number of drownings as if he were lauding a hair tonic.

As soon as the news was over, Lona and Jack left.

They walked to their trailer without speaking. Just wait until she sees that present, Jack told himself. Just you wait.

As soon as they got inside, still without speaking, Lona started picking up some of the stuff that littered the place, not to make order but to be doing something, absently.

He got the box in its fancy wrappings, wanted to hand it to her, but didn't know how. That she might refuse to unwrap it bothered him. So he said, 'Here's something for you,' and started jerking off the ribbon and the paper. He got the nightgown out. 'Take a look at this, would you,' he said, holding it up. And the festive quality he'd put in his voice, he didn't feel.

Lona dropped what she had in her hand and moved toward Jack – toward the black lace nightgown – as though mesmerized.

'Oh, it's *beautiful*!' Lona's face – so like a child's, he thought, for all that she was almost thirty – was wide-eyed and delighted. Her eyes explored the nightgown avidly. She touched her cheek to its softness, virtually embraced it.

'Lovely,' she said. 'It's lovely...'

'Glad you like it, honey,' Jack said, but he was aware that Lona was still so taken up with the beauty of her present that she hadn't heard him. He wanted to kiss her. But he couldn't let her think that he was buying her affection with the present. Slowly does it, he told himself.

'How about a drink?' he asked, louder this time. They'd celebrate the end of all bad feeling. And he, in addition, would celebrate the fact that his plan had worked – the end of his fear that it wouldn't. 'How about a little drink?'

Then – as suddenly as if a curtain had been pulled – the smile left Lona's face. 'Will one bottle be enough?' She didn't so much ask the question as throw it at him.

'I, ah, I guess so,' he answered, uncertainly. He was confused. 'What do you mean, doll?' he asked.

She stood there, stiff. Her face was cold, sullen. 'This lovely nightie.' There was a sneer in the way she said that. She pushed the nightgown from her, glowered at it. 'All this lace. The woman in me must have been carried away by it. Take the thing back. Go on, get your twenty-five dollars. That – that ought to buy enough liquor to get you good and drunk. I know if I were you I'd never want to sober up again as long as I lived.'

What *happened*? What made her change? Why had she – ? The, ringing like a bunch of jangly bells, the words – *Twenty-five dollars Twenty-five dollars Twenty-five* – He stared at her, swallowed. 'How'd you know?' he asked, his voice thick. He poured whiskey into the glass, tossed it down.

'How'd I *know*?' Her voice rose shrilly. 'Why, there won't be anybody around here tomorrow who won't know! Mrs. Cheener's son-in-law, the guard at the pen, called to give her the information. Did you forget about her son-in-law? He *saw* you there. Ugh!'

She looked at him with disgust and horror. He *had* forgotten. He never once thought of it. 'How could you *do* it?' Lona asked, her face twisted.

'I did it for *you*!' He cried his outrage aloud. '*That's* how I could do it! For *us* – to buy some nice present for you – to make you happy...' He moved toward her, his face hurt and baffled, his hands groping. They found the nightgown she had dropped, held it out to her in one last offering.

Lona stepped away. She shook her head. 'Oh, no,' she said softly, almost in a whisper. 'Not for me. I wouldn't touch it. What do you think I am?' And once again she cried, incredulously, 'How could you do it? *Oh!*'

His head was buzzing. The straight whiskey, no supper, the whole horrible business at the penitentiary, now this. But he had to answer her question.

'Well, uh... he had it coming to him. He killed someone. If it wasn't me, it would of been someone in my place, so what's the difference? That's the law.' And, pleased with this neat assumption, he cocked his head on one side and looked at her. For a moment there was silence. Then Lona moved away, began to pick up her clothes and fold them up haphazardly. She pulled a suitcase from its place. Her mouth was tight-pressed.

Jack looked at her in anguish. Ten minutes ago he'd thought, hoped, that their marriage was saved. Now... He wiped his face. 'Where're you – ? Lona? Please!'

She spun around and screamed at him, 'I'm packing up! I'm going to get out of here. And this – and this –' She pushed at the black lace nightgown which he continued to hold out to her in supplication. 'Get it away from me!'

Jack dropped the frothy garment and held her shoulders.

'Oh, no, you've got to stay – you've got to wear it, Lona! I only did it for you – only for you. It was awful, horrible – and if you don't stay, then it was all for nothing. I'll have helped kill a man I never knew, never even seen before, and all for nothing. All –'

She struck away his hands from her shoulders, and – when he touched her again – she clawed at him, spitting out ugly words. Then he knew that it had indeed been all for nothing, and a fury he had never known in his life took him.

'I'll kill you!' he cried. 'I'll kill you!' He hit her – once – twice. He lost count...

There were voices outside, old Mrs. Cheener's, the Roanes', others. What was he looking for?' he asked himself. A towel. There wasn't any. He knelt slowly to the floor, picked up the black lace nightgown, wet it at the sink, knelt again, began to wipe the blood away. The voices were baying outside, people pounding at the door, while he sponged his wife's face. 'Lona?' he said slowly. 'Lona?'

There was sawdust on the floor of the long room, just like in a butcher shop, bright lights, terribly bright, bore down from overhead on the far end. The near end was dark. The men there shifted from foot to foot, coughed nervously. The sound stopped abruptly and the door at the far end opened.

A group of people entered, but the men already waiting had eyes only for the one in the open shirt – the one who blinked, who ran the tip of his tongue along his lips. The man walked steadily enough and his head was up and he didn't say anything. But there was, suddenly, the sharp fresh smell of his sweat. It was the odor of fear. His face was paper-white.

The guards bound his arms, swiftly, tightly. One of them pinned a target over his heart. The chaplain murmured from his little book. These were the regular officials of the State and the State's justice and mercy. The men waiting at the far end of the room – the bright lights enabled them to see but not to be seen – were volunteers. They had driven up to the prison in their own cars. Later they would drive away, each one with twenty-five dollars in his pocket (two crisp tens and one crisp five); and many of them would drive away along the newly-built road. The road Jack Clauson had helped to build.

Jack Clauson blinked in the bright lights. The straps were very tight. His head moved from side to side – as if he was looking for an out – and knowing there wasn't any. He blinked and licked his lips and waited.

Murder #2

by Jean Potts

It would never have occurred to Rolfe Jackson to kill his mother if it had not been absolutely necessary.

He was not a criminal. He was an artist. (True, there were those who held that the pictures Rolfe painted were crimes of a particularly brutal sort. They were fools, of course; he had not yet found himself, that was all.)

Besides, he was really quite fond of the old girl. He had her to thank for his name, for instance. She might so easily have called him Henry or Albert, both of which were traditional family names. Henry Jackson. Albert Jackson. Why, with such a name he might never have had the heart to embark on his artistic career at all! Certainly the identity he had created for himself as Rolfe J. – which was the way he chose to sign his pictures – would have been inconceivable.

He was quite a character, this Rolfe J. who had been built up with such care and who would someday come into his own. Hard-boiled. Dedicated. A Hemingway among painters. There was his stubby beard to prove it, and his lumberjack taste in clothes. Without them, he would have looked what he was – short and pudgy. With them he was impressively burly. Rolfe J. talked tough. He had choice unprintable phrases for the critics and for the work of other artists. He sneered at creature comforts. Publicly, that is. Very few people ever saw the inside of his apartment, and so very few people knew how much he loved luxury.

None of it – his whole beloved, outwardly rough-hewn, secretly luxurious life – would have been possible without

Mother. Because it was Mother's father who had set up the trust fund, and the trust fund saved Rolfe J. from having to make a living.

Yet it was also the trust fund that made it absolutely necessary for him to kill Mother. The realization hit him, like a blow from a fist, while he and Mr. Webb were having their little talk. Mr. Webb was Mother's attorney, and a friend of many years' standing; he lived in an apartment just across the hall from hers. Rolfe was instantly wary when one night Mr. Webb asked him to come in. His own relations with the man had always been notable for their lack of cordiality. No open quarrels. Just a mutual case of low estimation. Mr. Webb looked like a Yankee farmer – stringly, lantern-jawed, granite-eyed. His study was just what you would expect. Rolfe had never in his life sat on a more uncomfortable chair.

'I've been meaning to have a little talk with you for some time,' Mr. Webb began. 'Ever since your mother had this stroke. How are things going with the nurse?'

Mr. Webb had found the nurse for Mother. An ugly, devoted woman named Stella, who came in every day. By now Mother could manage alone, at night. But she was never going to get beyond the wheelchair stage. Poor old girl. What a change after all the bustle and pressure of the job she had had for years with one of the ladies' magazines...

'Stella? She's a paragon,' said Rolfe. He felt, as usual, an impulse to shock Mr. Webb, jolt him out of his flinty composure. 'If she wasn't god-awful ugly I'd marry her, to save her salary.'

Mr. Webb just looked at him. He had a talent for the unsettling silence. Finally he said, 'That's what your mother's worried about. Money. She shouldn't be. But she is. So I thought we ought to get the whole thing straightened out.'

'What's to straighten out? She's got the pension from her office –'

'Peanuts,' said Mr. Webb curtly. 'Hardly pays the rent. That's why she's worried. She knows she's going to have to dip into your trust fund to pay the nurse and the doctors' bills.' He opened his brief case and spread some papers out on the desk in front of him. 'I don't know how familiar you are with the terms of your grandfather's will. It might be well to review them. He left his money in trust for you, with the proviso that your mother may draw on it, in case of emergency. Now I don't believe anyone would question the fact that your mother's illness constitutes an emergency.'

'Who's questioning it?' said Rolfe irritably. 'Not me.'

'I'm glad of that. It's only fair to warn you that the drain on your trust fund will be considerable. Very likely you will find it necessary to curtail your present and future expenses.' Mr. Webb said this with relish. 'Your living arrangements, for example, aren't exactly economical. My own suggestion would be that you move in with your mother. Why not? You're already living in the same apartment house. It would simply mean paying rent on one apartment, instead of two. As far as Stella's salary, and her appearance, are concerned' – he produced a wintry smile – 'it's not necessary for you to marry her. Since you don't go out to work anyway, I don't see why you shouldn't take over some of the care of your mother. Combine art and nursing say, two or three days a week. It would mean quite a saving.'

It was Rolfe's turn to just look at Mr. Webb. For once in his life he had nothing whatever to say. Mr. Webb did not seem to notice. Having curtailed living expenses to his Yankee heart's content, he was now proceeding to 'go over the figures.'

They appalled Rolfe. He had not realized their true nature until now; it was like the moment when the dentist's drill touches a live nerve, sending out shoots of excruciating pain. He sat bolt upright (there was no other way to sit in that contemptible chair of Mr. Webb's), his eyes riveted on Mr. Webb's bony face, while he watched his beautiful trust fund trickle away day after day, year after year. The doctor had said Mother might live for years. Fifteen, even twenty. And every day of every one of those years meant ten dollars for Stella, at least another ten for food and medicine and miscellaneous expenses.

And Rolfe was supposed to stand for this without a murmur of protest; he was – yes, Mr. Webb was making it quite clear –

he was supposed to stand for it *gladly*, just because Mother had gone out of her way to keep the trust fund intact, until now. As if that were Rolfe's fault! He hadn't asked her to pay for his education, the summers in France, all the rest of it, out of her own earnings. It was her business, how she chose to spend her salary. And yet, now that there was no more salary, he was to be penalized, his very life was to go down the drain!

Well, he *wouldn't* stand for it. They were dealing with a man, not a mouse. And no ordinary man, either; he would show them, once and for all, the caliber of Rolfe J. The dream, the vision of himself as a man among men, touched with genius, ruthlessly molding his own destiny, had never been more vivid. He would –

'As I say,' Mr. Webb was concluding, as he shuffled his papers back into their folder, 'I'm glad you're taking a sensible attitude about this. Even if you weren't, it wouldn't make any difference. There's not a thing you can do about it.'

That was what Mr. Webb thought. Rolfe knew better. It had hit him in the second before Mr. Webb stopped speaking: the flash of crystal understanding and the resolution.

Nothing he could do about it? Ah, but there was, there was. Something so obvious, so necessary and right (for why should Mother, simply by living, cheat him of what was rightfully his?) that even a fool like Mr. Webb ought to see it. He didn't though. There was a gleam of satisfaction in his granite eyes as he said good-night. He thought he had scored, in this little talk of theirs. He thought he had taken Rolfe down a notch or two.

Out in the hall, Rolfe paused a moment, waiting for his heart to stop pounding. Then he let himself into Mother's apartment and called cheerily, 'Anybody home? How about a glass of sherry?'

Mother was in bed – Stella always got her settled for the night before she left – but bright-eyed, obviously brimming over with news. She was a fat little woman, with a halo of white curly hair. 'You'll never guess what happened to me today,' she began, while Rolfe poured the sherry. 'I was approached by an ex-narcotics addict!'

'What? Now really, Mother –'

'Really. Oh, a strictly business approach. He wants me to help him write a book. "I Was a Narcotics Addict" – that sort of thing. I must say, he doesn't look like a man with a lurid past. Quite presentable. I don't know why I – Maybe it was his missionary zeal that put me off. This project seems to be kind of a crusade with him.'

'That's normal, isn't it?' said Rolfe. 'Look at the reformed drunks that go round spreading the good word. I suppose it works the same with dope addicts.'

'I suppose. Or maybe it was his name. It's Borden, and all I could think of was that little verse about Lizzie Borden taking an axe... It's awful to have a free-wheeling mind like mine.'

They both laughed. Rolfe became aware of a prickle at the back of his neck, a tremor of obscure excitement. But he kept his voice casual.

'You turned him down, then?'

'No, I told him I'd think it over and let him know tomorrow. It *would* be fun, you know.' Just the thought made her look, for a moment, quite like her old busy, enthusiastic self. 'And then supposing it turned out to be a best seller and we all got rich.'

'I wasn't thinking of the money,' said Rolfe truthfully. 'Nice as it would be. I was just thinking how much you'd enjoy having something to do again.'

'You think I'm being silly?' she asked wistfully. 'You think I ought to do it?' She waited for his answer, and at once the illusion of vigor vanished. For in the old days she would not have needed Rolfe's advice, she would have known her own mind. Now uncertainty clouded her eyes. Her whole face sagged into lines of doubt, almost of fear. But it was the delicacy of her temple that fascinated Rolfe. Above her plump cheek it was slightly sunken and threaded with blue. It looked fragile as an egg shell.

'Good Lord, Mother, I've never seen the man, so how can I tell? And I've been wondering, how'd he happen to get in touch with you?'

'Well, he works in a bindery, a book bindery. Someone there suggested an editor, who in turn suggested me. So he looked me up in the phone book –'

'If you want me to look him over when he turns up again tomorrow,' said Rolfe, 'I'll be glad to...'

The deal was clinched next day, on the spot. Mother, now that Rolfe had disposed of her original vague doubts, was frankly delighted at the prospect. So was Borden.

Only Stella held out. She cornered Rolfe as he left; she had been lurking in the kitchen, waiting to speak her piece. Which she did, in an ominous whisper. 'I don't like it, Mr. Jackson. I just think you and your mother are taking an awful chance, letting that dope fiend in here three evenings a week. Oh, I know. He claims he's cured. I've heard that one before. They're none of them ever cured. Not for sure. I don't like it. Not one little bit.'

Good old Stella. Under her white nylon uniform she wore what appeared to be a suit of armor; it jutted out in ridges across her meaty shoulders and back. Lumpy wriggles of varicose veins showed through her white stockings. And she dyed her hair shoe-polish black. As ugly as ever, and yet Rolfe regarded her with something very like affection. Good old doubting Stella.

'*Sh*,' he whispered back. 'The only reason I'm going along with it is that she needs something to keep her occupied. It's brightened her up already. Don't worry, I'll make sure she's never left alone with him. That's why I insisted on meeting the fellow, to make sure he seemed all right.'

'All right!' Stella snorted. 'With those gooseberry eyes of his, and those long twitchy hands? Gives me the shivers just to think of him.'

But even Stella seemed to forget her doubts as two weeks, three weeks, went by, with no danger signals from Borden. Rolfe found it necessary to remind her now and then, in an unobtrusive way.

He himself was busy exploring. He had been quick to sense Borden's potentialities. But they would remain only potentialities until he had found the way to use them. To use them he must know his man, through and through.

He found the whole project almost alarmingly easy. No one

could have been more cooperative than Borden, either in striking up a friendship or in promoting the exploration of his own character. The circumstances were favorable too. In his capacity as watchdog, Rolfe was always present on Borden evenings, for Stella – having first given Mother her early dinner and settled her in bed – left at seven thirty. Rolfe did not intrude on the book sessions, which were held in the bedroom; he lounged in the living room, pretending to read, waiting for Borden to emerge, ready with his suggestion – so natural – that they drop into the bar and grill next door for a sociable drink. Borden snapped at the invitation like a hungry dog at a bone. The drink or two often stretched out to dinner and beyond: a whole solid evening of analyzing Borden.

It was a subject that fascinated them both. Borden's experiences as a psychiatric patient had left him with an insatiable interest in his own mental processes. Sometimes he would work himself up into a transport of confession, like a religious convert glorying in the spectacle of his remembered sins. His prominent green eyes dilated even more than usual, and he would sway on his bar stool, making jerky gestures or running his hand through his lank blond hair.

At other times he was coldly objective. 'It's a classic type,' he would say. 'The rejected child.' And he would tick off the 'classic' elements – the family-deserting father, the indifferent mother, the succession of even more indifferent substitute parents. The few friends he had managed to make always ended by sloughing him off – frightened away, probably, by the violence of his attachment to them. For he was violent. He was so famished for affection that he could not help it.

'You'll never know what it's meant to me, meeting you and your mother. You've always had friends, so you can't possibly understand –' He broke off with an embarrassed laugh, and went on more calmly. 'You see, it's not just a question of getting cured of the dope habit. You've got to get cured of whatever it was that made you turn into a dope addict in the first place. That's where you can't ever be sure. I'm "cured" now, and I can stay "cured" as long as I've got my job at the bindery, and the book to work on, and most of all you and your mother. But let something go wrong, maybe the least little thing –'

It was the truth. When Rolfe tested it out a few nights later by breaking a dinner date they had made. Borden's face turned quite white and into his eyes flashed a look of desperate presentiment: here it was again, the pattern as before. Rolfe and his mother, like all the others, were going to cast him off. He wrote Rolfe a cringing, overwrought letter: What had he done to offend Rolfe? How could he make amends? It took Rolfe several days to quiet the fears he had set off with his trivial slight.

He was excited, even a little bit scared, at how easy it was going to be.

The crucial slight, he decided, must come from Mother, because the full force of Borden's devotion was focused on her rather than on Rolfe. It would have to be faked. Though Borden sometimes made Mother nervous ('He's so intense, poor fellow!') still she sympathized with him; she would stick with him as long as he behaved himself. Of course if she thought for one minute that he had gone back to drugs...

A little manipulation by Rolfe, and that was exactly what she thought. She couldn't understand it when Borden failed to turn up for three sessions in a row. (The doctor, Rolfe had explained to him, felt that Mother might be overdoing; she was showing signs of strain.) Why didn't Borden call? Why didn't he explain? ('Whatever you do, please don't call her,' Rolfe had cautioned. 'It would only upset her, and we're trying to keep her as quiet as possible.') She fretted. She hoped against hope – until Rolfe, commissioned to investigate, brought back a report that confirmed her worst fears.

Of course there was nothing to do but call the whole project off. They couldn't risk letting Borden come back now, under any circumstance. But Mother didn't know when she had been so disappointed in anyone. And just when she had thought he was doing so well! She had a good cry over it. Then – with Rolfe's help – she wrote the letter that had to be written to Borden.

It was all that was needed to push Borden over the edge. A prey, as always, to his own insecurity, he had been suspicious from the first. 'You're not telling me the truth,' he had raged to Rolfe. 'It isn't doctor's orders. She hasn't been overdoing. I've offended her somehow, the way I always do, with everybody I've ever cared about. She wants to get rid of me. Doesn't she? Doesn't she? Why won't you admit it?' And Rolfe had been just kind enough, just evasive enough, to keep him simmering.

He had expected an immediate explosion after the letter. But it was several days before he heard from Borden. No letter this time. None of the frantic telephone calls he had grown used to. His doorbell rang very late one night, and there was Borden – an ominously different, glassy-eyed Borden who at first seemed to have nothing to say and then suddenly burst into a flood of abject pleading. He couldn't stand it, that was all. They had to give him another chance. It was true that he had lost his job and hocked most of his clothes (he was not even wearing a jacket, though the night was raw and windy) but only because he couldn't stand it, they couldn't do this to him, another chance and he would be all right again.

'But that's why I've been trying to get hold of you!' Rolfe broke in – all sincerity, the distressed friend eager to help. 'I've told Mother all along she was being unfair. Only I didn't know where to find you, and here she is, all but convinced that she ought to give you another chance –'

'Let me see her! Now! Right away!' Trembling with excitement, Borden jerked himself out of his chair. 'I'll do anything, anything. Let me see her. You come with me, Rolfe, she'll listen to you –'

'Are you crazy?' said Rolfe coldly. 'At this hour of the night? And you in the shape you're in? We wouldn't have a prayer. I'll tell you right now, I'm not doing one thing for you unless you pull yourself together. Is that understood? You've got until tomorrow night. Let's say tomorrow night at nine thirty. We can meet next door at the bar, and if you're okay I'll take you to see Mother and I'll do all I can for you. But remember, it's up to you.'

'Anything, I told you I'll do anything –' Borden drew a long, shaky breath. 'Can't we make it earlier?' he whispered. 'It's so long to wait. Nine thirty. I don't know if I can wait.'

'You'd damn well better,' Rolfe told him. 'I can't make it till then.'

He thought he never was going to get rid of the fellow. Borden promised, over and over again. Agonized hope flared in his eyes; he knew that if he could just see Mother, speak to her for only a minute, he could convince her. He apologized, he explained, he all but licked Rolfe's hand in a transport of gratitude.

When he was leaving, as an afterthought, Rolfe lent him his own sports jacket. It seemed like the least he could do.

He may have slept some, during what was left of the night, but very little. Mostly, he paced the floor and planned. And as the hours of the next day slid by into afternoon, into evening, a mystical calm spread through him. Here was what he had waited for all his life – the moment (and of his own choosing, brought about by his own contrivance) that would change Rolfe J. in one incandescent flash from vision to reality. Soon, very soon. A bare half hour from now. He had only to slip down the fire escape and into Mother's bedroom through the window he had surreptitiously unlatched when he said goodnight to her, and then – and then –

It would take a very few minutes. He knew so well the exact location of the paperweight, on the desk beside her bed. He knew so well the way she would be lying, with the blanket pulled up to her chin and above it that egg-shell temple exposed, waiting for the blow. Asleep. She would be fast asleep. She would never know what hit her. Or who. Or why.

Back at the fire escape, because he could not afford the risk of being seen in the elevator. A few minutes later he would emerge from his own apartment quite openly, take the elevator to the street floor, and go into the bar next door. Most likely Borden would already be there, wild with anticipation. 'Come on,' Rolfe would say, 'Mother's expecting us.' And into the apartment house they would go, up in the elevator to Mother's door, where Rolfe would suddenly pause in the act of turning his key in the lock. 'Oh, damn!' (slapping his pockets) 'I forgot my pipe. I'll just run up to my place and get it. Go on in, I'll be right back.' Opening the door, he would call in to Mother the business about the pipe, just as though she could hear. Up to his own place again. Five, ten minutes.

When he came back, Borden would have discovered what had happened in the bedroom. He might be standing there, stunned; he might – even better – have fled in panic. Rolfe's story to the police would fit, in any case. 'I never trusted the guy,' he would say. 'Stella can tell you. I made a point of always being here, when he came for his sessions with Mother. But it never occurred to me – It couldn't have been ten minutes. Just while I went upstairs for my pipe. I shouldn't have left him there. God, if only I hadn't!' As for what Borden would try to tell the police – Well, who was going to take the word of a hophead? He didn't have a prayer. Like as not, before it was all over, Borden, along with everybody else, would become convinced of his guilt.

It had been snowing lightly, Rolfe found when he stepped noiselessly through his window. The fire escape steps looked ghostly under the thin white coat. The windows of the two floors between him and Mother's apartment were dark. So was the church next door. No one to see or hear him. Everything was just as he had planned: the swift, silent descent. Mother's window opening smoothly under his hands, his leg thrusting inside, feeling for the floor, avoiding the little chintz chair...

He was inside. And suddenly nothing was as he had planned: the paperweight was not there on the desk. He stumbled into the medicine table, setting off a nervous clash of silver against glass, and still there was no stir or sound from the hump in the bed. His own rapid breathing unnerved him; he could not make it slow down. He became aware of a smell in the room, and that too was wrong because it was unfamiliar – pervasive, yet not like Mother's medicine; sweetish, yet not like her dusting powder. The smell of fear? Might Mother, having heard the intruder, be lying there frozen with terror? It could not be that Rolfe himself was afraid.

It was just that he could not see to find the paperweight. But to turn on the lamp would be to meet Mother's eyes... Again he groped over the desk, for a moment he thought he had it, his fingers closed convulsively, and at once a snatch of wistful music tinkled out. Horrified, he clapped the lid back on the damned-fool contraption: one of those musical cigarette boxes. Mother loved such trinkets. He braced himself for what must surely come now – some movement, some sound from the bed. It did not come. He held his own breath, listening for hers. It was not there.

He turned on the lamp.

The shock came not so much from what had been done to Mother – after all, he himself had planned it – as from the fact that it had been done without him realizing it. For his first nightmarish conviction was that his memory had betrayed him, tricked him by blanking out. How could I have done it, he thought, and I have absolutely no recollection of it? Why, there I was, fumbling around for the paperweight, when all the time I had already...

The paperweight was on the bed, where it had been dropped once it had served its purpose. Mother's smashed-in head lay sideways on the pillow. She had put up quite a struggle for her poor life; one fat dimpled hand reached vainly toward the telephone, and her eyes, glazed and terrible with knowledge, stared up at him. She had known who hit her, and why.

It could not have been Rolfe. At last his mind grasped the truth. Memory was not playing tricks on him. Someone else had beaten him to it, had carried out his plan for him. A glance around the room, and he had the answer. The someone else was Borden. There across the chintz chair was Rolfe's jacket, the one Borden had borrowed last night. Maybe he had left it here on impulse – simply shucking off anything connected with Rolfe or his mother – or maybe on purpose in the hope (the dirty little rat) of implicating Rolfe. Well, Rolfe wasn't having any of that. He had come down in his shirt sleeves. With a feeling of triumph he slipped into the jacket. The comfortable set of it on his shoulders seemed to steady him.

Not that he was really shaken, of course. Not Rolfe J. Naturally it was a jolt, to find that Borden had come barging in ahead of time. But only a minor jolt, only momentarily.

How had the fellow gotten in? The open fire-escape window? No, Rolfe remembered. There had been a key to Mother's apartment, an extra one, in his jacket pocket. Finding it must have been the spark that set Borden off. There right in his hands was the means of cutting short the agony of waiting; he could not resist using it. And Mother – taken by surprise, unaware that she was supposed to be on the verge of giving Borden another chance – would not have minced words. A flat, harsh turndown. What followed was inevitable.

Yes, there was the key on the desk, where Borden must have tossed it when he came in. Rolfe reached for it. And hesitated.

Supposing the police didn't believe him? He had never doubted that he could convince them of a lie. But now, in a chilling flash, he saw the situation as it would look, for example, to someone walking in on him at that moment. Standing there with the weapon in his hand (hastily, he slipped it into his pocket), the open fire-escape window behind him...

But of course nothing like that was going to happen. It wouldn't take them long to catch up with Borden, and he would crack. He had none of Rolfe's stamina; he was sure to crack. Guilty as he was, he might already be turning himself in. He would spill everything – the jacket borrowed from Rolfe, the extra key accidentally left in the pocket.

So it was a mistake to wear the jacket away. He must leave everything just as it was. And it would be a mistake to call the police quite yet. Because the other key to Mother's apartment was upstairs, on his chest of drawers; and it would be hard to explain why, with it lying there, Rolfe had chosen to come down the fire escape. Thank God he had thought of it in time! He drew a breath of relief at the simplicity of what he had to do – another trip up the fire escape for his key, down again in the elevator, back here to the bedroom (he must remember to lock the fire-escape window) and then the distraught call to the police. He had it made.

All the same, he had one leg through the window when he realized he was still wearing the jacket. The near-blunder shook him; it gave him a grim glimpse of how treacherous his mind could be. But must not be. Would not be.

The trouble was that everything happened at once: he discovered in his hurry to shed the jacket why Borden had left it behind. There was blood on the sleeve; it was already beginning to stiffen. And he heard the voice and the footsteps. His whole body locked in a paralysis of listening. Someone was in the apartment. Someone who was moving through the living room, on toward the bedroom. That fool Borden must have left the door ajar, simply walked out and...

Move. Get out of here. But get out of the jacket too, the damning jacket, because the footsteps were appallingly close now! At the last moment his arms and legs unlocked, but only in a flurry of witless jerks that neither got him through the window nor out of the jacket. And it was all too late. He was lost. Ignominiously straddling the window sill, with one arm still trying to fumble its way out of the jacket, he looked into the granite eyes of Mr. Webb and knew that disaster was upon him.

Complete disaster. He felt Rolfe J. – the masterful man of destiny – disintegrate, once and for all, into the reality of what Mr. Webb saw – a pudgy, guilty wretch, caught red-handed and babbling (somehow that was the worst of all, that he could not stop babbling) an incoherent story that no one was going to believe.

'Tell it to the police,' said Mr. Webb, and reached for the telephone.

So Rolfe went on babbling to the police that they must find Borden, all they had to do was find Borden. He babbled on and on.

They found Borden. What was left of him. He had either fallen or jumped from the window of his room to the alley below. Nobody knew exactly when. Or why. And the police said, who knew what made hopheads do any of the screwball things they did?

Luck had been with Borden – until he went out the window, of course. Nobody had seen him entering or leaving Mother's apartment. Nobody had seen him wearing Rolfe's jacket; there was only Rolfe's word that he had ever borrowed it. Only Rolfe's word, which nobody believed.

Yet there was nothing else for Rolfe to do but to go on

hopelessly telling the truth. At the very end, while he was waiting in the death cell, he said, 'I am guilty. I did not do it, but I am guilty.'

A garbled sort of confession? Or just some more crazy babbling? No one recognized it for what it was. The deepest truth of all.

The Third Call

by Jack Ritchie

At 1:20 in the afternoon I phoned Stevenson High School and got through to Principal Morrison.

I spoke through the handkerchief over the mouthpiece. 'This is no joke. A bomb is going to explode in your school in fifteen minutes.'

There were a few seconds of silence on the other end of the line and then Morrison's angry voice demanded, 'Who is this?'

'Never mind that. I'm not fooling this time. A bomb is going off in fifteen minutes.'

And then I hung up.

I left the gas station, crossed the street, and returned to the main police station. I took the elevator to the third floor.

My partner, Pete Torgeson, was on the phone when I entered the squad room.

He looked up. 'Stevenson High School just got another one of those calls, Jim. Morrison is having the school evacuated again.'

'Did you get the bomb squad?'

'I'm doing that right now.' He dialed and completed the call to Room 121, giving them details.

The enrollment at Stevenson was 1800 and all the students were out of the building by the time we arrived. Their teachers, following the instructions we had given them the last two times the school had received phone calls, were keeping them at least two hundred feet away from the building.

Principal Morrison was a large graying man wearing rimless

glasses. He left the group of teachers at the curb and came forward. 'The call came at exactly 1:20,' he said.

The bomb unit truck and two squad cars pulled up behind our car.

My son David lounged against the wire fence with a half dozen of his buddies. He waved. 'What is it, Dad? Another bomb scare?'

I nodded. 'And let's hope it's nothing more than a scare this time too.'

Dave grinned. 'I don't mind a bit. We were just going to have a history exam.'

Morrison shook his head. 'I'm afraid that most of the students regard this as nothing more than a welcome break in the routine.'

Several more details of men arrived from headquarters and we began searching the building. We finished the job at 2:30 and I went back to Morrison. 'It was another hoax. We didn't find a thing.'

Morrison ordered the students back to their classes and then took Torgeson and me to his office.

'Did you recognize the voice?' Torgeson asked.

Morrison sat down at his desk. 'No. It was muffled and indistinct, just as before. But it was a male voice. That much I'm certain about.' He sighed. 'I'm having the attendance records checked right away. Are you sure it's one of the students?'

'In cases like this, it usually is,' Pete said. 'A boy decides he hates one of the teachers or the whole school because he's getting bad marks. So he uses this way to get what he thinks is revenge. Or maybe he just thinks the whole thing is a roaring joke.'

The attendance records were brought to Morrison. He glanced at them and then passed them over to us. 'Ninety-one absences. About average.'

Pete and I went over the names of the absent students. I knew that Bob Fletcher would be there, but that didn't matter. I hoped that Lester Baines had come back to school in the afternoon.

'Fletcher's here,' Pete said. 'But he's out, of course.' His eyes went back to the list. 'And Lester Baines was absent.' He ran down the rest of the names and then looked up and smiled. 'Just Lester Baines. He's our boy.'

Morrison had Lester's records brought in. He shook his head as he read. 'He's seventeen. No disciplinary problem at all, but he's absent a lot. His grades are pretty bad. He failed in two subjects last semester.'

Pete was looking over Morrison's shoulder. 'Do you know him?'

Morrison smiled wanly. 'No. A principal knows fewer of the students than any teacher.'

Torgeson lit a cigar. 'This looks like the end of this one, Jim. You should look more cheerful.'

I got to my feet. 'I just don't like to see any boy get into trouble.'

We drove to the Baines home. It was a medium-sized two-story house much like any of the others in the block.

Mr. Baines was tall and blue-eyed. The smile left his face when he opened the door. 'You here again?'

'We'd like to talk to your son,' Pete said. 'Lester wasn't at school today. Is he sick?'

Baines' eyes flickered and then he said. 'Why?'

Pete smiled faintly. 'The same thing we were here for before.'

Baines let us in reluctantly. 'Lester's at the drug store. He'll be back in a few minutes.'

Torgeson sat down on the davenport. 'He isn't sick?'

Baines watched us narrowly. 'He had a cold. I thought that it was best to keep him home today. But it wasn't so bad that he couldn't go down to the drug store for a coke.'

Pete's face was bland. 'Where was your boy at ten-thirty this morning?'

'He was right here,' Baines snapped. 'And he didn't make any phone calls.'

'How do you know that?'

'This is my day off. I was with Lester all day.'

'Where is your wife?'

'She's out shopping now. But she was here at ten-thirty.

Lester didn't make any phone calls.'

Pete smiled. 'I hope so. And where was Lester at 1:20'

'Right here,' Baines said again. 'My wife and I will swear to it.' He frowned. 'Were there two calls today?'

Pete nodded.

We sat in the living room waiting. Baines fidgeted nervously in his chair and then got up. 'I'll be right back. I've got to check some of the upstairs screens.'

Pete watched him leave the room and then turned to me. 'You're letting me do all the talking, Jim.'

'It doesn't take two for something like this, Pete.'

He lit a cigar. 'Well, everything turned out all right. We won't have to lose sleep on this one.' He picked up the phone on a table at his elbow and listened. After a while he put his hand over the mouthpiece. 'Baines is on the upstairs extension. He's calling around. He doesn't know where his son is.'

Pete kept listening and after a while he smiled. 'Now he's talking to his wife. She's at the supermarket. He's telling her about us. She's supposed to say that Lester was at home all day and made no phone calls.'

I was looking out of the picture window, when a blond teenage boy turned up the walk and came toward the house.

Torgeson saw him too and put down the phone. 'There's Lester now. We'll try to have a few fast words with him before his father comes down.'

Lester Baines had a new sunburn and he carried a rolled-up towel under his arm. His normally cheerful face sobered when he stepped into the house and saw us.

'Where were you today, Lester?' Pete asked. 'We know you weren't at school.'

Lester swallowed. 'I felt pretty rotten this morning and so I stayed home.'

Pete indicated the towel under his arm. 'Is there a wet pair of swimming trunks in there?'

Color came to Lester's face. 'Well – around nine this morning everything seemed okay again. Maybe I didn't have a cold. I mean, maybe it was just an allergy or something and it cleared up.' He took a deep breath. 'So I decided to go swimming, get some sun.'

'All day? Didn't you get hungry?'

'I took along a few sandwiches.'

'Who did you go with?'

'Nobody. Just me.' He shifted uneasily. 'Was there another one of those phone calls?'

Pete smiled. 'If you were feeling so fit, why didn't you go to school in the afternoon?'

Lester's hands worked on the towel. 'I was going to. But the next thing I knew it was after one o'clock and I couldn't have got back in time anyway.' He went on lamely, 'So I just decided to swim some more.'

'If you were just going to be away for the morning, why did you take the sandwiches along?'

Lester's color deepened and he finally decided to tell the whole truth. 'I didn't have a cold today. I just stayed away from school. Mom and Dad don't know that. There was going to be a civics test this morning and a history test in the afternoon, and I knew I'd flunk them both. I figured that if I studied tonight I'd be able to pass make-up tests tomorrow.'

We heard the footsteps coming down the stairs and waited.

Baines stopped when he saw us with his son. 'Don't tell them anything, Lester. Let me do the talking.'

'I'm afraid it's too late for that now,' Pete said. 'Your boy admitted that he wasn't in this house today.'

Lester's voice showed panic. 'I didn't make any of those calls. Honest, I didn't!'

Baines moved beside his son. 'Why keep picking on Lester?'

'We're not picking on Lester,' Pete said. 'But we're reasonably certain that one of the students did the phoning. However, all of the calls came during times when classes were in session. And that means that only a student who was absent could have made them.'

Baines wasn't impressed. 'I'm sure that Lester wasn't the only student absent today.'

Pete conceded but went on. 'The first of the three phone calls came eighteen days ago. We checked the attendance records at Stevenson at that time and found that ninety-six students had been absent at the time it was made. Sixty-two of those were boys and we talked to all of them – including your son. Your boy was home at that time with a cold... and alone. You were at work and your wife was attending the birthday party of a friend. However, your son denied making the call and we had to accept his word for that.'

Lester appealed to his father. 'I *didn't* make that bomb call, Dad. I wouldn't do such a thing.'

Baines met his eyes for a moment and then turned back to us, his face expressionless.

Pete continued. 'The second phone call came this morning at ten-thirty. We went over the attendance records again and discovered that only three boys had been absent on both this morning and on the day of the first phone call.'

Baines' face showed a faint hope. 'Are you checking the other two boys?'

'We were about to do that, but then another bomb scare call was made this afternoon and we were saved the trouble. We went back to the attendance records. One of our three suspects had returned for the afternoon session and therefore could not have phoned.'

'What about the other boy?' Baines demanded.

'He's in a hospital.'

Baines grasped at that. 'Hospitals have phones.'

Torgeson smiled faintly. 'The boy caught scarlet fever while he was out of the state with his parents last weekend.. He's in a hospital five hundred miles away from here – and the phone calls were all local.'

Baines turned to his son.

Lester paled. 'You know I never lie to you, Dad.'

'Of course you don't, son.' But there was doubt on Baines' face.

The front door opened and an auburn-haired woman stepped inside. Her face was pale, but determined, and it took her a moment to get her breath.

'I just stepped out for a moment to go shopping. Otherwise I was here all day. I'm sure I can account for every moment of Lester's time.'

'Mom,' Lester said miserably. 'It's no use. I played hookey all day today and they know it.'

Pete reached for his hat. 'I'd like both of you to talk to your son tonight. I'm sure you can do that much better than we can.' He put one of our cards on the table. 'We'd like to see all three of you tomorrow morning at ten.'

Outside, when he pulled our car away from the curb, Pete said, 'We might find ourselves in for a hard time, if they decide to keep lying for their son.'

'Suppose it wasn't somebody from the school?'

'I hope it wasn't. But you and I know that the chances are ninety-nine out of a hundred that it was.' Pete sighed. 'I don't like to see things like this. The bomb scare is bad enough, but what's happening to that family now is a lot worse.'

I checked out of the station at five and got home a little after five-thirty.

My wife, Nora, was in the kitchen. 'I read in the paper that there was another bomb scare at Stevenson this morning.'

I kissed her. 'And one this afternoon. That one happened too late to get into the paper.'

She lifted the cover off the pot roast. 'Did you find who made the calls?'

I hesitated a moment. 'Yes I think we have.'

'Who was it?'

'One of the students. A Lester Baines.'

Her face showed pity. 'What would make him do something like that?'

'I don't know. He hasn't admitted making the calls yet.'

She studied me. 'You look tired, Jim. Is something like this a little worse than usual?'

'Yes. A lot worse.'

Her eyes showed worry, but she smiled. 'Supper's just about ready. Why don't you call Dave? He's out in the garage trying to get that car of his to run.'

Dave had the carburetor on the work bench. He looked up. 'Hi, Dad. You look beat with the heat.'

'It was a hard day.'

'Find the fiend?'

'I hope so.'

Dave had his gray eyes of his mother. He frowned. 'Who was it?'

'A boy named Lester Baines. Do you know him?'

Dave peered down at the parts before him. 'Sure.'

'What kind of boy is he?'

Dave shrugged. 'I just know him to talk to. Seems like he's all right.' He still frowned. 'Did he admit making the calls?'

'No.'

Dave picked up a screwdriver. 'How did you narrow it down to him?'

I told him the method we had used.

Dave seemed to have trouble with an adjustment. 'Is he in a lot of trouble?'

'It might turn out that way.'

'What do you think will happen to him?'

'I don't know. He's never been in trouble before. He might get probation.'

Dave thought about that. 'Maybe he did it as a joke. I mean nobody got hurt. All he did was stop school for awhile.'

'A lot of people could have gotten hurt,' I said. 'It wouldn't have been a joke if there had been a panic.'

Dave's face seemed slightly stubborn. 'We have fire drills all the time. Everything goes off okay.'

Yes, and that was what I had counted on when I called. I didn't want anyone to get hurt.

Dave put down his screwdriver. 'Do *you* think Lester did it?'

'He could have.'

Yes, Lester Baines could have made those first two phone calls. And I had made the third.

Dave was silent for a while. 'Dad, when the school got the first phone call, did you talk to all the boys who were absent?'

'Not myself. But the department got around to seeing all of them.'

Dave gave a faint wry smile. 'I was absent that day, Dad. Nobody talked to me.'

'I didn't think it was necessary, son.'

And I hadn't. Other men's boys might have done such a thing, but not my boy. But now I waited.

Dave spoke reluctantly. 'I was absent this morning too.'

'Yes,' I said.

He met my eyes. 'And that narrowed it down to how many boys?'

'Three,' I said. 'But we discovered that one of them couldn't possibly have made the call. He was in a hospital out of the state.' I watched Dave. 'And that left us with just two suspects. Lester Baines – and you.'

Dave had trouble manufacturing a grin. 'Some luck, huh? I was at school this afternoon when the third phone call came and so that left just poor Lester.'

'That's right. Poor Lester.'

Dave licked his lips. 'Is Lester's dad standing by him?'

'Of course. That's the way dads are supposed to be.'

Dave seemed to be perspiring slightly. He worked silently at the carburetor for a minute or two. Then he sighed and met my eyes. 'Dad, I think you'd better take me down to headquarters. Lester didn't make those bomb calls. I did.' He took a deep breath. 'I did it as a joke. I just wanted to pep things up. I didn't mean anything wrong.'

I hadn't wanted to hear those words, and yet now I felt a pride that I had a son who wouldn't let someone else suffer for his own mistakes.

'But, Dad, I just made the first two calls. Not the one this afternoon.'

'I know. I made that particular call myself.'

His eyes widened. And then he understood. 'You tried to cover up for me?'

I smiled tiredly. 'It was something I shouldn't have done, but a father doesn't always think too clearly when it involves his son. And I was hoping that it might turn out to be Lester after all.'

Dave wiped his hands on a rag and there were a few moments of silence.

'I guess I ought to tell them I made all the calls, Dad,' Dave said. 'There's no sense in all of us getting into trouble.'

I shook my head. 'Thanks, son. I'll tell them what I did.'

And now when Dave looked at me, I had the feeling that

134 The Third Call

somehow he was proud of me too.

'We'll have supper first,' I said. 'And then we'll phone Lester's father. A half an hour won't make much difference.'

Dave smiled wryly. 'It will to Lester and his dad.'

I made the phone call as soon as we got back to the house.

A Home Away From Home

by Robert Bloch

The train was late, and it must have been past nine o'clock when Natalie found herself standing, all alone, on the platform before Hightower Station.

The station itself was obviously closed for the night – it was only a way-stop, really, for there was no town here – and Natalie wasn't quite sure what to do. She had taken it for granted that Dr. Bracegirdle would be on hand to meet her. Before leaving London, she'd sent her uncle a wire giving him the time of her arrival. But since the train had been delayed, perhaps he'd come and gone.

Natalie glanced around uncertainly, then noticed the phonebooth which provided her with a solution. Dr. Bracegirdle's last letter was in her purse, and it contained both his address and his phone-number. She had fumbled through her bag and found it by the time she walked over to the booth.

Ringing him up proved a bit of a problem; there seemed to be an interminable delay before the operator made the connection, and there was a great deal of buzzing on the line. A glimpse of the hills beyond the station, through the glass wall of the booth, suggested the reason for the difficulty. After all, Natalie reminded herself, this was West Country. Conditions might be a bit primitive –

'Hello, hello!'

The woman's voice came over the line, fairly shouting above the din. There was no buzzing noise now, and the sound in the background suggested a babble of voices all intermingled. Natalie bent forward and spoke directly and distinctly into the mouthpiece.

'This is Natalie Rivers,' she said. 'Is Dr. Bracegirdle there?'
'Whom did you say was calling?'
'Natalie Rivers. I'm his niece.'
'His what, Miss?'
'Niece,' Natalie repeated. 'May I speak to him, please?'
'Just a moment.'

There was a pause, during which the sound of voices in the background seemed amplified, and then Natalie heard the resonant masculine tones, so much easier to separate from the indistinct murmuring.

'Dr. Bracegirdle here. My dear Natalie, this is an unexpected pleasure!'

'Unexpected? But I sent you a 'gram from London this afternoon.' Natalie checked herself as she realized the slight edge of impatience which had crept into her voice. 'Didn't it arrive?'

'I'm afraid service is not of the best around here,' Dr. Bracegirdle told her, with an apologetic chuckle. 'No, your wire didn't arrive. But apparently you did.' He chuckled again. 'Where are you, my dear?'

'At Hightower Station.'

'Oh, dear. It's in exactly the opposite direction.'

'Opposite direction?'

'From Peterby's. They rang me up just before you called. Some silly nonsense about an appendix – probably nothing but an upset stomach. But I promised to drop round directly, just in case.'

'Don't tell me they still call you for general practise?'

'Emergencies, my dear. There aren't many physicians in these parts. Fortunately, there aren't many patients either.' Dr. Bracegirdle started to chuckle, then sobered. 'Look now. You say you're at the station. I'll just send Miss Plummer down to fetch you in the wagon. Have you much luggage?'

'Only my travel-case. The rest is coming with the household goods, by boat.'

'Boat?'

'Didn't I mention it when I wrote?'

'Yes, that's right, you did. Well, no matter. Miss Plummer will be along for you directly.'

'I'll be waiting in front of the platform.'

'What was that? Speak up, I can hardly hear you.'

'I said I'll be waiting in front of the platform.'

'Oh.' Dr. Bracegirdle chuckled again. 'Bit of a party going on here.'

'Shan't I be intruding? I mean, since you weren't expecting me –'

'Not at all! They'll be leaving before long. You wait for Plummer.'

The phone clicked off and Natalie returned to the platform. In a surprisingly short time, the station-wagon appeared and skidded off the road to halt at the very edge of the tracks. A tall, thin, gray-haired woman, wearing a somewhat rumpled white uniform, emerged and beckoned to Natalie.

'Come along, my dear,' she called. 'Here, I'll just pop this in back.' Scooping up the bag, she tossed it into the rear of the wagon. 'Now, in with you – and off we go!'

Scarcely waiting for Natalie to close the door after her, Miss Plummer gunned the motor and the car plunged back onto the road.

The speedometer immediately shot up to seventy, and Natalie flinched. Miss Plummer noticed her agitation at once.

'Sorry,' she said. 'With Doctor out on call, I can't be away too long.'

'Oh yes, the house-guests. He told me.'

'Did he now?' Miss Plummer took a sharp turn at a crossroads and the tires screeched in protest, but to no avail. Natalie decided to drown apprehension in conversation.

'What sort of a man is my uncle?' she asked.

'Have you never met him?'

'No. My parents moved to Australia when I was quite young. This is my first trip to England. In fact, it's the first time I've left Canberra.'

'Folks with you?'

'They were in a motor smashup two months ago,' Natalie said. 'Didn't the Doctor tell you?'

'I'm afraid not – you see, I haven't been with him very long.' Miss Plummer uttered a short bark and the car swerved wildly across the road. 'Motor smashup, eh? Some people have no business behind the wheel. That's what Doctor says.'

She turned and peered at Natalie. 'I take it you've come to stay, then?'

'Yes, of course. He wrote me when he was appointed my guardian. That's why I was wondering what he might be like. It's so hard to tell from letters.' The thin-faced woman nodded silently, but Natalie had an urge to confide. 'To tell the truth, I'm just a little bit edgy. I mean, I've never met a psychiatrist before.'

'Haven't you, now?' Miss Plummer shrugged. 'You're quite fortunate. I've seen a few in my time. A bit on the know-it-all side, if you ask me. Though I must say, Dr. Bracegirdle is one of the best. Permissive, you know.'

'I understand he has quite a practise.'

'There's no lack of patients for *that* sort of thing,' Miss Plummer observed. 'Particularly amongst the well-to-do. I'd say your uncle has done himself handsomely. The house and all – but you'll see.' Once again the wagon whirled into a sickening swerve and sped forward between the imposing gates of a huge driveway which led towards an enormous house set amidst a grove of trees in the distance. Through the shuttered windows Natalie caught sight of a faint beam of light – just enough to help reveal the ornate facade of her uncle's home.

'Oh, dear,' she muttered, half to herself.

'What is it?'

'The guests – and it's Saturday night. And here I am, all mussed from travel.'

'Don't give it another thought,' Miss Plummer assured her. 'There's no formality here. That's what Doctor told me when I came. It's a home away from home.'

Miss Plummer barked and braked simultaneously, and the station-wagon came to an abrupt stop just behind an imposing black limousine.

'Out with you now!' With brisk efficiency, Miss Plummer lifted the bag from the rear seat and carried it up the steps, beckoning Natalie forward with a nod over her shoulder. She halted at the door and fumbled for a key.'

'No sense knocking,' she said. 'They'd never hear me.' As the door swung open her observation was amply confirmed. The background noise which Natalie had noted over the telephone now formed a formidable foreground. She stood there, hesitant, as Miss Plummer swept forward across the threshold.

'Come along, come along!'

Obediently, Natalie entered, and as Miss Plummer shut the door behind her, she blinked with eyes unaccustomed to the brightness of the interior.

She found herself standing in a long, somewhat bare hallway. Directly ahead of her was a large staircase; at an angle between the railing and the wall was a desk and chair. To her left was a dark panelled door – evidently leading to Dr. Bracegirdle's private office, for a small brass plate was fixed to it, bearing his name. To her right was a huge open parlor, its windows heavily curtained and shuttered against the night. It was from here that the sounds of sociability echoed.

Natalie stared down the hall toward the stairs. As she did so, she caught a glimpse of the parlor. Fully a dozen guests eddied about a large table, talking and gesturing with the animation of close acquaintance – with one another, and with the contents of the lavish array of bottles gracing the tabletop. A sudden whoop of laughter indicated that at least one guest had abused the Doctor's hospitality.

Natalie passed the entry hastily, so as not to be observed, then glanced behind her to make sure that Miss Plummer was following with her bag. Miss Plummer was indeed following, but her hands were empty. And as Natalie reached the stairs, Miss Plummer shook her head.

'You didn't mean to go up now, did you?' she murmured. 'Come in and introduce yourself.'

'I thought I might freshen up a bit first.'

'Let me go on ahead and get your room in order. Doctor didn't give me notice, you know.'

'Really, it's not necessary. I could do with a wash – '

'Doctor should be back any moment now. Do wait for him.' Miss Plummer grasped Natalie's arm, and with the same speed and expedition she had bestowed on driving, she steered the girl forward into the lighted room.

'Here's Doctor's niece,' she announced. 'Miss Natalie Rivers, from Australia.'

Several heads turned in Natalie's direction, though Miss Plummer's voice had scarcely penetrated the general conversational din. A short, jolly-looking fat man bobbed toward Natalie, waving a half-empty glass.

'All the way from Australia, eh?' He extended his goblet. 'You must be thirsty. Here, take this, I'll get another.' And before Natalie could reply, he turned and plunged back into the group around the table.

'Major Hamilton,' Miss Plummer whispered. 'A dear soul, really. Though I'm afraid he's just a wee bit squiffy.'

As Miss Plummer moved away, Natalie glanced uncertainly at the glass in her hand. She was not quite sure where to dispose of it.

'Allow me.' A tall, gray-haired and quite distinguished-looking man with a black moustache moved forward and took the stemware from between her fingers.

'Thank you.'

'Not at all. I'm afraid you'll have to excuse the Major. The party spirit, you know.' He nodded, indicating a woman in extreme décolletage chattering animatedly to a group of three laughing men. 'But since it's by way of being a farewell celebration – '

'Ah, there you are!' The short man whom Miss Plummer had identified as Major Hamilton bounced back into orbit around Natalie, a fresh drink in his hand and a fresh smile on his ruddy face. 'I'm back again,' he announced. 'Just like a boomerang, eh?'

He laughed explosively, then paused. 'I say, you *do* have boomerangs in Australia? Saw quite a bit of you Aussies at Gallipoli. Of course that was some time ago, before *your* time, I daresay –'

'Please, Major.' The tall man smiled at Natalie. There was something reassuring about his presence, and something oddly familiar too. Natalie wondered where she might have seen him before. She watched while he moved over to the Major and removed the drink from his hand.

'Now see here –' the Major sputtered.

'You've had enough, old boy. And it's almost time for you to go.'

'One for the road –' The Major glanced around, his hands waving in appeal. 'Everyone *else* is drinking!' He made a lunge for his glass, but the tall man evaded him. Smiling at Natalie over his shoulder, he drew the Major to one side and began to mutter to him earnestly in low tones. The Major nodded exaggeratedly, drunkenly.

Natalie looked around the room. Nobody was paying the least attention to her except one elderly woman who sat quite alone on a stool before the piano. She regarded Natalie with a fixed stare that made her feel like an intruder on a gala scene. Natalie turned away hastily and again caught sight of the woman in décolletage. She suddenly remembered her own desire to change her clothing and peered at the doorway, seeking Miss Plummer. But Miss Plummer was nowhere to be seen.

Walking back into the hall, she peered up the staircase.

'Miss Plummer!' she called.

There was no response.

Then from out of the corner of her eye, she noted that the door of the room across the hallway was ajar. In fact, it was opening now, quite rapidly, and as Natalie stared, Miss Plummer came backing out of the room, carrying a pair of scissors in her hand. Before Natalie could call out again and attract her attention, Miss Plummer had scurried off in the other direction.

The people here, Natalie told herself, certainly seemed odd. But wasn't that always the case with people at parties? She crossed before the stairs, meaning to follow Miss Plummer, but found herself halting before the open doorway.

She gazed in curiously at what was obviously her uncle's consultation room. It was a cozy, book-lined study with heavy, leather-covered furniture grouped before the shelves. The psychiatric couch rested in one corner near the wall and near it was a large mahogany desk. The top of the desk was quite bare, save for a cradle telephone, and a thin brown loop snaking out from it.

Something about the loop disturbed Natalie and before she

was conscious of her movement she was inside the room looking down at the desk-top and the brown cord from the phone.

And then she realized what had bothered her. The end of the cord had been neatly severed from its connection in the wall.

'Miss Plummer!' Natalie murmured, remembering the pair of scissors she'd seen her holding. *But why should she have cut the phone cord?*

Natalie turned just in time to observe the tall, distinguished-looking man enter the doorway behind her.

'The phone won't be needed,' he said, as if he'd read her thoughts. 'After all, I *did* tell you it was a farewell celebration.' And he gave a little chuckle.'

Again Natalie sensed something strangely familiar about him, and this time it came to her. She'd heard the same chuckle over the phone, when she'd called from the station.

'You must be playing a joke!' she exclaimed. 'You're Dr. Bracegirdle, aren't you?'

'No, my dear.' He shook his head as he moved past her across the room. 'It's just that no one expected you. We were about to leave when your call came. So we had to say *something*.'

There was a moment of silence. Then, 'Where *is* my uncle?' Natalie asked at last.

'Over here.'

Natalie found herself standing beside the tall man, gazing down at what lay in a space between the couch and the wall. An instant was all she could bear.

'Messy,' the tall man nodded. 'Of course it was all so sudden, the opportunity, I mean. And then they *would* get into the liquor –'

His voice echoed hollowly in the room and Natalie realized the sounds of the party had died away. She glanced up to see them all standing there in the doorway, watching.

Then their ranks parted and Miss Plummer came quickly into the room, wearing an incongruous fur wrap over the rumpled, ill-fitting uniform.

'Oh, my !' she gasped. 'So you found him!'

Natalie nodded and took a step forward. 'You've got to do something,' she said. 'Please!'

'Of course, you didn't see the others,' Miss Plummer said, 'since they're upstairs. The Doctor's staff. Gruesome sight.'

The men and women had crowded into the room behind Miss Plummer, staring silently.

Natalie turned to them in appeal. 'Why, it's the work of a madman!' she cried. 'He belongs in an asylum!'

'My dear child,' murmured Miss Plummer, as she quickly closed and locked the door and the silent starers moved forward 'This *is* an asylum...'

The Handyman

by Clayton Matthews

The man in the witness chair twisted the stained, broad-brimmed hat in big-knuckled hands. His weathered features took on a pale hue. 'Well, sir, it was pretty bad. About the worst I've ever seen, I reckon, in all my years lawing.'

The prosecutor asked, 'Bad in what way, Sheriff?'

'Why, the blood. Blood on the bed, even on the walls...'

At the defense table the defendant shuddered, drew a deep breath, and shuddered again. He leaned over and whispered to his attorney, 'I remember.'

The defense attorney swiveled his head. 'You remember? Everything?'

'It was his mention of blood that brought it all back.'

The lawyer shot to his feet. 'Your Honor! I beg the court's pardon for this interruption, but I would like a short recess. My client is... uh feeling ill.'

There was a brief silence, then the gavel fell. 'Very well. Court will stand in recess for fifteen minutes.'

Quickly the lawyer hustled his client into the anteroom off the courtroom. When the door was locked behind them, he said, 'Then this amnesia, or whatever it is, was real? You haven't been faking?'

'I haven't been faking.'

'All right. Then talk. But if you're lying to me –'

'I'm not lying. I remember everything. I wish to God I didn't!'

Spring weather in north central Texas is deceptively mild. The days of March can be quite warm, but a blue norther can boil up any time and send the temperature plummeting thirty degrees within an hour.

On such a day it was that Cliff Dandoy first saw the Ledbetter place. He had left the main highway, as he liked to do, some miles back and was hiking down a gravel road, khaki shirt open at the throat, shoulders loose under the warm sun, knapsack strapped to his back, canvas-cased guitar slung over one shoulder.

Cliff was slender, quick, rawhide-tough, with eyes a deep blue and hair as blond as harvest wheat, and was just short of thirty. By many he was considered a transient farm worker. To Texas folk, he was a handyman, an extra hand hired to do seasonal farm labor. Cliff thought of himself as a troubadour, an unfettered soul, going where the wild goose goes.

At the last farmhouse where he had inquired about a job they hadn't needed a hand, but the woman had provided him with a lunch of cold fried chicken, cold biscuits and a slab of peach pie. He sat under a tree beside the road and ate the lunch. Finished, he smoked his pipe and dosed for a little while. When he awoke, he saw the norther, stretching from horizon to horizon, a solid blue cloud moving fast like smoke billowing in advance of a prairie fire.

Cliff knew what a norther could do. He had wintered in the Rio Grande Valley where winter clothes were rarely ever needed. One of his traveling-on moods had seized him, and he had walked north early. He had no warm clothes with which to weather the norther. He had to find shelter before nightfall or risk freezing to death, but there wasn't a farmhouse in sight.

He started walking. After an hour he rounded a bend in the road and saw the Ledbetter place. The house, he learned later, was close to a hundred years old. It looked it. It hadn't been painted recently, if ever. A porch ran the length of the house, with a rain cistern at the east end. Fifty yards behind the house was a steep-roofed red barn not over a year old. Involuntarily he glanced up at the parallel-bar patterns of wires overhead, leading both to the house and the barn. At least the place was electrified, and there was a new, rubber-tired tractor standing before the barn.

146 *The Handyman*

Cliff, wise from experience, went around back. At this hour of the afternoon, a rap on the front door would most likely be considered a peddler's knock and be ignored. He knocked on the kitchen door, waited a moment and knocked again.

The door swung open, and he saw the heat-flushed face of Kate Ledbetter for the first time. She was tiny, lithe, with long blonde hair and eyes the color of wood smoke. She wore a shapeless housedress that nonetheless revealed a figure adequately curved. She couldn't have been much more than twenty.

She pushed a strand of moist hair out of her eyes, saying, 'Yes?'

'Ma'am, I was wondering if you'd be needing a hand around the place?'

'You'd have to speak to Troy about that. Troy's my husband.' Then, as though fearful she had somehow discouraged him, she added quickly, 'We did let a man...go, just last week.'

She smiled shyly, and it seemed to Cliff that the smile cost her an effort, as though she hadn't smiled for some time.

'I reckon your husband's out in the fields?'

'He's somewhere on the place, but I can't say just where.' She shivered suddenly, hugging herself, and Cliff realized that the front of the norther had struck. The sun had disappeared, and a cold wind was pushing against the house.

She stepped back inside. 'It's going to be freezing out there soon. Why don't you come into the kitchen and wait? Maybe you'd like a bite?'

Cliff never turned down food, no matter how recently he'd eaten, the involuntary omission of meals being commonplace in his life. Her pecan pie was delicious, the glass of milk cold and foaming fresh.

The kitchen, while sparkling clean, had a primitive air about it. There was an ancient refrigerator that, when on, thumped like a jukebox; it was the only electrical appliance in sight. The cookstove was a huge wood range, and in the sink was a hand pump, not faucets. On the stove a tub of water heated. The splintery floor was slightly damp, and Cliff surmised she had been scrubbing it, hence her heat-flushed features when she answered the door.

Apparently she spoke only when spoken to and, since reticence was a normal condition with Cliff, they waited mostly in silence. Yet it wasn't at all uncomfortable. Cliff fired his pipe and smoked while she worked about the kitchen. Once or twice he heard her sigh and looked up to find her standing at the window over the sink, gazing out. The full fury of the norther worked on the old house now, setting up ghostly creakings and groanings.

Then, again at the window, she said, 'He's coming. Troy's coming.'

Troy Ledbetter wasn't at all what Cliff had been expecting. He was a slight, wiry man, an inch shorter than his wife, and, it was Cliff's guess, perhaps twenty years older. His features were pale. Most men who spent their working days in the fields under the scald of the Texas sun had skin a dark red, the backs of their necks also red and cracking like baked earth. Ledbetter's expression was mild, and gentle brown eyes peered out at Cliff from under the bill of a baseball cap.

When his wife had explained Cliff's purpose. Ledbetter said, in a voice as mild as his manner, 'I reckon I still do the hiring, Kate.'

Her hands fluttered. 'I know, Troy, I know. But I just thought you'd –'

'You just thought,' Ledbetter said tonelessly. He switched his gaze to Cliff. 'It so happens I do need a man. Handle an axe?'

'I've used one.'

'Not much field work this time of the year, reckon you know, but I'm clearing timber off thirty acres by the river for fall planting. If you want to work the timber, I might keep you on until fall harvest time, which means you have a job until winter sets in, you care to stay that long.'

Cliff didn't take offense. A transient farm hand was expected to move on whenever a whim struck him. He said, 'All right, you've hired a hand.'

Ledbetter's nod was meager. 'There's a spare room down the

hall you can use, and you'll take your meals with us. Supper soon ready, Kate?'

His wife, at the stove with her back to them, said in a muffled voice, 'Yes, Troy.' There was a fear in her. It didn't show in the way she spoke or acted but in a certain tenseness that had come over her the moment her husband had entered the kitchen.

As Cliff picked up his knapsack and guitar case, she faced him. 'You play and sing, Mr. Dandoy?'

'A little of both,' he smiled. 'Dogs howl and cats scamper, but I manage to entertain myself.'

He felt certain she wanted to return the smile, but her husband was watching, and she didn't.

Cliff awoke sometime in the night. The norther had blown itself out, and the old house was still. He thought a cry had awakened him. He dismissed it as the residue of a dream, and yet, just before he drifted into sleep again, he thought he heard muffled weeping.

Kate Ledbetter was an excellent cook. Breakfast was a stack of wheatcakes and thick slabs of smokehouse ham. Ledbetter ate with his eyes cast down, rarely speaking. Kate didn't sit with them. She moved back and forth from the table to the stove, serving them. Cliff knew this wasn't a cruelty practiced by Ledbetter; it was customary. She would eat later, when they were gone.

He wanted to ask her to sit and eat with them, but he knew it wouldn't do. He did say, leaving the table, 'Best-tasting breakfast I've had in a while, Mrs. Ledbetter.'

She didn't blush coyly and look away. She met his gaze levelly, searching for mockery. Finding none, she did, then, glance away with a flutter of hands.

To ease her embarrassment Cliff turned aside, fumbling for his pipe, and saw Ledbetter watching them, a slight smile curving his thin lips.

The day was clear, the sky scoured clean of clouds, and a little crisp. Cliff was given two sharpened axes by Ledbetter and shown the area to be cleared of timber, an S-shaped section of river bottom. The river was a narrow, deep-running stream. The timber was live oak, black oak, a scattering of mesquite and a snarl of underbrush. It took Cliff a couple of hours to settle into a working rhythm. By mid-morning he had warmed up enough to remove his shirt.

At noon Kate came out with a hot lunch. She stared at the smooth skin of his heaving chest, then quickly averted her gaze.

Cliff accepted the lunch with a grave, 'Thank you... Kate.'

She nodded, smiled briefly and fled. He stared after her for a moment, shrugged, and sat down to eat.

The Ledbetters baffled Cliff more and more as the days passed. They didn't speak a dozen words to one another during the day, at least not in his hearing, and Cliff very much doubted they were more loquacious when he wasn't around.

Their evenings were spent in the parlor, Kate with a lap piled high with mending, Ledbetter poring over farm journals or equipment catalogs. They didn't have a television set, not even a radio. Cliff owned a transistor radio and he brought it into the parlor on the third evening. At the sound of music Kate glanced up from her mending with an anticipatory smile, a smile that quickly died as she looked at her husband. Cliff was stubborn: he stayed for an hour. Ledbetter didn't say a word; as near as Cliff could ascertain he never once glanced up from his journal perusal, but Cliff felt his disapproval as powerfully as if the man had shouted at him.

Cliff never carried the transistor into the parlor again. In fact, he never went into the parlor again. He remained in his room, listening to the radio or idly strumming on the guitar and singing softly to himself.

The morning after that particular evening, he managed a moment alone with Kate. He said, 'Would you like to listen to my radio here during the day?'

Eagerness swept her face, was instantly gone. 'No, Mr. Dandoy. It's nice of you to offer, but I have too much to do to bother with such things.'

Most farmers Cliff had worked for had possessed a radio to catch weather reports and crop prices; even those too stingy or too poor to own a TV had that, at least. Then he discovered that Ledbetter had a radio on his tractor on which, apparently, he received all the reports he deemed necessary.

That, of course, was only another bafflement. Ledbetter owned the latest in farm equipment: two tractors, disk plow, row-top planter, hay baler, and others, but the very few appliances in the house were falling apart and the furniture was ancient and worn thin with repeated polishings. Kate housecleaned with a broom, dust mop and dust cloth. And their only means of transportation was a ten-year-old pickup.

Cliff's first conclusion was that Ledbetter was of some religion that frowned upon electrical appliances and electronic entertainment. But his first Sunday there disabused him of that notion. The Ledbetters didn't go to church. After breakfast Ledbetter went to the fields and Kate worked around the house. Their only concession to the Sabbath was Ledbetter's gruff remark, 'It's Sunday, Dandoy. You don't need to work today.'

It was on the tip of Cliff's tongue to say, 'Well, thanks a *heap*,' but he doubted it would be received in the proper spirit.

It wasn't a household he would ordinarily be happy in, and he would, ordinarily, have taken his leave after the first week. Yet he remained, angry with himself for doing so, and even more furious because of the reason. He was in love with Kate Ledbetter. It was ridiculous, idiotic, insane. She hadn't given him the slightest encouragement, yet he sensed she somehow knew.

By June the weather had warmed sufficiently for Cliff to sit on the porch evenings, and play and sing. He knew Kate was listening. He halfway expected Ledbetter to object, but the man said nothing.

It was a week before Kate ventured out to sit on the porch and listen, hands folded in her lap. The light was out in the parlor. Ledbetter had gone to bed, which he did early seven nights a week.

This also puzzled Cliff – that Ledbetter would go off to bed and leave Kate alone with the hired hand – but he didn't question his good fortune.

Kate said nothing at all during those first few evenings. Then one night Cliff stopped playing and leaned back to gaze dreamily at the full moon, and Kate said softly, 'Play another sad song for me, Cliff.'

It was the first time she had called him by his first name. Cliff turned to her and said urgently, 'Ah-h, Kate, Kate!'

He half-started to his feet, but she was gone with a pale flutter of hands, vanishing into the dark innards of the house like a wraith.

Weeks passed. The weather heated steadily, and then it was summer. Cliff's axe flashed in the sun, and trees fell like columns of soldiers shot down one by one. Crops grew toward the sun. Thirty acres of alfalfa Ledbetter had planted on the river-bottom land would soon be ready for mowing and baling.

Evenings, Cliff played and sang on the porch, but to himself, Kate didn't join him again, and didn't call him Cliff again. Always 'Mr. Dandoy.'

Cliff wanted to leave. He stayed on, cursing himself for a fool.

One unusually hot day, Kate was a little late bringing his lunch. He had been burning piled underbrush near the river and was sweaty, covered with a dusting of ash. The water looked cool and inviting. Every night now he swam awhile in the river before going up to the house.

On an impulse he stepped out of his shoes and socks and dived into the water. The trousers didn't matter; they would dry within a matter of minutes in the sun. He came up snorting, blowing water. He heard clear, ringing laughter. He saw Kate on the river bank. It was the first time he'd heard her laugh.

She said, 'You look like a little boy caught playing hooky.'

It was never quite clear in his mind what prompted him to say what he did next, but something told him this was the right time, the right moment for them. He said, 'Come play hooky with me, Kate, dress and all. The sun'll dry it before you get back to the house.'

Without hesitation she set the lunch pail down, unlaced and removed her sneakers, then cut the water in a perfect dive.

For a time they frolicked like children. Kate was good in the water. Cliff was sure she forgot everything but that moment in that little time. She laughed and yelped and splashed.

Finally they staggered up the slippery bank. Her hair clung to her head like seaweed. Her dress was plastered to her figure. She was a mess.

She was the loveliest thing Cliff had ever seen.

With a groan he reached for her, 'Kate, Kate, I love you. You *must* know that!'

She came into his arms willingly, her mouth raised, seeking. Then she tore away with a strangled cry. 'No, no! I won't be responsible for another death!'

He stared at her, blinking. 'Kate... What in God's name are you talking about?'

She stood with her face turned away. 'There was another man before you came...'

'I know that. You told me your husband let him go.'

'That's what I told you,' she whispered, 'but I think Troy killed him!'

'Killed...' Cliff caught her chin and forced her face around. Her eyes were clenched shut. 'What are you talking about? Why would he do a thing like that?'

'Troy caught us laughing together. That was all it was, Cliff. I swear there was nothing else!'

'All right, I believe you. Go on.'

'Well, the next morning Joel was gone. Troy told me he had left in the middle of the night.'

'How do you know he didn't?'

'He left a suitcase full of his things.'

'That could well be, if your husband scared him enough. Why do you think Ledbetter killed him?'

'Because...' She shivered. 'I just know!'

'That's only a woman's reason, Kate.'

'He was a drifter. No folks, nobody. No one would ever miss him.'

'Kate, I don't like Troy Ledbetter, but that could be because of the way I feel about you. Even so, I can't see him killing a man.'

'You don't know him, that's why. He's stingy and mean, all knotted inside like a fist!'

'Why did you marry him, Kate?'

Orphaned and left penniless when her parents were killed in an automobile accident four years ago, Kate had looked upon Troy Ledbetter's proposal of marriage as her salvation. At seventeen, in her last year of high school, she hadn't known which way to turn. Troy was well thought of, a prosperous farmer; he was clean, frugal, and seemed a kind and gentle man. She hadn't loved him, but maybe love was for the storybooks and the movies. Four years of marriage had taught her that the frugality was stinginess, the gentle manner a façade concealing an infinite capacity for small, subtle cruelties. For instance, they lived seven miles from town; twice a year Troy drove her into town and allowed her to buy a few clothes. He did all the other shopping, and all spare money went for machinery and farm improvements. Too, of late he had become unreasonably jealous.

It was a story as old as time and as such was suspect. Cliff couldn't keep the skepticism out of his voice. 'If he's like you say, why didn't you leave him? Run away, if nothing else?'

'I've thought of it many times, but he swore he'd find me and kill me. I believe him.'

Cliff knew that she did believe this. Whether it was true or not really didn't matter. She was just as frightened.

'Kate, you haven't yet said. Do you love me?'

'I...' She gazed up at him, eyes suddenly enormous. 'I don't ... It's wrong, Cliff!'

'It's no more wrong than you being married to him,' he said soberly, 'not loving him and believing the things you do about him. Look, I'll go to Ledbetter and tell him about us, then I'll take you away.'

Her hands fluttered wildly. 'No! He'll kill you, Cliff!'

'Kate, listen to me now,' he said gently. 'I've been a drifter too. I've had no reason to settle. Now I do.'

Apparently those were the words she needed to hear. Her resistance crumpled. In his arms she still trembled, and he knew she hadn't overcome her fear of Ledbetter, but she obeyed him without question when he told her to put on her sneakers, and she snuggled her hand trustingly in his as they walked back to the house.

They didn't have to look for Ledbetter. He had started baling hay that morning. Cliff didn't hear the tractor motor as they walked to the house; evidently Ledbetter had gone in for lunch. He came out of the kitchen to meet them as they approached.

Kate's hand leaped like a frightened bird, and Cliff's closed tightly over it. 'Ledbetter, Kate and I love each other...'

'Just like those songs you sing, eh, singer?' Ledbetter said mildly. The man's eyes had the glassy, bottomless look of marbles, and Cliff knew that Kate had reason to fear him.

Cliff said, 'We're leaving together. This afternoon.'

'That so?'

Cliff stood away from Kate, stood loosely, ready to meet Ledbetter's attack. He was confident he could defeat the man in a fair fight.

But Ledbetter was looking at Kate. 'You're my wife, Kate. You belong to me, just like this farm and everything on it. I'll kill the man who tries to take anything of mine.'

'You can't stop us, Ledbetter, with threats or anything else.' Cliff glanced at Kate. 'He's just trying to scare us, Kate.'

Ledbetter still didn't look at him. 'Kate, you know I mean what I say.'

Kate's hand fluttered. One went to her mouth. She gnawed on her knuckles. She stared at Cliff, her eyes alive with fear. 'Cliff... I'm sorry! I can't! I just can't!' Her breath caught in a sob. She broke toward the house, running awkwardly.

Cliff took a step after her, then turned toward Ledbetter.

The man's features were void of triumph. He could have been discussing the weather. 'I'll expect you gone, singer, when I come in tonight. You have a month's salary coming. Why don't you try singing for it?' He wheeled and started off, never once looking back.

Cliff gazed after him for a moment, then plunged into the house. Kate had barricaded herself in the bedroom. Through the door he pleaded, cajoled and threatened.

Over and over she said the same thing, 'Go away, Cliff! Please go away!'

Finally he knew he had lost. Maybe she had never intended going away with him at all. He trudged to his room, packed his knapsack and left.

As he walked up the road, he heard the tractor chugging down by the river.

After an hour's walking, he began to think more clearly. Slowly the realization came to him that Kate's fear had been more for his safety than her own. He should have known that all along. His anger had blinded him.

He turned and started back. He would take her away with him even if he had to carry her.

He had been gone over two hours by the time he saw the house again. He heard the stutter of the tractor in the field long before he glimpsed the house.

The back door was open, but Kate wasn't in the kitchen. He went through the house calling her name.

There as no answer.

He found her in the bedroom, almost cut in half by a shotgun blast.

Cliff groped his way outside and was violently ill. The distant whine of the tractor motor, rising and falling, rasped across his raw nerves. He knew Ledbetter had killed her. He would come home tonight, pretend to find Kate dead and blame it on his hired hand who had fled.

But why? Why had he killed her?

Cliff started toward the field, staggering at first but gaining strength as he went.

The tractor pulling the hay baler was at the end of a windrow and was executing a wide turn to start a new one. At the sight of Cliff, Ledbetter halted the tractor, but didn't shut off the motor. As a result the baler, connected to the tractor drive shaft, continued to run, the auger flashing in the late afternoon sun.

Ledbetter said calmly, 'I didn't expect to see you again, singer.'

'Why? Why did you do it, Ledbetter?' Cliff had to shout to be heard over the tractor motor and baler. 'She wasn't going to leave you!'

'Oh, but she was. She was packing to leave when I went back to the house for a minute.' For one of the rare times Cliff saw the man grin. 'She waited until she was sure you'd gone. Didn't want you hurt, she said. She was going off by herself.'

Through a shimmering haze of hurt Cliff reached up and caught Ledbetter by the shirt front and hauled him down off the tractor seat.

His lawyer said, 'Then you killed him?'

'Yes, I killed him,' Cliff said. 'Oh yes, I killed him.'

'But the body? It was never found. The sheriff looked everywhere. You're being tried for killing Kate, I guess you know. Since you wouldn't, or couldn't, tell us what happened, the sheriff figured you also killed Ledbetter and buried him somewhere.'

'The baler? Is it still in the field?'

'No, the tractor and the baler were driven into the barn the next day. But the hay's still there. It rained that same night and ruined the hay.'

'The rain,' Cliff mused. 'I guess it rinsed away the blood.'

'The blood?'

'Ledbetter loved his machinery, you know, more than he ever did Kate.' Cliff looked at his lawyer without expression. 'When I pulled him off the tractor, I hit him once, knocking him into the hay baler. I could have saved him, I guess, but I didn't try. Tell the sheriff he'll find what's left of Troy Ledbetter in the last two bales of hay from his machine.'

Nothing But Human Nature

by Hillary Waugh

Captain of Detectives Mike Galton, or 'the old man' as he was known to his underlings, looked down at the woman's body. It was dressed in a nightgown and a blue flannel robe and lay on the kitchen floor in a crumpled heap. The woman was a brunette, thirty-three years old, and perhaps twenty pounds overweight. Whether she was pretty or not was hard to tell from the way her head was smashed. The instrument that did the damage, a length of lead pipe, lay beside her. There was a bag of groceries on the kitchen table, and the back door was open.

'Photo been called?' the old man asked William Dennis, the young detective beside him.

'Yes, sir, and the M.E.'

The old man turned and went back to the little front parlor where Joseph Eldridge, the dead woman's husband, sat twisting his hands between his knees. A policeman stood nearby, trying to look invisible.

'That piece of pipe,' the old man said to the husband. 'Did that come from somewhere in the house?'

Joseph Eldridge focused on the detective's face. He was a lean, handsome man in his mid-thirties though now he looked harrowed and white. 'No,' he said, shaking his head. 'I never saw it before.'

'You want to tell it again – exactly what happened this A.M.?'

'I went to do the marketing, same as every Saturday morning –'

'You do the marketing?'

'My wife teaches school all week. I want – wanted her to relax on weekends.'

'You work, Mr. Eldridge?'

'Me?' He looked startled. 'Yeah. I sell insurance.' Then he said, 'I didn't touch her money, if that's what you mean. We lived on what I make.'

'But she taught?'

Joseph Eldridge nodded. 'She taught because she loved teaching. She didn't want to give it up when we married, and I didn't make her.' He sighed deeply.

Mike Galton nodded. 'And you do the marketing Saturday mornings. Tell me about this morning.'

Eldridge shrugged and looked down at the floor. He spoke in a choked voice. 'There's nothing to tell, really. I went to the supermarket, I bought the week's groceries, I drove home, came in the back door and – and found her.'

'Any idea who did it?'

He shook his head slowly. 'I can't imagine.'

Detective Dennis said, 'Did you go into the bedroom?'

Eldridge nodded. 'When I called you. The phone's in there.'

'You touch anything?'

'No.'

Dennis said to the old man, 'The bedroom's been ransacked, Captain. The bureau drawers, the closets.'

Galton said, 'You have valuables in the house, Mr. Eldridge?'

'Not anything much. A few dollars maybe, and May had a couple of rings that might have been worth a little – a hundred bucks or so.'

The photographer arrived and Galton and Dennis took him out to the kitchen. Then the medical examiner came and was also shown the scene.

Galton returned to the husband. 'What time did you go to the store, Mr. Eldridge, and what time did you get back?'

'I left the house around nine o'clock, give or take ten minutes. I wasn't noticing the time.'

'Somewhere between eight-fifty and nine-ten, then?'

'That sounds about right.'

'And you got home?'

'I didn't notice. I came in. I saw her. I guess after that I just stopped thinking.'

'Can you give me a rough idea what the time was?'

Eldridge tried to think. 'About half an hour ago, I suppose. I phoned the police, and then –' He looked up. 'Wait, I do remember. The clock in the store said twenty of eleven when I was checking out. Five minutes to load the car and five minutes to get home here – Call it about ten minutes of eleven when I found her.'

'How long have you been married, Mr. Eldridge?'

'Ten years in June.'

'No children?'

'No.'

'Did she have any enemies that you know of?'

'She couldn't have. Everybody loved her.'

'Any relatives?'

'Her mother, two brothers, and a sister. But they live on the west coast.'

The old man went back to the kitchen. The medical examiner told him the woman had been beaten to death with the pipe. The photographer said he'd got his pictures and did the captain want him to dust for fingerprints?

'See if you can get anything off the pipe,' the old man said. 'And the drawers in the bedroom. I understand the bureaus have been ransacked.'

Dennis said, 'Do you believe the burglar theory?'

The old man shrugged. 'It's possible there was a burglar. It's possible Eldridge killed her and faked the burglary. It's possible someone else killed her and faked the burglary.' He said to the doctor, 'Do you think she was beaten unnecessarily – by someone who hated her rather than someone who wanted to rob her?'

The doctor said he couldn't venture an opinion. He sat down at the kitchen table to fill out his papers.

The body was lying face up now, and Captain Galton said to Dennis, 'See if you can find a sheet or something and cover her.'

Policewoman Jenny Galton came through from the living-room. She was a young and pretty redhead, but poised and experienced despite her youth, for she was Mike Galton's daughter.

'Hi, Pops,' she said. 'I hear I'm to search a body.' Then she saw the dead woman and she sobered. 'That's not very pretty,' she said. 'It's a homicide, then?'

Galton said, 'It's a homicide, pet, and a nasty one.'

While Jenny searched the apparel on the body, Galton went outside for a look around. The house was a tiny brick bungalow in an area of tiny brick bungalows, packed together on midget lots with one-car garages in back and just room for a driveway between. Joseph Eldridge's station wagon was standing in front of the garage and two steps from the stoop. In the back were two more bags of groceries like the one on the kitchen table.

Detective Dennis came out to join him. 'No fingerprints on the pipe,' he said, 'and it doesn't look like there's going to be anything on the bureau knobs either.' He smiled wryly. 'We aren't left with much.'

'We never are when there are no witnesses.' Galton sighed and turned to the porch steps. 'Well, I guess the next step is to canvas the neighborhood, see if there's been any strangers around – salesmen, vagrants, and the like – and see if anybody can tell us anything about the Eldridges. I'd like to know whether his grief is as real as it looks.'

A sheet was over the body when they came back in, and Jenny told them the woman was missing her wedding and engagement rings. Otherwise there was nothing to report.

'You get any ideas when you examined the body, kitten? Any female intuition?'

She said, 'If you mean do I think Mr. Eldridge is telling the truth, I don't know. Nothing I found is inconsistent with his story. It could have happened like that.'

The captain went on into the little bedroom. The police photographer was putting away his fingerprint equipment and shaking his head. 'Just smudges,' he said. 'One partial on the bureau top but it looks like the woman's.'

The old man and Dennis brought Mr. Eldridge into the bedroom then to make a search. He looked through the drawers and his wife's purse. He found there was no money in the purse and her jewelry box was missing from the drawers.

'You got any insurance on the jewelry?' Dennis asked him.

Eldridge shook his head. 'It wasn't worth that much.'

The old man showed him a note on the telephone pad. It said: 'Membership comm. Tues. at 4:00.'

'May wrote that,' Eldridge told him. 'They usually meet at the church on Mondays. I guess it got changed.'

'Do you know when she received the call?'

'I don't have any idea. It wasn't when I was around.'

'Do you know who would have made the call?'

Eldridge said it was probably the committee chairman. Her name was Mrs. Bertha Crump, and the old man found her number in the address book on the phone table.

Dennis took Eldridge back to the living-room while Galton got the woman on the line. Yes, she told him, she was the one who called May Eldridge about the change. She'd called her just that morning, in fact.

'Do you know what time this morning, Mrs. Crump?'

'About quarter past nine. Why, is something the matter?'

'Yes, something is the matter. But can you say for sure that you made the call at quarter past nine?'

'Well,' Mrs. Crump said hesitantly, 'I wouldn't want to swear to it. But I do know that I don't make phone calls before nine o'clock, and Mrs. Eldridge was the fourth person I talked to about the change. It couldn't have been before quarter past nine. Of that I'm sure.'

'It was Mrs. Eldridge who answered the phone?' Galton said.

'Yes.'

'How long did the two of you talk?'

'Oh, perhaps two minutes. Usually I'd talk longer, but I had five others to call so I didn't want to dally.'

'Did she mention her husband at all?'

Mrs. Crump said no, and asked again what the trouble was.

Galton told her, helped her over her shock, and questioned her some more, but the answers didn't change.

When he hung up, Galton went back to Eldridge and had him tell the story over again two more times. It came out the same way, but with two additions. He knew nothing of Mrs. Crump's phone call, for he had already left. He knew of nobody who could support his alibi.

The hearse pulled into the drive and two morgue attendants came through the back door with a stretcher. Galton watched them lift the body onto it with practised precision and take it out. He sent the patrolman back to his beat and, with Detective Dennis, started a canvass of the neighborhood to see what they could learn.

The brick bungalow abutting the Eldridges' driveway was their first stop and the door was answered by a trim young bottled blonde in shorts and halter. Galton showed his badge, apologized for the intrusion, and explained about the death next door.

'Yeah,' the woman said. 'I saw the hearse. You say she was killed, huh? Gee, that's terrible.'

'Did you know them well, Mrs. – ah –'

'Jenks. Mimi Jenks. No, I didn't know them except to say hello to.'

'What about Mr. Jenks?'

The woman laughed. 'Mr. Jenks sends me an alimony check once a month. That's all I know about him or care.'

Galton said, 'Oh.' Then he said, 'Can you tell me anything about this morning? Did you see anybody or hear anything next door?'

Mrs. Jenks frowned in thought. Then she said, 'I heard their car go out at nine o'clock. I can't think of anything else.'

'Did you say nine o'clock?'

She shrugged. 'Well, it might not have been exactly nine o'clock. It might have been two or three minutes after.'

'How do you remember the time so well?'

She laughed. 'That's easy. I got up at nine. I looked at the clock. And I had just got out of bed when I heard their car start up.'

'And you saw or heard nothing else?'

'Nothing else. Until the hearse.'

'You didn't hear his car return?'

She shook her head. 'I only heard it go out because the bedroom's on that side of the house and the window was open.'

'I see.' Galton pursed his lips. 'One more question. You know anything about what kind of a marriage they had? Did they get along or fight, or what?'

Mrs. Jenks said she didn't have any idea. All she knew was she never heard them fight. She never heard anything from them at all.

'I see. Now, one last thing. It's very important. Are you absolutely sure it was nine o'clock when he drove away?'

'Absolutely, because I looked at the clock when I got up and then I did my exercises by the window for fifteen minutes and I remember the car wasn't there. Why is that so important?'

'Because it supports his own story that that's when he went shopping.'

'I see. I'm his alibi, in other words?'

'Yes, you could call it that.'

'I'm glad I can help.'

'So are we. You'll be asked to testify, of course.'

She smiled. 'Any time.'

Galton and Dennis tried the family on the other side of the Eldridges' but they could not help at all, nor could anyone else in the neighborhood. No one had noticed suspicious strangers around. No one had seen Eldridge go to the supermarket.

The old man and his youthful companion returned to police headquarters at half past twelve. The chief was there and so was Jenny.

'We're up a tree,' Dennis told the chief. 'Absolutely no clues.' He went on to explain the problem. Mr. Eldridge left the house between nine and nine-five. Mrs. Eldridge received a phone call from Mrs. Crump between nine-fifteen and nine-twenty, between nine-twenty when she hung up, and ten-fifty, when Mr. Eldridge returned, someone came in the back door, beat Mrs. Eldridge to death with a pipe, ransacked the bureaus in the bedroom, and made off with a box of inexpensive jewelry and the few dollars in Mrs. Eldridge's purse.

The chief said, 'Is that how you see it?' to the old man, but Galton's attention was on his daughter.

'You're a right pretty girl, kitten,' he said. 'Now that I notice, I'm struck by that fact.'

She laughed and told him he was dotty.

'No, I'm not dotty, I'm serious. What are your measurements, thirty-eight, twenty-three, thirty-six?'

'That's reasonably close. Why?'

'Because when you go home for lunch, your going to change into your prettiest dress. Then we're going to see what kind of an actress you are.'

Jenny, the chief, and William Dennis all were curious, but the old man merely said very mysteriously, 'Wait and see.'

At half past two that afternoon, the old man rang Mrs. Jenks' doorbell again. He smiled and said he was sorry to trouble her but could she come down to headquarters so they could take her statement? She said she'd be glad to oblige and got her coat.

On the way he told her how much he appreciated her cooperation and she said she was only doing her duty. As an innocent man's only alibi, she had to testify.

'Yes,' the old man said, 'except, you will be pleased to learn, the burden is no longer solely on your own shoulders. We've found someone else to verify his alibi.'

'Oh?' she said, and turned to look at him. 'Who?'

'A young woman he knows. She's come forward to testify that she saw him enter the supermarket at ten minutes past nine.'

Mrs. Jenks said, 'Oh,' again, in a strange voice.

The chief and William Dennis were in the squad room when the old man brought Mrs. Jenks in. He introduced her and told her that they'd take her statement in just a few minutes, and if she'd wait in the other room... He took her to the door and there was Jenny, sitting on the couch in her prettiest dress, her hair just so, looking as luscious as chocolate cake. 'This is Miss Murphy, Mrs. Jenks, the old man said. 'She's the one I was telling you about, the one who saw Mr. Eldridge in the supermarket. Isn't that right, Miss Murphy?'

Mrs. Jenks stopped dead in the doorway but 'Miss Murphy' didn't seem to notice. 'That's right,' she said brightly. 'Joe came in at exactly ten minutes past nine. I know because I was looking at my watch.'

Captain Galton smiled with approval, but Mrs. Jenks didn't smile at all. 'She's a liar,' she said.

Miss Murphy put her nose in the air. 'I ought to know when Joe came in,' she said. 'I'm the one who was looking at my watch.'

'She's a liar,' Mrs. Jenks repeated in a louder voice. 'Because Joe Eldridge didn't leave his house until half past nine.'

'Half past nine?' the captain said.

'Half past nine,' she told him. 'Because that's how long it took that two-timing cheat to bash in his wife's head. And he didn't go to the store for five more minutes after that because he got blood on his shirt and had to change it. I know, because the bloody one is in the bottom of my laundry bag, wrapped around her jewelry box.'

Captain Galton said, 'Is that right?' but Mrs. Jenks wasn't paying any attention to him.

She was pointing at 'Miss Murphy' and saying, 'So if you think you're going to run off with him to the Virgin Islands while I'm left holding the bag, forget it. He's going to jail. And I'm going to put him there.'

She told it all to the detectives and a tape recorder, how Eldridge promised her marriage and a life of Caribbean luxury in return for a murder alibi. Then they got the district attorney in and she went over it again. After that, they sent two policemen out with a warrant for Mr. Eldridge's arrest.

In the squad room Detective William Dennis and the chief of police looked at Captain Galton and shook their heads. 'Absolutely amazing,' they said.

'It's nothing but human nature,' the old man replied. 'I figured the moment she thought a younger and prettier girl was also lying to save Eldridge's neck, she'd blow his alibi to kingdom come.'

Dennis said, 'That, I understand. But how did you know she and Eldridge were a twosome to begin with? That's what amazes me. What tipped you off?'

The old man said, 'Human nature again, Bill. Put a sexy young grass widow next door to a handsome free-lance insurance agent whose wife is away at work all day and you can expect there's going to be a situation. And when the wife has ten years' worth of teaching salary lying around unspent, you know the answer to that situation isn't going to be divorce, it's going to be murder.

'We had the murder, so one look at the woman next door was all I needed to know the whole story. It wasn't the piece of pipe or the missing jewelry or the stories they told that gave it away. It was her shorts, her halter, and her bleached hair.'

Murder, 1990

by C.B. Gilford

The case of Paul 2473 really began when he discovered the old book. He recognized it instantly for what it was, because he had once been through the Micro-filing Section where they were recording some old-fashioned but worthy volumes on genetics before destroying them. But the sight of this book, obviously an uninspected relic of the dim past, provoked a simultaneous curiosity and dread in him.

He'd been marching with the Thursday Exercise Platoon over a country back road, and now they were enjoying their ten-minute rest period, lying by the roadside among the grass-strewn brick ruins of some ancient building. Paul was bored – Thursdays always bored him intensely – and both his mind and eye were casting about for something of interest to focus upon.

Which was why his gaze had roamed over the crumbling, disintegrating wall beside him. He saw the aperture almost immediately. At this particular spot, the bricks seemed to have fallen down against a still standing portion of the wall so as to make a small igloo or cave. A tiny, cozy, rain-proof den, he thought, for some small wild thing. A few of the little beasts always seemed to survive the best efforts of the decontamination squads which constantly scoured vacant areas.

Paul turned over and lay on his stomach so that he could peer into the dark hole, and saw the book. He knew instantly, of course, what the proper procedure was. He should take the thing, not open it, but hand it over instead to the Platoon Leader. He'd been taught that all such objects pertaining to the former civilization could be either valuable or dangerous. He had no more right to destroy the book than he had to look at it.

Half-intending deceit but not fully decided, he checked first to see if he was being observed. The Leader was nowhere in sight. The members of the Platoon were all prone, none of them close to Paul, and none of them playing the least attention to him. Tentatively, still not committed to disobedience, Paul reached into the hole, grasped the book and drew it out.

It was small, light, and seemed ready to fall apart at his touch. Trembling, but overwhelmed by curiosity, he lifted the cover and glanced at the fly leaf. *The Logic of Murder*, he read.

For a moment, he experienced a dismal disappointment. The word 'logic' had some meaning for him, though vague. The last word, 'murder,' was completely and totally mysterious. The book was useless if he knew absolutely nothing of its subject matter. But as he pondered it, he was not so sure. The book might teach him what 'murder' was. And 'murder' might be something vastly entertaining.

'Everybody up!' The Platoon Leader's shrill bark of command came from far away through the trees.

In the instant before the somnolent members of the Platoon could rouse themselves and stir from the matted grass, Paul 2473 came to a momentous decision. He thrust the little book inside his shirt. Then he got up, stretched, and walked back to the road where the files were forming.

In his cubicle, Paul 2473 re-invented the ancient stratagem of schoolboys. Every evening during the few minutes he had to himself, he held the little book behind the afternoon edition of *The News of Progress*, and thus, while seeming to be immersed in the sort of reading that was his duty, he was actually engaged in a forbidden pastime. He practised this little deception in case the wall television screen chose at any time to look in on him.

As he read, though more and more conscious of the dangers involved, he grew more and more fascinated by what he found in the little book. Gradually, by piercing together scattered references, he began to arrive at some conclusions.

Murder, he discovered with something of a shock, was the taking of a human life. It was a completely new and hitherto undreamed-of idea to him. He knew that life did not go on forever. He knew that elderly people sometimes got sick, were carted off to some medical building or physiology laboratory or clinic, and then were never seen again. Death, he also knew, was usually painless – unless there was a specific, scientific reason for the authorities to decree it should not be – and so he had neither considered death much nor feared it.

But murder had apparently been a phenomenon of the previous civilization in which the authorities not only did not arrange human death, but were actually opposed to individuals who took such matters into their own hands. Yet the practice, though accompanied by danger, seemed to have been amazingly popular. Paul 2473 shuddered at the barbarism of it, but could not stop reading.

But as he came to understand the title of the book, he discovered that although murder was hideous, it had been in its own past environment rather understandable. In a society where people had chosen their own mates at random, murders had been committed out of sexual jealousy or revenge. In a society where the authorities had not provided sustenance for the population, murders had been committed to acquire wealth.

As he read on, Paul was treated to the full panorama of homicidal motivations, both sane and insane. There was a chapter on methods of murder. There were sections of the detection, apprehension, and punishment of murderers.

But the conclusions of the book were the most amazing part. 'Murder,' it was stated emphatically, 'is a much more widespread crime than statistics indicate. Many murders are committed without premeditation, in the heat of emotion. Those who commit such murders are quite often brought to justice. Much more successful at evasion, however, are the murderers who plan their crimes beforehand. The bulging files of unsolved murders are predominantly of this variety. In the battle of wits between murderer and policeman, the former has all the advantage. Although the findings of various statistical studies have varied somewhat, they all point inescapably in one direction. Most murders go unsolved. Most murderers live out their natural lives in peace and safety and the enjoyment of the fruits of their efforts.'

Paul 2473 was thoughtful for a long time after he finished the book. He recognized the peril of his own position more than ever. The new civilization simply could not afford to let this book be disseminated, to allow humanity to realize how recently it had emerged from primitive savagery. He himself had therefore broken an important rule in reading the book, and he saw now why it was an important rule. If he were found out, he would surely be reprimanded, demoted, perhaps even publicly disgraced.

But he did not destroy the book. Instead he hid it inside his mattress. The notion of murder, like some inventor's dream, intrigued him, and he devoted all his spare time to thinking of it.

He even considered mentioning it to Carol 7427. He saw Carol 7427 almost every evening at Recreation, and on many occasions had gone into the Caressing Booths with her, and more often than with any other girl. He had taken Compatibility Tests with Carol 7427, and was hoping for a Three-Year Assignment with her, a Five-Year if he could get it.

That first evening after he had finished the book, he came very close to confiding in her. She came into the Recreation Center still in her work slacks, but they fitted her so neatly and snugly that he did not mind. He gazed at her close-cropped blonde hair, at her bright blue eyes and clear skin, and he thought about the Mating Assignment. It would be very nice to share a double cubicle with someone, to have someone to talk to, really talk to, someone to whisper to, out of reach of the microphones, someone with whom to discuss strange and fascinating and bizarre ideas, such as murder and what civilization must have been like when individuals dared to murder one another.

He maneuvered her over into a corner, away from the Group Conversation on Radiation Agriculture. 'Would you like to know a real secret, Carol?' he asked her.

Her long lashes blinked at him, and her color heightened prettily. 'A secret, Paul?' she breathed. 'What kind of a secret?'

'I've broken a rule.'

'Really!'

'A serious rule.'

'Really!' She was enthralled.

'And I've discovered something that's terribly interesting.'

'Tell me!' She leaned closer to him. She had taken a perfume tablet, and her exhalations enchanted him.

'If I told you, you'd either have to report me, or you'd be in the same dangerous position I'm in.'

'I'd never report you, Paul.'

'But I wouldn't want to get you into trouble.'

She looked disappointed and began to pout. But her reaction pleased him. They shared the same spirit of adventure and curiosity. He wouldn't tell her now. But when the Mating Assignments came out – next week for sure – when they shared a cubicle, then he would give her the book to read, and they could discuss the wonders of homicide for hours and hours.

That was the day that Paul 2473 definitely decided he was compatible with Carol 7427. And surely the Tests, scientific as they were, would bear him out.

But the Tests didn't. He saw the results on a Thursday, as he came back from Exercise. The enormous poster almost covered the bulletin board, and it read, 'Five-Year Mating Assignments for Members of Complex 55.' Confidently he raced down the list. But it was with horror that he made two discoveries. Carol 7427 was paired with Richard 3833, and he had drawn Laura 6356.

Laura 6356 for five years! A simpering, dumpy little thing with mouse-colored hair. Was she the sort with whom they thought he was compatible? And Richard 3833, who was to have exclusive possession of Carol for five years, was a beast, a swaggering, arrogant beast.

Paul contemplated his future with indignation. He was now in the age group to which the Caressing Booths were no longer allowed. The authorities had found that at this age a worker would be more productive if he had a settled and well-defined social pattern. Therefore, the mating Assignment meant that he would be tied exclusively to Laura 6356, while Carol would be just as exclusively the companion of Richard 3833.

He and Carol would scarcely see each other! There would be no cozy cubicle for them. No stealthy little discussions after hours about his wonderful book.

The book!!!

It was by no devious, hesitant line of reasoning that Paul 2473 came to a conclusion about committing murder. It posed itself instantly as the solution to his problem. His mind traveled briskly through the checklist – motives, methods, risks.

Certainly the motive was there. He was to be mated with an incompatible person, while his compatible person was to be mated with someone else. As he referred to his handbook for possible variations to remedy this situation, he perceived that a purely emotional murderer might choose to eliminate Carol to prevent Richard's getting her. But that line of action would not obtain Carol for himself, and it would leave him with Laura.

A double murder was necessary then. Richard and Laura. A bit more complicated in the execution, but the only procedure that would guarantee satisfaction.

The details of the method he left for later. But he did choose a weapon. Or rather, necessity chose it for him. He had no gun, nor means of obtaining one. He had no knowledge of poisons, nor access to any. Richard 3833 was bigger and stronger than he, and Laura 6356 was hardly a frail creature, so strangulation and all such feats of overpowering violence were impossible to him. But he could get a knife, and he could sharpen it adequately. And he knew enough physiology to know how a knife should be used against the human body.

Finally, he tried to calculate the risks. Would they catch him? And if they did what would they do to him?

It was then that something really amazing occurred to him. As far as he knew, there was no crime called murder in the statutes. If there were, he surely would have been aware of it. They were lectured often enough on things they should do and things they shouldn't do. At the head of the list, was treason to the state. This included such things as sabotage, insurrection, and subversive activities of all sorts. Below treason on the list were the crimes of sloth, failure to fulfill work quotas, failure to attend meetings, failure to maintain mental and physical health.

And that was it. Murder wasn't listed, nor any of the other

crimes often connected with murder – no fraud, none of the old attempts to gain material wealth by violence. Paul realized that he lived in an ideal civilization, where there was an absolute minimum of motivation for crime. Except the one that he had found – when some official made an obvious error in grading the Compatibility Tests.

Now the amazing thing then was simply this. Without the crime of murder even mentioned in the law books, the state simply possessed no apparatus for dealing with murder. There was no organization, no experienced detectives, no laboratory scientists trained in sifting clues, none of the things or people that the book had said existed in the old civilization. With just a little reasonable caution and planning then, the murderer of this new, enlightened age could take the authorities completely by surprise, catch them utterly unprepared. And he could commit his crime in absolute safety!

This realization set Paul's heart to beating fast, and set his mind to scheming. The Mating Assignments would go into effect just as soon as the plan for the shifting of cubicle occupancy could be drawn up. This would, he knew, take a week. As it turned out, he had plenty of time. He was ready to begin operations in two days.

His job gave him an initial advantage. As an air filtration maintenance engineer, he was free to rove throughout the entire area of Complex 55. No one would question his presence in one place or his absence from another. All he needed was a work schedule that would take him on a route in the vicinity of first one of his victims and then the other.

Thursday came, and he had to waste a whole afternoon trudging about with the Exercise Platoon. On Friday, however, luck turned in his favor. As he glanced at the sheet which listed the air filtration troublespots he was to visit that morning, he knew the time had come.

He carried his sharp steel blade tucked into his belt under his shirt. In his soft-soled, non-conductive shoes he padded noiselessly along the antiseptic corridors. His work schedule was tight, but the route was perfect. He could spare a minute here and there.

He arrived first in the vicinity of Richard 3833. The latter worked in Virus Chemistry, had his own private corner where he could work more efficiently out of sound and view of his fellows. Paul found him there, absorbed in peering through a microscope. 'Richard,' Paul greeted him softly, 'congratulations on your Mating Assignment. Carol's a fine girl.'

There was always a chance, of course – perhaps one in fifty, or a hundred – that a microphone would be eavesdropping or a television screen peeking in on them. But Richard – and Laura too, for that matter – had never caused any trouble. So they would not be under special surveillance. And very seldom did the guards monitor anyone during working hours. The small risk had to be taken. He would conduct his business as quickly as possible though.

'Thanks,' Richard said. But his mind wasn't on Carol. 'Say, while you're here, take a look at this little beast on this slide.' He climbed off his stool and offered his place to Paul.

Paul took an obliging look, and managed surreptitiously to turn a couple of adjustment knobs while he was doing it. 'I can't see a thing,' he said.

Richard patiently went back to re-adjusting the knobs. His broad back was turned to Paul, all of his attention concentrated on the microscope.

Paul slipped the knife from under his shirt, chose the exact point to aim at, and struck hard.

Richard's reaction was a startled grunt. His hands clutched at the counter top. Before he sagged, Paul withdrew the blade, then stood and watched as his victim slumped into an inert heap on the floor. Then very carefully he wiped the bloody knife on Richard's shirt, and left the laboratory immediately afterward. No one saw him go.

Within four minutes from the time he stabbed Richard 3833, Paul arrived at the Mathematical Calculation Section where Laura 6356 tended one of the huge machines. As in the case of Richard, Laura worked practically alone, out of contact with the other girls who did similar work on similar machines. Her only companion was the moniter itself, an enormous panel of switches, buttons, dials, and blinking lights of all colors.

Laura saw her visitor out of the corner of her eye, but her fingers continued to type out information for the machine. She was a very conscientious worker.

'Hello there, Paul,' she said with a little giggle. She had scarcely noticed him before the Mating Assignments came out, but since that time she had grown very feminine. 'Don't tell me our cubicle's ready to move into!'

Did she imagine that he would make a special trip to bring her news like that? He maneuvered to a position behind her and groped under his shirt for the knife.

Possibly she imagined he was going to caress her, despite the fact that such things were strictly forbidden during working hours. Her chubby shoulders trembled expectantly, awaiting his touch. He plunged the knife in quickly.

She did not sag to the floor as Richard had done, but instead fell forward over her keyboard. The machine continued to hum, its lights continued to flash, as Laura's dead weight pressed down upon the keys.

The machine will be giving some inaccurate answers, Paul thought with grim amusement as he withdrew the knife and wiped it on the sleeve of Laura's blouse.

But then as he went away and back to his own work, another, pleasanter thought occupied his mind. Carol 7427 and Paul 2473 now had no mates. Surely it would be logical – and the easiest thing to do in view of the compatibility scores – for the Committee to assign these two orphans to the same cubicle. For five years, subject to renewal, of course.

He had not known what to expect. He could not predict how the rulers of Complex 55 would react. The book was an inadequate guide in this respect, since it dealt with the phenomenon of murder in the old civilization.

Murder always had the power to excite interest, the book said. Especially if the victim was well known, if the method of murder was particularly gruesome, or if there was some sensational, scandalous element involved. The newspapers featured detailed description of the crime, then followed along as it unraveled, and finally – if the murderer was caught – reported on the trial. The whole thing could drag on for weeks, months, even years.

But in Complex 55, *The News of Progress* was circulated that afternoon without containing any mention of an usual happening. At Recreation that evening, nothing seemed amiss, except that Richard 3833 and Laura 6356 were missing.

Paul saw Carol there, and realized he had not spoken to her since the Mating Assignments were published. He managed to detach her from her companions, and carefully asked her:

'Where's Richard?'

She shrugged.

'I don't know. I haven't seen him.'

He was overjoyed at her attitude. Richard was missing and she didn't seem in the least concerned, as if she had never read the Mating Assignments. Probably she didn't care for him at all. When this was all straightened out, she'd be quite willing to accept a new arrangement without mourning for Richard.

He stayed with her most of the evening, in a happy, languorous state. He was even beginning to believe that the authorities, confronted with a new problem outside the realm of their rules and experience, might even decide to hush the matter up, pretend it never happened, in the hope that the rank and file, if kept ignorant of the idea of murder, would never think of indulging in it.

By the time he retired that night, Paul had convinced himself of the soundness of this theory.

Reveille on Saturday morning shattered his illusions. In fact, he wasn't even certain it was reveille because the high-pitched buzzer seemed to sound louder and more insistent. And also at an earlier hour. It was still dark outside his single window.

He climbed into his clothes quickly and joined the others out in the corridor. They were all as startled as he was, very meek, slightly uneasy.

'Forward... march!'

They tramped in long files to the end of the corridor, plunged down the iron stairs on the double, emerged into the courtyard where light awaited him. All the floodlights on the roofs and the high walls had suddenly been turned on. In their harsh glare platoons and companies formed quickly and stood at stiff attention. There was no talking in the ranks, no complaining at being routed out at this early hour. An atmosphere of fear and foreboding settled over the whole place.

Paul felt it. Even if he had known of no reason to be afraid, the others' fear would have communicated itself to him. Nothing quite like this had ever happened before. Surely nothing pleasant was in store.

What were they going to do? There would be an announcement probably, stating that two people had been killed. And what then? Would they ask the guilty party to identify himself? Or ask if anyone could volunteer any information?

Then quite strangely, he felt calm. If they had brought everybody out here, that meant they didn't know who was responsible, didn't it? That was encouraging. Of course it appeared now that there would be an investigation of some sort. Questions asked. Whereabouts checked. He would have to be careful. But the main thing to remember was that the authorities did not yet know who the murderer was. And if he could keep his wits about him, they need never know.

But there was no announcement from the loudspeakers. The long ranks of silent men were left to contemplate the unknown, to nurse their fears. Perhaps the authorities had planned it this way, to let those fears wreak their psychological mischief for a little while before the questions began.

Half an hour went by, and still the dawn did not appear. Yet no one broke ranks. No one coughed or shuffled his feet. The only sound was the moan of the night wind over the high walls.

What bothered Paul the most were the floodlights. They seemed to be shining directly into his eyes. He could blink against the glare, but he discovered that if he tried to close his eyes for a few seconds, his body had a tendency to sway. He didn't dare call attention to himself by falling down or even by swaying too much. So he tried to endure the glare, tried to think of the pleasant things that would happen when this ordeal was over.

And it had to be over sometime. The whole machinery of Complex 55 with its hundred thousand members could not be halted and disrupted indefinitely because two of those members had been murdered. People were taken off to die every day, and their places were filled with recruits from the Youth Farms. There would be some excitement and tension for a while, but sooner or later things would have to return to normal.

Normal... a mating cubicle with Carol... somebody to talk to... talk to privately... an end to the deadly aloneness... even with the microphones and the television screens, he knew that mated couples could manage a certain degree of privacy.

'Company Number One! Right face! Forward march!'

A sound of trampling feet, and a hundred men left the courtyard.

By listening to the shouted commands that followed, Paul could estimate where they had gone. To the Recreation Hall adjoining the Dormitory. Whatever was happening to them, whatever processing they were going through, was being done in the Rec. That didn't sound too ominous. If they had marched out the gate, he might have felt more uneasy.

A few more minutes passed. Possibly a quarter of an hour. The lights were becoming unbearable, and there was still no sign of dawn. But Paul was in the second company. Perhaps he could manage. But there were pains shooting up and down his legs. A slight dizziness attacked him momentarily. The floodlights danced before him. He closed his eyes tightly, but they could not be shut out. The dance became weird.

'Company Number Two!'

He marched, fawningly grateful for the exquisite feeling of being able to move again. Yes, they were going to the Rec. Two guards held the doors ajar, and the entire company tramped into the big place.

More lights, but no longer painful. A buzz of human voices pitched low. The company was taken to the far end, then formed in a single file. They were held at attention no longer, but still the men could not relax. Their fears had been worked on too long. They were silent, refusing to speculate among themselves.

Finally, the single file became a queue, and began moving through the small door. Paul was perhaps the twentieth man in line. It seemed to him that the men ahead of him moved through the door at a rate of one every thirty seconds or so. He awaited his turn, still calm, confident that the huge scale of this maneuver indicated desperation and helplessness on the part of the authorities.

Then he saw around the shoulders of the man ahead of him, saw through the door into the room beyond. There was no one and nothing there, but a nurse with a tableful of hypodermic needles beside her.

He could have either laughed or cried with relief. They were only giving shots. Oh, of course, it perhaps meant a plague scare. Or a test of some new serum. Or even a possibility of bacteriological warfare – and they were being given a precautionary antidote. It had nothing at all to do with his two insignificant little murders.

When his turn came for the needle, he endured the small sting with supercilious disdain. After the long ordeal in the courtyard and his occasional uneasy imaginings, this was a small enough price for reassurance.

Yet the effect of the shot was rather strange. There was scarcely any pain in his arm, but there was an odd lightness in his head. Surely, he thought, he wasn't going to faint in this moment of triumph.

But then he lost all awareness of himself as self. He did as a guard told him. He walked into the next room. There a man in a white coat and a very penetrating stare confronted him.

'Did you stab two people to death yesterday?' the man asked.

Somehow there didn't seem to be any choice, but to answer with the truth. Perhaps it had been the shot.

'Yes,' he said.

There was a big trial. He was dazed throughout most of it. But it wasn't for his benefit anyway. It was rather for the edification of all the members of Complex 55.

Then afterward they put him in a glass cage at one end of the courtyard. He was strapped there in an upright position. More than a hundred wires were inserted into various portions of his body, and ran down through the floor and thence out into a control box where there was a button for each wire. His torturers were the members of Complex 55 themselves, who were expected to display their devotion to civilization by pausing in front of the cage whenever they had a moment and pushing a few of the buttons. The result was exquisite pain, which made him scream and writhe inside his bonds, but which was never fatal.

Once a day, of course, the loudspeaker reminded him and all the others why he was there. 'Paul 2473,' it would intone, 'in wantonly and wilfully destroying two pieces of valuable state property, Richard 3833 and Laura 6356, committed sabotage, and is a traitor to the state.'

But his miscalculations had not ended there. One of the most frequent visitors to the cage, and one of the most enthusiastic button-pushers, was Carol 7427.

Panther, Panther in the Night

by Paul W. Fairman

If this final account – the end of the Cozenka story – satisfies you, you're an exceptional person. It didn't come anywhere near satisfying me. But then, I'm a pretty ordinary person. I like things neatly tied up and rounded off at the corners.

And I don't like murder.

Or at least I keep telling myself that I don't. But the fact remains – I'm a writer. I make my dubious living reporting on extraordinary people and places and things. So perhaps I was subconsciously conditioned to stand back and let it all happen.

I hope not, but I can't be sure.

I was even witness to the tragedy in a professional capacity. I'd interviewed Cozenka in New York on her arrival from Africa and had been invited to drop out to 'their little hideaway,' as she termed it, to look over the animals she'd brought back.

She and Peter Wyndham.

And I certainly had no reason to suspect that I was being invited for any other reason.

I was getting the story for a top magazine and had a liberal expense account, so the trip into the Southwest, halfway across the country, was no problem – merely a pleasant excursion on someone else's money.

Thus, a week later, I was picked up at a lonely whistle stop and driven twenty miles to Ken Bender's place by a chauffeur in a custom-built station wagon, a pith helmet, and what appeared to be the hiking uniform of an African scoutmaster.

Of course, Cozenka is no stranger to you, her picture having appeared in every important magazine and newspaper in the nation, the sultry Eurasian beauty's romance with Ken Bender holding the national spotlight strictly upon its own merits.

A natural glamour, the merging of oriental loveliness with Texas oil millions; east is east and west is west and the twain meet head on to make a fool out of Kipling.

There was plenty of post-marriage ammunition too. Cozenka's love of Africa, the safari, and all the noble beasties of jungle and veldt. Ken Bender's apparent acceptance of handsome Peter Wyndham as Cozenka's guide and companion both here and abroad. The money he poured out like water at her slightest whim, turning a portion of his endless lands into an African replica as a sanctuary for the animals she brought back and couldn't bear to part with.

A colorful background with ever-potent possibilities newswise.

So the three of them were in the papers as often as Khrushchev and that was the situation when the knobby-kneed chauffeur dropped me off in front of Bender's twenty-room lodge.

Bender himself was waiting for me and there was nothing stiff about our meeting because I'd interviewed him several times before and we'd gotten on well together.

A big, shapeless man without veneer or polish; no touch of the sophistication one would expect in the man Cozenka chose as a husband.

He seized my bag and crushed my hand and bellowed, 'Marty, you old wrangler! Great to see you. Zenka's down at the sheds with Pete. A sick monkey or something. How about a brandy? And by the way, you've never seen this place before. How do you like it? Great place, isn't it?'

That was Ken Bender; a man who seemed always to be tumbling eagerly forward through life; a study in clumsiness, physical and otherwise. But honest, open, and as friendly as a stray pup.

'Nice of you to let me come,' I said. 'I'm finishing up a piece on Cozenka's latest trip and I'm out here to check on the deer and the antelope, African style.'

'Great,' he boomed. 'Stay a month. Stay a year. But now, how about that brandy?'

So we had a couple of Texas-sized snifters and then – because it never occurred to Bender that anyone ever got tired – we headed for the sheds.

The trip was a five-minute drive into the heart of the Dark Continent – a million-dollar never-never land carefully recreated out there in the middle of nowhere.

And there were animals to go with it. I saw a pair of sullen water buffalo, a giraffe nibbling its mate's ear way up there in the stratosphere, a rhino in its own private puddle, and a zebra that looked completely bored with the whole impossible business.

Cozenka and Wyndham were not in the monkey house, but in a shed further out where we found them standing very close together in front of a cage that housed a gorgeous black leopard.

Very close indeed, I thought. But Bender took no notice at all and I couldn't help wondering about his blindness. I couldn't help thinking also what the scandal sheets would do with an eyewitness account of this situation.

Not that I'd ever had any dealings with such outfits. I merely wondered about the true relationship between Bender and the woman he'd married.

Nor did Cozenka react from guilt. As we approached, she dazzled us with her famous smile and flowed into Bender's arms and when he kissed her I envied him.

There was something about Cozenka that conjured up visions in a man's mind – in my mind at any rate; thoughts of Javanese dancing girls, ancient temples, orange-robed Buddhist monks, and fragrant tropical nights. Arrestingly attractive, she still symbolized beauty rather than radiated it; a beauty so fragile I was loath to reach for it even with my mind for fear it would shatter like a Ming vase.

Moreover, Cozenka needed no atmospheric background. She could produce this illusion in riding britches, a cocktail gown, or – so I suspected – even an old flour sack.

She turned from Bender's kiss to give me her hand and say,

'How wonderful of you to find us way out here, Marty darling. You must stay a long, long time. You know Peter of course.'

I knew him mainly as Cozenka's eternal shadow. He was a striking brute of a man who'd proved it wasn't necessary to look like Gregory Peck in order to fill the white hunter role to perfection. He was blond and made the most of it; a shock of carelessly perfect sunbleached hair conspired with bushy, overhanging eyebrows to give him just the correct touch of masculine ruggedness. Yet he would have been at home in a dinner jacket at the Savoy.

He took a bulldog pipe from his mouth just long enough to say, 'Payne, old fellow – delighted to see you looking so fit,' and put it back again.

I replied in kind and we turned our attention back to Cozenka. She was gripping Bender's arm and staring into the leopard's cage as though hypnotized. 'Darling,' she said, 'if I'd lived in pagan times I'm sure I would have worshipped the cat god. Just look at him crouching there in all his savage black symmetry! What murderous thoughts he must be thinking. How he must hate us!'

Bender smiled, more at Cozenka than at the cat, and said, 'I sure wouldn't want to meet him on a dark night with a gun in my –'

'Watch it, Payne! Stand away! Have a care, man!'

The warning came from Wyndham – rapped out sharply – and I jumped as though bee-stung.

'Sorry,' he went on. 'Didn't mean to frighten you, but those cats are the soul of treachery – that one in particular. A little closer and you could have lost an arm. You certainly could have.'

'Sorry,' I mumbled, still shaken.

'Not the right kind of cage for his breed. He should really be paneled off with steel netting.'

I viewed the beast with new respect. It lay facing us, satiny black except for the white star on the sleek head that rested gracefully between its barbed front paws, looking more classically beautiful than dangerous.

But I saw that Wyndham could well have been right. The

animal's eyes, though motionless, were pools of living green flame and I was able to read into them all the hatred and treachery of which Cozenka and Wyndham had spoken.

Cozenka broke the silence with a laugh.

'Come, darlings,' she said, 'Marty will give us a bad press – bringing him here to be scared to death by our lovely Demon. We must try now to be good hosts and perhaps he will forgive us.'

'Right you are,' Bender said heartily.

'Quite,' Wyndham intoned and put a match to his pipe.

And good hosts they were, with a dinner few cosmopolitan restaurants could have hoped to match; with coffee and brandy on the screened patio later, where Bender – boring and voluble – told of his pre-millionaire struggles; where Wyndham's manner implied he was graciously contributing his presence: and Cozenka, without effort, overshadowed everyone and everything with her electric aura.

It was either a trio that represented rarely achieved compatibility, or a lot of color and personality wasted on the desert air – I couldn't tell which.

But late the following afternoon, a new insight into the picture was furnished by Bender himself. He and I had ridden out together, Bender acting as guide so that I might get some idea of how much land he owned.

We each had a canteen strapped to our saddles and gradually it dawned on me that Bender's had been filled with brandy, most of it having gone into the big man by the time we started.

I realized this when he began swaying in his saddle and we were drawn down to a walk. Then he stopped his horse and got off and sat down on a rock and said, 'They're going to kill me, Marty old pal. They're going to kill me as sure as –'

He stopped and rubbed a big hand over his face as I got off my own horse and sat down on the rock beside him.

'I think maybe you've had a little too much sun and brandy,' I said.

'Sure, I'm drunk – as drunk as I ever get – but I always keep my head.' He shook it groggily as though to prove it hadn't gone anywhere, and said, 'Were you ever in love, Marty?'

'A couple of times. But I was always too busy to follow it up.'

'There's love,' he said, 'and then again – there's love.'

'I don't quite follow you.'

'The kind that's a good thing and the kind that's dope, a drug – all the drugs on earth rolled into one. And when this second kind hits you, you're done, man – finished – all washed up for good.'

It was beginning to be a little embarrassing, but I could hardly ride away and leave him there; at least, that was the excuse I gave myself for sitting tight with both ears wide open. 'You were pretty lucky in that particular department,' I said.

'You're crazier than a spooked herd.' And there seemed to be more weariness in his voice than drunkenness. 'I got cursed the day I set eyes on her and I've been cursed ever since.'

I measured my next question carefully. On one side, I put the wisdom of minding my own business; on the other, the fact that he'd opened the subject, not I, and I asked, 'Is it Wyndham?'

He thought that over, giving the impression of a bewildered man trying to penetrate the logic behind a swarm of flies. 'No. He's incidental. It's me – the way I feel about her – because if I didn't feel the way I do, I'd throw him right out and kick him clear back to Africa.'

'Exactly how *do* you feel about her?'

'Like I said – she's dope to me. I want her so bad it makes me sick – so bad I ain't been the same man since I met her. She's so damned important to me that I'm afraid to open my mouth about Wyndham or that idiotic zoo or traipsing off to Africa or anything else. Scared for fear she'll walk out on me. The way it is now I'm willing to settle for whatever little bit of affection she'll give me.'

'I'd say that's a pretty dangerous attitude. Aren't you afraid it's just the kind of thing that might kill her love for you altogether? I don't think a woman like Cozenka could care a great deal for a spineless man.'

He looked at me in disgust, for being so stupid. 'Her love for me? Why, you fool – there isn't any. There never was. She told me that when I chased her all over the world, begging her to marry me. But I was willing to settle for any scraps she was willing to kick my way, so long as she'd give me a chance to make a fool of myself on a permanent basis.'

'I don't think that's the situation at all. I think that somehow you've completely lost your perspective. What actual proof do you have that she doesn't love you?'

'Are you blind? Look at me. I know what I am. A big loudmouthed slob – not her kind at all. The only excuse for me being in the same county with her is that I've made a lot of money and Cozenka needs money like she needs God's breath.'

I raised a hand in protest. 'Now wait a minute –'

But he rushed on. 'I know how she looks to you, Marty. The way she looks to all men she isn't married to – a woman of beauty and warmth – but that's only on the outside. Actually, she takes everything she can get and gives nothing in return.'

'Then why don't you face up to what you've got to do. Get her out of your system. Divorce her. Pay her off. You can afford to make it worth her while.'

'Sure I can – financially, but that's not how it is. In plain words, I can't. If I sent her away, I'd be on her heels begging her to come back before she'd gone no more than a mile.'

So this was the reason for his blindness where Wyndham was concerned. Not blindness at all, but a fear of accusing Cozenka of anything lest she walk out on him.

I could partially understand his position, having been around Cozenka's beauty enough to realize it would be dangerous to fall in love with her. I said, 'Look here, Bender. You've got to take hold of yourself. Because one thing is certain, the answer doesn't lie in the direction you're going. In fact, I think you're distorting the whole situation.'

He was a man who needed reassurance and he snatched pathetically at what I was offering.

'Do you really think so?'

'It's obvious. Give things a little more time. Then, if you can't see that you're wrong, go away alone somewhere and think it all out. You'll land on your feet, believe me.'

'That's a good idea.'

'And forget this nonsense about your life being in danger. You're way off base with that kind of thinking.'

He jerked suddenly to his feet and said, 'Sure – sure. Sorry, Marty – putting my problems on you this way.'

I wanted to make him understand that I thought none the less of him for it; that I saw the outburst for what it was, not the maudlin whining of a weak man, but rather, the blowing of a strong man's safety valve. 'You needed to get it off your chest,' I said.

'We can forget it then?'

'Of course.'

He scowled. 'Look if you've got any idea of putting this little talk into the piece you're writing about my wife –'

'Now you know I wouldn't do that.'

Again he was abjectly sorry. 'Sure you wouldn't. Forget I said that too.'

He grinned now. 'I really do things up right, don't I? When I sound off, I pick a writer out here for a story –'

'You did nothing of the kind. You picked a friend.'

'Thanks, Marty. And now we'd better get back to the lodge. You'll be plenty saddle sore tomorrow, I bet.'

We headed back and I was glad he'd blown off. I was sure it had done him some good, especially getting that murder fantasy out of his system.

But it wasn't fantasy at all.

They killed him that night.

They killed him right under my nose.

The evening began pleasantly enough. We had as fine a dinner as the night before and another session on the patio with Bender having sprung back to his old self. The way he felt about Cozenka was quite obvious.

Cozenka fairly outdid herself as the gracious hostess and showed Bender such marked affection that I felt he had to be wrong in his doubts of her love.

'Darling, shall I change? Shall I look beautiful for you and our guest in an exquisitely beautiful evening gown?'

'You look just fine in that riding outfit, honey, and I know

Marty feels the same way about it.'

That sort of thing, with Wyndham sitting back – as he had the night before – and generously lending his presence and its continental glamor.

It was Bender who suggested the movie, an hour-long affair that we watched in his den; the color-film record of Cozenka's last trip; a dazzling parade of lions, tigers, zebras, monkeys, and ton after ton of elephant with Cozenka and Wyndham always showing off to good pictorial advantage.

Cozenka tiptoed out before the film ended. The three of us watched it to the finish, then went back to the patio to wait for her.

I visualized her returning in some ravishing Parisian creation and looked forward to it with anticipation. But I was disappointed. When she came back, a little while later, she was still wearing the riding habit.

Then, some ten minutes later, the curtain came up on the heart of the drama.

It was raised by a running man, a man in coveralls, who rushed into the patio breathing heavily, his voice reflecting unrehearsed fear.

'The leopard, Mrs. Bender! The black cat! It got loose! It ain't in its cage!'

Cozenka stiffened and Wyndham sprang to his feet.

She asked, 'You mean he's out and running around in the shed?'

'He's running around loose on the grounds – anywhere. I came by on my midnight check and –'

'You went into the shed and baited him!' Cozenka shrilled, and it was the first time I had ever heard her speak in other than throaty, liquid tones. 'You disobeyed orders, you stupid, senseless clod!'

'I didn't –'

'You angered him.'

'No. No. Why should I?'

'Because you are a fool! You know Mr. Wyndham and I are the only ones who tend him. All others are ordered away. He was quiet as a lamb when we left him at five o'clock.'

The man wouldn't be cornered into any damaging admissions. He shook his head stubbornly. 'I just did like I always do – opened the shed door and flashed my light – no more. And the first thing I saw was the cage door open. I stayed just long enough to make sure he wasn't anywhere in the shed. Then I ran here to tell you.'

Wyndham's eyes met Cozenka's. 'The cat could have broken out,' Wyndham said.

'Not unless he was annoyed. This fool –'

'I'm not so sure. We debated putting a heavier lock on the cage – don't you recall? And the upper windows were open. Fifteen feet would have been no problem to Demon.'

'This oaf is to blame,' Cozenka insisted.

Wyndham turned to the man. 'Go around to the kitchen and wait there until you're sent for. We don't want anyone roaming the grounds until something's done.'

The man left, obviously hurt by Cozenka's ill-treatment, and Wyndham tried to smooth her down.

'It doesn't really make any difference who's to blame,' he said. 'We both know what has to be done now. We'd better get at it.'

He didn't have to draw her a picture, for her anger flared even higher.

'No! I refuse. I will not see him destroyed – shot down like a common alley cat. He is the royalty of his kind. It would be a sacrilege.'

Wyndham's face was grim. 'I agree. It's a bloody shame. But better the cat than –'

'Not so fast,' Bender cut in. He'd remained silent, leaving decisions to the experts, but as Cozenka's shoulders drooped he put his arms around her and scowled at Wyndham. 'Zenka loves that cat. We aren't going to just walk out and kill it simply because you think that –'

'But Peter is right, my love. Demon is a killer. It is his nature to kill. We must think of the helpless human life at stake. We have no other choice.'

Wyndham knocked the ashes from his pipe. 'You people stay as you are. I'll go and get a wind on him. It shouldn't take very long to do that.'

But Cozenka objected. 'Alone? You would leave me here to wait and suffer? Peter, sometimes you have no regard for how —'

'But this is a man's job.'

'When have I not done as well as a man? I am as capable as you.'

Wyndham shrugged, appealing silently to Bender as the latter said, 'You and I will handle it, Pete. Zenka stays here with Marty.'

Cozenka brightened as she kissed Bender. 'No, you and I, my love. We two – together. We will find our beautiful Demon. Our bullets alone will destroy him.'

She appeared to be throwing this challenge at Wyndham. The Englishman shrugged again. 'Very well. Let's get about it. No telling what devilry that killer is up to. I'll swing to the west of the sheds. You two take the eastern side. We should turn him up in fairly short order.'

So they trekked off into the night with lights and rifles. I stayed behind, happy to agree that my experience with an air gun at the age of ten hardly qualified me for a job Wyndham wouldn't even allow the animal handler to attempt.

I saw them off, three flashlights bobbing in the gloom, and then sat back to wait.

But no finishing shots broke the heavy silence and it grew lonely there on the patio. I waited a while longer and then got up and went back into the den where we'd left the brandy.

It was more comfortable there – and safer, with four stout walls around me instead of the patio screening. Much safer, until I raised my eyes and looked straight into those of the black leopard.

It had come in the window; the soft thud of its four paws on the thick carpeting and there it was, death in a satiny black skin.

I dropped my brandy and my first thought – when my brain functioned again – was why had the beast sought me out? There must have been others far more conveniently located.

Then a lot of thoughts skittered through my head: disgust with myself for not having had the sense to close the window; resentment at my hosts for not realizing I wouldn't have the sense and had to be reminded; anger at the leopard for looking so incredibly evil as it squatted there obviously understanding my predicament and enjoying it.

There was no chance to reach the door even if I'd had the strength to get up out of my chair. There was nothing in my favor except a faint hope – something I'd heard somewhere – that certain animals ignore you if you remain motionless.

I remained motionless, but the cat did not ignore me. It came up on its four sturdy legs and stretched fore and aft as it contemplated the coming slaughter. It opened its maw and showed me its fine white teeth.

It moved toward me, slowly, gracefully.

Then, as its whiskers practically brushed my paralyzed knees, a suspicion was born in my mind. It was soon quite clear to me that the ape-jawed expression was only a grin, that the menacing rumble in its throat was not a snarl, but a purr.

And immediately the cat verified my dawning doubt as to its ferocity by rolling over on its back to make kittenish passes at me with open paws.

The animal was as tame as a house cat. Lonely out there in the dark, it had seen my open window and come in search of company. It quite obviously wished misfortune to no one.

Reaction drained me of what little strength I had left, and I was on the verge of a nervous giggle as I extended a timid hand of friendship and actually patted the beast's head.

But we were given little time to cement relations because a few moments later a shot sounded somewhere out on the grounds – a sharp report that brought the cat to its feet, and sent it back to the window where it crouched, a black bundle of uneasiness.

Then scream upon scream from the same direction as the gunfire sent the leopard back out the window into the protecting night.

I left also, through the patio, guided by the continuing screams, until I saw a light to the east of the sheds. I ran hard and came finally upon Cozenka crouching over the still body of Ken Bender. They were both within range of a flashlight that lay on the ground nearby, its beam marking the bloody wound in Bender's chest.

It took no medical experience – only common sense – to know that Bender was dead.

Cozenka had stopped screaming. Her face was empty, her eyes stared and she swayed rhythmically back and forth.

'I killed my love. Oh! Oh, God forgive me, I killed him.'

I knelt down. 'How did it happen?'

She stared at me as though not comprehending. I shook her, rather roughly, by the shoulder. 'How did it happen?'

'We were hunting separately. I was not using my light – watching for the glow of Demon's eyes. My darling must have veered over – gotten in front of me. But Demon was here. I swear it – I swear it. I saw the green of his eyes. I was sure he charged me as I fired. But of course it was –'

A pounding of feet cut off her flow of words and Wyndham arrived. He took in the scene like a white hunter should – no panic, no shock. 'What's happened here?'

'Cozenka shot Ken. She thought he was Demon. She thought he had green eyes.'

If Wyndham found my tone sarcastic, he gave no sign as he turned away to sweep his light in a circle. 'The cat isn't here now,' he said. 'Go to the sheds. Bring a blanket to cover the body and someone to stay with it. Leave him one of the guns. Then you take Cozenka back to the lodge. I've got to keep going until I find that bloody cat.'

'It shouldn't be too difficult,' I retorted. 'Just sit by an open –' But he'd trotted off into the night and I went about obeying orders.

Ten minutes later, leaving a stunned guard with the body, I led the now-silent Cozenka back to the lodge. As we entered the patio, we heard the bark of Wyndham's gun from beyond the lodge. A few minutes later, he returned to find us waiting for him in the den.

He knocked off a stout shot of brandy before saying, 'What a mess! What a bloody mess!'

Both Cozenka and I asked the obvious question silently, with our eyes, and Wyndham nodded. 'I found him in that brush patch, out away from the house – on the den side. I got in a good, clean shot. He's dead.'

Cozenka had recovered somewhat, to just the extent that would be expected after what she'd been through. I paid her unspoken tribute as an actress when she said, 'My love is dead. My beautiful, beautiful love.'

'Are you referring to your husband, or the cat?' They both looked at me sharply. I wondered suddenly about my own chances of surviving the night, and pondered the wisdom of keeping silent.

But my sense of outrage was too great. 'I should have paid more attention to what Ken told me this afternoon,' I said.

Wyndham waited.

Cozenka asked, 'What did my darling tell you?'

'Your darling said you two were planning to kill him. I think he was indirectly asking me for help, but I was too thick to understand. And by the way, I don't like to seem pickishly technical, but shouldn't someone call the police?'

'I took care of that on the way in,' Wyndham said. 'The County Sheriff. He comes from Kenton – a small village. A half hour's drive.'

'You were speaking of Ken,' Cozenka said. 'But you're lying, of course. What sort of nonsense are you –'

'I took it for that, but I was wrong. I thought he was a little drunk and emotionally upset. But he obviously knew more than I let him tell me.'

At this point, Wyndham won my respect as a cool operator if not as a human being. He sat back, masking the concern he must have felt, listening, saying nothing.

Excitement intensified Cozenka's foreign way of speaking. 'Marty, darling – has this terrible tragedy shocked away your reason? What madness in heaven's name is this – what delirium?'

'Stop it. Your whole murder plot went down the drain. The cat that Wyndham was so desperate to shoot just now paid me a visit earlier – just before you shot Ken Bender down in the coldest kind of blood. The cat was lonely. It wanted to be petted and played with. It was as tame as a kitten.'

'What utter insanity. If Demon was here, you're fortunate to be alive!'

'Perhaps I am. But I was never in any danger from the cat. The soul of treachery Wyndham spoke of out in the shed lies elsewhere – the cat never possessed it.'

Wyndham was still content to let me do the talking, but Cozenka had assumed the role of a cruelly persecuted innocent. 'But why, Marty? Why? What motive could I have had? Why would I kill the man who gave me everything?'

'He did give you everything. But all his love and money couldn't change the fact that he was a crashing bore – a big, clumsy, childlike man with only one qualification for your exquisite attentions. He was rich as Croesus. He, in short, had plenty of dough – you know, money. So you were quite willing to take everything he had except the one thing he wanted you most to accept. Himself.'

'Marty – please –'

'So you figured out a foolproof way to kill him and have it called an accident. So foolproof it almost worked.'

Wyndham had exhibited only one sign of uneasiness. He'd let his pipe go cold. He took it out of his mouth, now, and said, 'Do you plan to tell all this to the sheriff, old man?'

'I do. That is, unless you feel you can explain away two corpses as easily as one. There's a rifle standing two feet from your hand.'

Wyndham smiled a thin smile.

'Good heavens, no. In fact with things as they are now, it will be deuced difficult to explain away one.'

Cozenka had no doubt been frightened, but she drew courage from Wyndham's refusal to panic. 'Marty, you're being very, very foolish.'

'That's right, old fellow,' Wyndham added. 'I don't think you'll get very far with the constable – not with that silly yarn.'

'I see no reason why he shouldn't be interested.'

'Oh, no doubt he will be, but the cat's dead. And the law likes witnesses to such startling bits of revelation.'

He was right, of course.

I began to realize how right, when I talked to the sheriff. He was a small man with a hat and boots that appeared too large for him. He came to the lodge in an officially marked station wagon, and the first thing he did after looking at the body was to go to the phone and call the coroner.

He talked to Cozenka privately, then to Wyndham. I had no opportunity to learn what they'd said, although I was inclined to think they would both stick to their original story.

He questioned me last, in the den, also alone, and I told him the whole miserable story, beginning with Bender's fears and ending with my accusations before he'd arrived.

He listened politely, putting in a question here and there. Then, when I'd finished, he said, 'Those are pretty grave charges, Mr. Payne.'

'I'm aware of that.'

'And are you aware that you have nothing with which to support any of it?'

'There's my word as a reasonably honest citizen.'

He'd spent a great deal of time outdoors and there were skeins of tiny wrinkles at the corners of his clear blue eyes. These made him appear to be looking into a high wind as he studied me and said, 'A newspaperman too.'

'I beg your pardon?'

'I said you are a newspaperman.'

Not quite that, but I saw no point in explaining the difference. 'What's that got to do with it?' I asked.

'Nothing, maybe. But you *are* out here looking for a story. These poor people haven't been left alone ten minutes since they got married. Writers and newshawks snooping around – snooping in their business – practically peeking in their bedroom windows.'

I could have explained also that the publicity they gave her was very important to Cozenka, but the sheriff was too close to antagonism as things now stood. 'I don't see what that's got to do with the case. I really don't.'

'Well, you might find it real easy to exaggerate – make yourself a sensational story. The leopard, for instance. Are you sure it was tame? Are you dead certain you know the difference between a purr and a snarl?'

'If it wasn't tame, why didn't it attack me?'

'Conceding it was there in the first place, I can't say. Maybe it was blinded by the light and didn't see you. Or maybe it was more interested in hiding than in killing someone at that particular time.'

'All right. Suppose we concede that it was vicious and I was just lucky. That still puts the cat in the den with me when Cozenka claims she saw it out by the sheds.'

The sheriff shook his head. 'She didn't tell me that. She said she *thought* she saw it. She's making no claim that it was actually there.'

I began to heat up under the collar. 'Sheriff, tell me. Are you on their side?'

'I'm not on anybody's side. I'm interested only in the facts. But you don't have to worry about that. You'll get a chance to tell your story at the inquest tomorrow – that is, if you still thinks it's a good idea.'

'Why shouldn't I tell the truth?'

'You should, by all means. But in matters of this kind, the truth has to be supported by a little tangible evidence and I don't think you've got much.'

'It seems to be my word against theirs.'

'And I'd give a little thought to the libel laws, Mr. Payne. You can be certain Mrs. Bender's legal battery will know all about them. They might take a dim view of unsupported accusations. You could get into serious trouble.'

'I'll think it over.'

'In the meantime, it's Mrs. Bender's wish this tragedy doesn't leak out – at least until after the inquest tomorrow.'

'And you're cooperating with her?'

'Why not? She has a right to privacy. So don't try to use a telephone tonight. If a mob of reporters flood down on us, I'll know who to blame.'

I was angry with him even while knowing I had no right to be. Actually, I'd given him nothing to sink his teeth into. The 'word of a decent citizen' bit wouldn't hold water in court. I'd suspected that even before talking to the sheriff. But to let those two icy-veined killers get away with it –

I boiled over that for a while and then remembered what he'd said about the inquest.

Put up or shut up.

He was right. If I went ahead with my accusations, I could get myself into a serious jam.

I retired to my room before the coroner arrived and no one bothered me any more that night. Only my conscience, as I pondered the advisability of keeping my mouth shut.

Ken Bender, a fine man who hadn't deserved it, had been murdered by two calculating killers. I knew it. Yet there was absolutely nothing I could do.

Nothing except pace the floor all night thinking about the old chestnut – *there is no perfect plan for murder*. The killer always makes a small mistake – one that gets him convicted and hung.

But where was the mistake here? This one was so good, they could get away with it even when luck turned against them. Certainly it was only their bad luck that had sent that black cat into the den.

And yet their plan hadn't been seriously damaged.

I knew now the reason for Wyndham's almost casual attitude when I'd accused them. A much faster thinker than I was, he knew instantly that things would work out as they'd planned.

Of course, he hadn't threatened my life. There was no need for him to.

And I realized that the perfect murder was not only a possibility, but a fact. The fallacy in the old saying was that the perfect ones were never uncovered.

Fuming and fretting, I finally got to sleep – so late I didn't wake up until ten the next morning. I showered and shaved and went downstairs to find the sheriff alone in the dining room with a cup of coffee and a notebook.

He was neither friendly nor hostile as he looked up. Simply impersonal.

'Good morning, Mr. Payne. Sleep well?'

'Not very, but that's beside the point. Do you still think the death of Ken Bender was nothing more than an accident?'

'Nothing's happened to change my mind.'

'By the way, I didn't get your name last night. You do have a name, don't you?'

'Henderson – Milt Henderson.'

His answer was annoyingly mild, and I was fully aware that I was deliberately trying to irritate him – using him as a target for my own frustrations.

And the keen-eyed little lawman sensed the same thing because he said, 'I don't want you to misunderstand what I said last night, Mr. Payne.'

'Misunderstand? Why should you care one way or the other?'

'For two reasons. I do my job and I don't want anyone to think otherwise.'

'And the other?'

'This case is going to cause a national stir when it breaks. As a reporter on the scene, your copy will be in demand and you could easily make me the goat. You could make it look like I covered up for Mrs. Bender – that her money and position made me tip my hat and say yes, ma'am, and no, ma'am. Do you see?'

'And that isn't true?'

He scowled for the first time since I'd known him. 'You're damned right it isn't. Mrs. Bender and Wyndham get no more from me than any other resident of my county. You know yourself you've got nothing that will stand up. So go find something that will hold up in court, Mr. Payne. You do that and I'll back you to the limit. But don't expect me to accuse people of murder when it isn't proved.'

He was right, of course, and maybe what he said was just what I needed. At any rate, it started me thinking along positive lines instead of sitting around feeling sorry for myself because nobody would believe me.

Not that it reaped any immediate harvest. With Sheriff Henderson's parting instructions to be on hand for the inquest that had been scheduled for two o'clock, I wandered out toward the sheds trying to figure out a way to back my story with some proof the law would recognize as such.

There had to be a hole in their scheme somewhere.

I think now my anger was centered mainly around having been played for a fool. Cozenka's invitation, putting me on the scene at the time of the murder, had not been coincidental. I'd been carefully chosen as an amiable, not-too-bright slob who would automatically back up their play and give it the prestige of a witness whose copy appeared nationally in top magazines. An accessory, in essence, to bolster the vicious plot with blindly sympathetic testimony after the fact.

This made me mad. Together with the sheriff's prodding, it forced my mind to labor mightily and bring forth a hunch, one that sent me rushing back to the lodge and up to Cozenka's room.

She answered my knock, incredibly beautiful in a black lace gown. She'd done something to her eyes to make them appear red from weeping, and the sight of her – even with what I knew – was a strain on my determination. Could this sorrowing creature be anything but a grieving wife? I had to bring in a quick image of her as she must have looked with her rifle aimed at Bender's chest.

'You have come to apologize, Marty dear? Then I will accept your sorrow. I will forgive you. Do come in.'

I went in and found Wyndham sitting on the edge of the window seat with a scotch in his hand. The streaming sun turned his blond thatch into a halo. He looked like a good friend for one to have in time of grief.

He said, 'Hello, Payne,' and then knocked off the rest of his drink.

With what I had in mind, I didn't want their antagonism. All I wanted was a little time alone in Cozenka's room. Not that I was sure I would find what I hoped to, but it was the logical place to look and the sooner the better.

So I smiled engagingly at Wyndham and patted Cozenka's hand. 'I guess I was a little cruel last night, but Ken was my friend. Perhaps we can –'

Wyndham, pipe in hand, suddenly turned serious, the first hint of hostility that he'd shown. 'I'm afraid it isn't quite as simple as that, Payne.'

'I don't understand.'

'Good lord, man! You aren't so stupid as to believe you can throw vicious charges all around the place and walk off scot-free, are you?'

'But we were all upset last night. I –'

'You called us murderers to our face. You also gave the same ridiculous story to the sheriff. That means it will get around. Your ugly accusations are no doubt on every tongue in the place right this minute. Do you think we can just stand by under such circumstances?'

'What do you plan to do?'

'Drag you into court. Sue you to the limit. Any other course would indicate fear of your charges on our part. Therefore, in countering, we must strike deep, so the magazine you're representing must also be named as a defendant.'

Wyndham took a balefull puff on his bulldog.

'I wouldn't be surprised if when we get through with you, you'll not only be a pauper, but you'll be blackballed in every editorial office in the country.'

Obviously, Wyndham had considered all aspects and decided they had nothing to fear from me. That made his sudden turn to the offensive entirely logical. An attack of the sort he'd outlined would block me off permanently from gaining any official sympathy. I would become a persecutor of upstanding manhood and the defamer of a woman crushed by tragedy.

I wondered who the executive of this steam was – Wyndham or Cozenka? The turnabout could have been advocated by either of them. I turned to Cozenka.

'Do you really think I deserve this?'

She chose to pout. 'But, Marty darling, you said cruel things to Pete and me. We have our good names to think of. And the world must know how deeply I loved the man I married.'

'I think I know. And there's something else. I think you loved Demon. I think you truly grieved for the animal when he had to be sacrificed.'

'I did love him because I love beauty. And Ken loved him too. I loved Demon, yet I did not flinch from turning my rifle on him to save human life.'

'And the fact that you hit Ken only added to your grief.'

'Marty – you are so cruelly sarcastic.'

She was right. I was doing a bum job of placating them and I knew I had to get out of the room or there would be fists flying. 'I'm sorry it sounds that way.'

'You are cruel – cruel –'

Then my clumsy approach worked inadvertently in my favor and Cozenka flared into sudden resentment. 'We were waiting here for a visit from Mr. Henderson. He has been so kind – so thoughtful. But we will not wait. We will go to him. I cannot stand your presence a moment longer.'

'She's telling you to get out, Payne. That should be clear, even to you.'

I got out, hoping Cozenka meant what she said about going to the sheriff. I was in trouble – with only the slimmest chance of clearing myself, and very little time left for even that.

I went back to my own room at the end of the hall where I could watch Cozenka's door through the keyhole. And a few moments later, she and Wyndham emerged and went downstairs.

The moment they vanished, I was out of my own room. And before they reached the bottom of the stairs, I was snooping through Cozenka's personal belongings like any other common sneak thief. I didn't enjoy it.

It was a big room and there was a lot to go through and I spent the most uncomfortable fifteen minutes of my life. I heard them back at the door every time I opened a fresh closet, but I kept on, reconciled to being caught in the midst of things if it should happen that way.

They didn't return and I found what I was looking for – or hoped I had. There was no way of really telling. I didn't have enough time, because my discovery, like the hunch it had sprung from, came too late to give an opportunity for complete investigation. I could only sneak out of the bedroom and trot downstairs with my find in my pocket – before they came hunting for me – to attend the inquest.

I only had time enough to say a small prayer and hope I had

what I needed to trip up Cozenka, Wyndham and Company.

There were six men in the coroner's jury – all recruited on the premises from among the help – the coroner himself being a Doctor Wendell whom – I later learned – hadn't even told his wife what had happened there at the Bender lodge.

Such was the prestige and power of Bender's millions. The same millions, I thought nervously, that might soon be turned like cannon in my direction.

Doctor Wendell was a man in his sixties, quietly efficient, with something of a judicial bearing. He was admirably suited to the job of presiding. He'd obviously been briefed by the sheriff as to my contribution to the general confusion, because he regarded me with marked interest as I entered and took my seat.

But there was no over-leaping of routine procedure. He questioned Cozenka first, and she did very well, so well that every man in the room wanted to come forward and comfort her personally. Not that they were callous and unmindful of Bender's tragic taking off, but he was dead and absent and Cozenka was very much alive and present.

And she was Cozenka.

Wyndham came next and he also handled himself beautifully. They both stuck to the story as it was originally laid out in their plan. Cozenka tearfully admitted her carelessness in acting hastily – admitted it most convincingly – and they lied with sincerity about the exceptional viciousness of the cat, giving justification to Cozenka's nervousness and fatal mistake.

In short, they stuck to their story right down the line.

Then the slightest of chinks appeared in their armor, the first one since Cozenka's shot had rung out the night before. This when Wyndham leaned casually forward and placed his lips close to my ear.

He said, 'A deal, old man. You can only hurt yourself with that fool yarn about a tame cat, so let's call it a stalemate. Forget the nonsense and I'll forget what I said upstairs. No point in our flailing each other.'

'You're scared,' I whispered.

'Not scared. Just sensible. And you should follow suit, because you know damned well that if you open your mouth I'll crucify you.'

With that cheerful reminder, I was called to the stand.

Doctor Wendell, possibly from a keen sense of the dramatic, worked backwards in his questioning. He started with my hearing the shot and the screams and running out to investigate. I verified everything Wyndham and Cozenka and the watchman had told him of the actual tragedy, a girl – recruited from the late Mr. Bender's small office force – taking down every word meticulously. Then Doctor Wendell jumped clear over to the arrival of the sheriff and the removal of the body.

After that, he fired a question that was the business, the showdown. 'I understand that shortly after Mr. and Mrs. Bender and Mr. Wyndham left the lodge to hunt down the leopard, you had an extraordinary experience. I'd like to hear about it.'

This was my last chance to back down.

And I won't deny that I was frightened for my career and future as I agreed with Doctor Wendell that it had been most extraordinary and gave it out, for the record, exactly as it had happened.

There was a time of silence after I'd finished, probably longer to me than anyone else. I used the time to steal glances at Cozenka and Wyndham. Cozenka was crying softly into her handkerchief, crying in a way that made the coroner's jury hate me and my story – I was sure of that.

Wyndham took it with perfect aplomb, tamping tobacco into his pipe as though he had been indirectly accused of nothing more than swatting a troublesome fly.

Finally Doctor Wendell spoke. 'Mr. Payne, do you have any proof whatever, other than your unsupported word, that the incident in the den, the coming and going of the leopard, actually occurred?'

'I hope so, but at the moment I can't be sure.'

'That's a pretty ambiguous statement.'

'I realize that, but it's all I can tell you at the moment.'

'When do you expect to be able to tell us more?'

'When we run this off and see what's on it,' I said, and took from my pocket the reel of sixteen-millimeter film I'd found in a shelf in one of Cozenka's closets.

'You don't know what's on it?'

'No. I haven't had time to check.'

'How did you happen to come into possession of this film?'

'As a result of what I hope will turn out to be logical thinking on my part. From observation, I believed that Mrs. Bender entertained a definite affection for the black leopard named Demon, that she was sincerely sad when the cat had to be sacrificed as a part of her plan.

'So it seemed strange to me that the leopard did not appear anywhere in the hour-long film covering her last trip to Africa. I viewed the film last night, and saw enough to convince me that Mrs. Bender considered motion pictures of her activities over there and the animals she captured as being very important.

'So why no pictures of the animal she obviously regarded more highly than any of the others?

'From that point I proceeded on the belief that such films or stills actually existed and went about hunting for them. This is what I found and only viewing them will prove me right or wrong.'

But I knew I was right. Cozenka went pale as death and while Wyndham didn't jump up and break any windows, he tightened up in a manner that was almost the equivalent for a man of his self-control.

Cozenka did spring to her feet.

'No! No! He is wrong. He is deliberately torturing me. That film is most personal. I beg you not to run it off. You have no right to shame me!'

She was making a desperate all-out effort and Doctor Wendell was most polite in his ruling. 'I'm very sorry, Mrs Bender, but this is an investigation into a man's death and as such takes precedence over any personal feelings. Grave charges have been raised. Is there a film projector available?'

It was all there: highlights in the taming of a black leopard named Demon; shots mainly of Wyndham and the cat that could probably have been used in a course of instruction on how to take the viciousness out of jungle cats; a record from the time Wyndham first entered Demon's cage, somewhere in Africa, to the high point where Cozenka frolicked with the happy and gentle beast on the sylvan meadow.

There was a sound track, too, and during the final sequence I couldn't resist turning to Sheriff Henderson to say, 'I think you will agree, Sheriff, that the cat is purring, not snarling.'

I was instantly regretful. After all, Henderson hadn't been against me. He'd only been doing a difficult job as well as he could.

The verdict said nothing about accidental death. It merely stated that Kenneth Bender had died of a gunshot wound under circumstances that warranted further investigation, and it enjoined Sheriff Henderson to continue with that investigation.

I wish I could report that the film did the trick – confounded two vicious murderers and that full payment was demanded.

But I can't. That wasn't how it finally worked out.

I left the lodge, of course, but I stayed on a few days in the sheriff's town. Some disturbing rumors made me seek him out.

He was busy in his office and so I got right to the point. 'What's this I hear about charges being dropped against Mrs. Bender and Wyndham?'

'Nothing was dropped. Charges were never made. The grand jury, upon advice of the County Attorney, refused to indict.'

'And how did that gross miscarriage of justice come about?'

'Through orderly, logical thinking.'

I was thoroughly disgusted.

'Then we'd better have more disorderly and illogical thinking. It's an outrage.'

'I can understand your point of view,' Henderson said, 'but let's look at facts as they really are.'

'I've looked at them.'

'But you haven't seen them as they are. What was there,

really, that would have a chance of getting a guilty verdict from twelve jurors?'

'Proof that their vicious cat was as tame as a kitten.'

'Sure, but that isn't proof. It's merely a point for argument in court. Bender and Wyndham would have had a battery of the country's finest defense attorneys, but even a mediocre one would have thrown doubt upon whether a black leopard, regardless of the evidence, is ever really tame.

'And their reason for hiding the fact could have been any of several that would have nothing to do with murder. Mrs. Bender could admit not being the hunter she claimed to be; that she wanted the prestige of owning a vicious cat without the danger.'

He stopped to light a cigarette and then added, 'Do you see my logic?'

'I'm beginning to.'

'And your story about Bender's fear of death probably wouldn't even be admitted as evidence.'

'I see.'

'And one last point. Would you care to go before a jury made up principally of men and try to get Cozenka Bender convicted on the evidence we have?'

I thought it over for a moment. 'No, but just the same they're both guilty.'

'I think you're right,' he agreed. 'And now, how about a drink? I'll buy.'

Perhaps there is some consolation in the fact that Cozenka and Wyndham gained nothing but tragedy from the tragedy they instigated. So it seemed.

They were both dead within six months after Cozenka fired the fatal bullet.

Wyndham, in Africa where he was pounded into the mud by a water buffalo after he missed a hundred-foot shot and had no time for a second.

He went back there, alone, two months after Bender's death. And three months later, Cozenka was killed when her sports car rocketed off the road one dark night.

It would be nice to think that she did away with herself because she couldn't face the guilt of her crime. But if her death was other than an accident, it was probably because Wyndham refused to step into Bender's shoes, and she realized that his clinging to her had been for the money she no doubt settled on him, not for love of her.

I think she truly loved Wyndham; ironically, in the same hopeless way Bender had loved her. And perhaps realization that Wyndham was the one man in this world that she couldn't have was sufficient grounds for suicide.

Then too, there's another possibility. Could I have been wrong from the beginning?

As Sheriff Henderson said, my conversation with Bender probably wouldn't have been allowed in court, and there were many reasons why Cozenka could have covered the true situation relative to Demon.

One thing is certain. Even though I was sure of their guilt, I wouldn't have wanted to pull the switch personally on either of them. Not on the evidence that I actually had.

So, in the final summing up, I was sure of only one thing.

The cat was tame.